A Perfect Fit

By Kellan McKnight

©2023 Kellan McKnight

All rights reserved. No part of this publication may be reproduced, distributed, or transmitted in any form or by any means, including photocopying, recording, or other electronic or mechanical methods, without the prior written permission of the publisher, except in the case of brief quotations embodied in critical reviews and certain other noncommercial uses permitted by copyright law. For permission requests, write to kellan.mcknight.author@gmail.com

Quantity sales. Special discounts may be available on quantity purchases by corporations, associations, and others.

Interior formatting and cover design by:

Tara Sullivan, The Write Gal Co.
www.thewritegal.com

Printed in the United States of America

Acknowledgements

So many folks to thank... There will never be enough time or space to say all that needs to be said.

From the very beginning S, you have been my rock. None of this happens without your unyielding support and love. You are my safe space.

To T, C, B, A, J, and R... You are all my inspiration and make me a better person.

To those who have helped me along the way, your help and expertise is greatly appreciated. Willie, you were the first one to provide advice when I wanted to make this happen. I can't tell you how much I value your friendship. Melissa (kismet), you're the best in the world. I truly believe it. Tara, the service you provide is priceless (and thank you for not killing me with my eighty daily questions). Your patience-plus-professionalism formula sets my mind at ease.

To all authors who have provided advice wrapped in kindness, this also doesn't happen without you. For those of us who must just psych ourselves up to actually send a message to someone we venerate, it means the world.

To all those who read this and might be inspired: Do it. Whatever your "it" is. Life's just too damn short. Some of us learn that lesson the hard way. Stop putting it off. You can do it. I believe in you because someone (several someones, actually) believed in me and I want to pay it forward. YOU'VE GOT THIS.

— KM

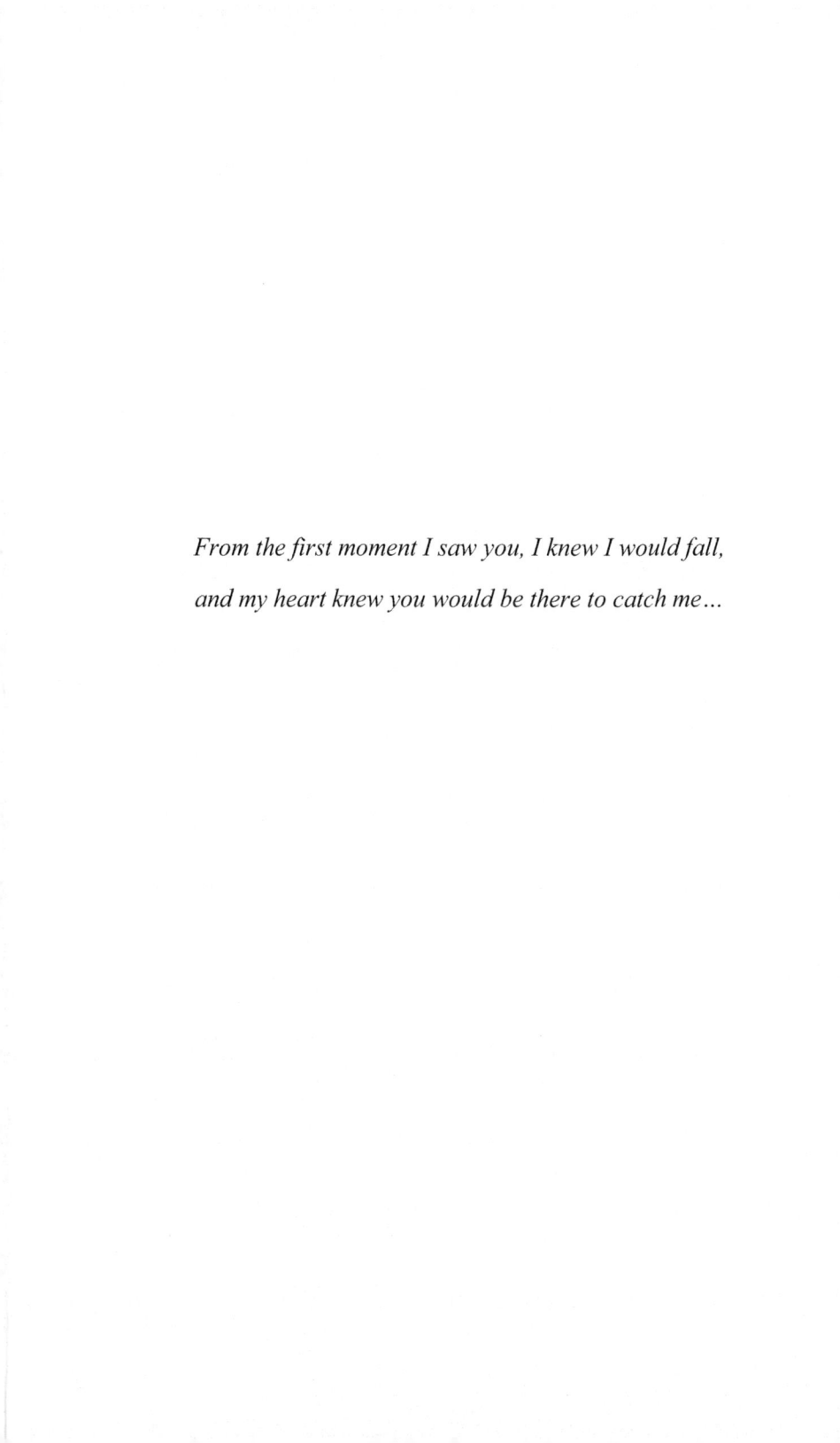

From the first moment I saw you, I knew I would fall, and my heart knew you would be there to catch me…

Table of Contents

©2023 Kellan McKnight v

Chapter 1 1

Chapter 2 7

Chapter 3 17

Chapter 4 29

Chapter 5 35

Chapter 6 55

Chapter 7 67

Chapter 8 83

Chapter 9 97

Chapter 10 123

Chapter 11 143

Chapter 12 179

Chapter 13 211

Chapter 14 215

Chapter 15 235

Chapter 16 245

Chapter 17	263
Chapter 18	281
Chapter 19	299
Chapter 20	311
Chapter 21	327
Chapter 22	341
Chapter 23	351
Chapter 24	363
Chapter 25	369
Epilogue: One year later	393
About the Author	399

Chapter 1

"Let's do this," Ella Gardner said out loud to no one in particular as she opened up her laptop with the intention of researching the best places to meet women online. Her cat Narcissus blinked and turned away disinterestedly.

Ella was divorced and looking. After seventeen years of marriage to her husband, she finally decided to deal with what was wrong in her life. She had always known she was gay, but it wasn't something she could accept.

After she realized she was developing troubling feelings for the new girl in high school, Ella got together with her best friend Alex in their senior year to prove to herself and everyone else that she was straight. Super straight. She and hot women were like two parallel lines, going on forever never to cross: therefore, never to gay. This mentality earned her a lot of self-loathing and an unplanned teenage pregnancy. As a volleyball star, Ella's post-high school plans were to play four years at a university while earning a teaching degree. After AJ was born, she and Alex got married and the families united to help with childcare while she completed her teaching certificate.

Now, at thirty-five years old, Ella was ready to start living her life, but wasn't sure how to go about meeting women. There was only one gay bar in the area, which was a few towns over. But there was no way she would be able to walk in there alone. She opted to make a profile on lesbefriends.com complete with pictures and as much information as she could think of. It had been a disastrous experience thus far.

Where most women her age were listening to pop radio and watching rom-coms, outsider Ella preferred things a little more off-kilter. In her humble opinion, grunge from the '90s was still the best music, and there was no convincing her otherwise. It seemed like most people she ran across while scrolling through profiles wanted to watch *Friends* and listen to Miley Cyrus. Why couldn't she find someone who wanted to curl up and watch a horror flick and listen to Nirvana?

Ella stumbled across a brand-new profile for Danna, who was thirty-two, liked Alanis Morrisette and R.E.M., and cited her favorite movie as the *Rocky Horror Picture Show*. This could work.

Ella sent Danna a 'zing'; this site's way to let someone know you are interested. She received a response a few hours later.

Danna, 10:23 p.m.: "So, you're only my second zing. Is that good news or bad news?"

She was funny. This had potential.

Ella, 10:25 p.m.: "I guess that depends. Did you respond to the other one?"

Danna, 10:26 p.m.: "Nah. She listened to Taylor Swift."

Oh, she *was* funny. She didn't overuse emojis, which said to Ella that there was real potential for some fun, acerbic banter.

Ella, 10:28 p.m.: "Okay you're my new favorite person. It is so hard to find people on these sites who aren't just in it for hook-ups, threesomes or have shitty taste in music."

Danna, 10:32 p.m.: "How do you know I'm not in it for a hook-up or a threesome?"

Whoa. Hang on. Ella knew she wasn't into anything like that. But, moments later, she was relieved to receive a winky-face emoji. She had to give it to Danna, her interest was piqued.

Ella, 10:33 p.m.: "Okay, you scared me for a sec. Thanks for the emoji lifeline."

Danna, 10:36 p.m.: "Yeah I'm a comedian at heart."

Ella, 10:38 p.m.: "I'm going to go out on a limb here because you're the first person I have talked to on this site who I've related to. Would you like to meet up for a drink soon?"

There you go, Ella. Just go with the first thing that comes to mind. Put yourself out there. Good stuff.

Danna, 10:41 p.m.: "Same here. Although my profile is new so I guess I can't say much. How about the new Puerto Rican place that opened just across from Sparkle? Maybe tomorrow if that's not too soon?"

Being a teacher made your schedule a little bit difficult to deal with. Being a mom made it worse. But today was Thursday. Tomorrow meant Friday. AJ had already made plans to stay at her dad's house for the weekend, so she was free. Perhaps, if everything went well, Ella could make her first trip to a gay bar.

Ella, 10:44 p.m.: "That would be great. It's your lucky day!"

Danna, 10:45 p.m.: "Well now that sounds hopeful. Let's say eight then. We'll start with a drink then if things go well, we can talk about dinner...and possibly breakfast."

Hold the phone. What was that? Ella reread that last line a few times before the site's bouncing, pride-flag-colored double-ellipsis told her that Danna was still typing.

Danna, 10:46 p.m.: "That was supposed to be funny. I figured that my sense of humor kept you talking, so I would flex my comedy muscle."

Ella liked her a lot already. Drinks and dinner sounded perfect.

Ella, 10:48 p.m.: "Okay you got me there. Yes, let's do it. Breakfast to be considered on date two...?"

Two can play that game, Miss Danna.

Danna, 10:51 p.m.: "I like you already, Ella. I look forward to seeing who can be funnier tomorrow night."

Danna understood her sense of humor, which was very refreshing. They traded phone numbers just in case, and Ella couldn't stop smiling. Tomorrow, she would go on her first real date ever. With a woman. With Danna. Funny Danna with the good taste in music and movies. She couldn't stop herself from thinking this could be the start of something wonderful.

Chapter 2

It didn't take long for Ella to realize that there was zero romantic chemistry between her and Danna. She was beautiful to be sure, shorter than Ella with full breasts and hips and luscious lips, but there was just no spark. The night was salvaged by a budding friendship. They were on the same wavelength in their senses of humor, and the date turned into a laugh riot. Both agreed that you couldn't have too many friends, and that they would be hanging out a lot more in the future.

After learning Ella had never been to Sparkle, Danna offered to reach out to her friends to see who was going to be there. Ella drained her drink and ordered another because she had every intention of cutting loose for once in her life.

Danna's friends Wendy and Valerie were already there, so they paid their bill and headed across the street. Danna was a regular and spoke candidly with the front door bouncer on the way in. This had the makings of a fun night, even if she was finding it hard to walk a straight line. The good news is they were in a gay bar. *Straight* lines need not apply!

Wendy and Val seemed very nice. Wendy sported a blond ponytail that bobbed with every nod of her head as introductions were made. Val had a neatly maintained pixie cut that suited her face and chestnut hair. Both were all smiles and agreed that shots were to be had before the night could continue. Ella had already lost track of the number of drinks she had consumed, but the buzz she was feeling was too good for her to spend much time thinking about it.

Val returned with a tray of what Ella assumed were tequila shots as they were accompanied by lime wedges and a saltshaker. If she were sober, she would not have done shots on top of the alcohol she had already consumed. But she and sober were not currently acquainted.

"Here's to the newest member of our crew!" Wendy said, clapping Ella on the back and picking up her shot. Everyone else followed suit, and cheers were had all around.

"Guys, I ate a lot of mofongo and need to make up for it with some bumping and grinding," Danna said, taking Ella by the hand and dragging her to the dance floor. Wendy and Val were right behind them.

Ella did her best to weave her way through the sea of bodies as beautiful woman after beautiful woman brushed against her in the crowd. She made eye contact with a lovely, ochre-skinned woman with fire-engine red hair. They made meaningful eye contact as she moved to the music, but there was no time to talk as Danna made a beeline to the action. She made a mental note to try to find the woman later to see if she wanted to dance.

Is that how you do that sort of thing in the lesbian community? She had no dating experience on either side of the fence, of course, having married right out of high school.

When they found just the right spot, Ella leaned over to yell-whisper into her new bestie's ear as they swayed, jumped, and bopped to the music. "Hey, so, how do you get these women to dance with you? Do you just ask?" Danna looked back at her quizzically, but nodded through what must have been a light-bulb moment. They had discussed her lack of dating history in depth during dinner.

"Yeah, I mean, gay bars are different. There's no pressure here. A lot of straight women come here because they're not going to get hit on relentlessly like they do when they're at straight bars."

Ella stared at her in confusion, but Danna put an arm around her and pulled her in for a side hug.

"I know, I know. Why do they come here and tease us, right? In all seriousness, it's just a fun environment. You are free to ask anyone to dance. Women know they can just tell you yes or no, and you will respect their decision," Danna said.

It was in that moment that Ella decided that lesbians and women in general were mystical creatures. But then, she took a moment to think about her chosen outfit, comparing it to the other women dancing around her. She was such a mom. A teacher-mom. With mom-clothes and teacher-mom clothes. Ugh.

When dressing for her date, Ella had settled on a fitted, lightweight V-neck navy blue sweater paired with a pair of AJ's slim-fit jeans that had a stylish rip in the knee and a small cuff at the bottom for this evening's attire. She wore her shoulder-length blond locks loosely curled and parted on the side and just a touch of natural makeup and lip gloss.

"Hey, you have some good moves, my friend," Val said as she paired off with Ella for a dance.

"Thanks. I just love losing myself to the music. I always do this on the weekends when I have the house to myself."

It was so easy to just go somewhere else on the driving beat and not have to worry about anything. Time just melted away. After a few songs, Danna made a show of wiping her brow and fanning herself before suggesting they get another drink. Wendy and Val said they would meet up in a bit as they were focused on a lovely auburn-haired woman who moved seductively between them.

The line at the bar was moving quickly as the team of bartenders operated like a well-oiled machine to keep the patrons liquored up. Ella perused a list of drinks on her phone's web browser because tonight was a night of firsts, and she wanted to try some new libations. When she looked up from her phone, she felt herself swaying a bit on her feet and reconsidered. "I think I may just get some water. I have had quite a bit to drink already," she said as she leaned towards Danna's ear.

Danna looked at her with an overexaggerated pout. "The night is still young, newbie! Come on, one more drink. Then we can switch to water like old ladies," she said, receiving her whiskey and Coke and scooting to the side so Ella could step up to make her order.

Ella heard "what'll you have?" just before she looked up from the drink menu on her phone. Time stood still, and the noise of the room faded away.

In front of her was the most beautiful woman she had ever seen. Dark, wavy locks cascaded over her shoulders and down her back, framing her heart-shaped face. Smoldering eyes the color of dark chocolate stared back into Ella's sea-green ones as one side of her mouth curled up into a wry, knowing smile.

"Uh…" Ella stuttered as she ripped her eyes away to look down at her phone. The delicious-looking drink she had been pondering was no longer there. Frantically, she scrolled and ordered the first drink that popped up while her brain functioned on autopilot. "A Screaming Orgasm?" she said, and as soon as the words fell from her mouth, she felt the blood drain from her face. Danna elbowed her incredulously from the side as the beautiful bartender laughed out loud.

"Really, now? You did mean the drink, right?" she said with a wink.

It was just then that Ella snapped out of her trance and realized what she said. "Wait, no, sorry. I've lost my page here. Just a second," she said as she tried to scroll back. No matter what the striking drink-maker thought, the folks behind her started to voice their wishes for her to get her drink and go...now. Ella couldn't function. She couldn't make the page come back up on her phone, so she opted to order something she knew she would enjoy for the first drink and perhaps she could get creative when she came back through the line. Danna made it obvious she wanted them to drink more.

"Let's just do a vodka soda with lime," Ella said to the lovely woman in front of her, who smiled and nodded and went about crafting the drink. "Make it a double, please," she added as she stood red-faced and ready to sink into the floor.

The bartender nodded and, without looking up, added, "Do you want to pay for it or leave your card and cash out at the end of the night?"

Ella dug her credit card out of her back pocket and handed it over. She had come to the bar with the intention of hanging out with Danna and her friends for a while, but she now had a new objective: to drink more than she ever had in her life in order to lose herself in those eyes as often as possible.

The bartender picked it up and nodded, sitting it on a shelf behind her before tucking the drink receipt under it. She handed the drink over, and for the briefest of moments, their fingers brushed. Ella drew in a deep breath to steady herself.

"Here you go. You didn't specify your brand of choice, but the well vodka we have here is terrible. So, I substituted something top-shelf for you, no charge," she said with a beaming smile, showing off pearly-white teeth. "My name's Parker Chase. It was very nice to meet you, Ella Gardner." Parker said *very* in an alluring way that made her pulsate deep in her core. "Come see me if there's a new drink you're wanting to try. I have many recipes I want to try and am always looking for a willing participant," Parker continued.

She let go of the drink, and Ella took a sip. It was just strong enough without being overpowering. Parker had traced the lip of the glass with the lime wedge before dropping it in the drink for a refreshing sour explosion in her mouth each time she sipped. This was the most perfect vodka soda in the history of the world; she was sure of it. "Oh, I will. I would love for you to try your recipes out...on...me." Ella could no longer form cogent thoughts. Parker laughed heartily and winked at her again before Ella left the line with Danna.

"Girl, what in the world was that!" Danna said with a kindhearted chuckle.

"So, apparently, I still interact with hot people like an awkward seventeen-year-old, too," Ella said, placing her forearm over her eyes in exasperation. She wondered if the gods would just strike her dead if she asked nicely.

"It was cute. That was one of the most honest reactions to Parker I've seen, and she loved it," Danna said.

Curiosity stirred in Ella. Remembering this was a place which Danna frequented, she decided to probe a little further for information on the sultry Miss Parker.

Danna held up a hand, stopping her questions before they even started. "She has worked here for about a year. Everyone is in love with her, and she takes full advantage of their affections, if you know what I mean," Danna said. Ella raised her eyebrows and shook her head. Danna sighed.

"She's a bit of a...heartbreaker," Danna said. "She doesn't always take a woman home when the night is over, but if she does, it's always someone new. This causes problems. I mean, just look at her. They can't seem to stop themselves from falling hard."

Ella searched Danna's eyes, but Danna wrinkled her nose and shook her head.

"No, that's not my style. She is one of the most beautiful women in the bar, but I am not a one-night stand kind of girl. I'm looking for wifey," Danna said with a grin.

Ella smiled back and nodded, because isn't that what she wanted, too? Did she even know what she wanted? She took another sip of her drink and looked back to where Parker stood as her fans fell over themselves trying to get her attention. She looked up at the same time and met Ella's gaze with an amused smile. She held up her hand as if there were a drink in it, pointed at it, and gave a thumbs-up before raising her eyebrows in question. Ella nodded with vigor, assuring her that the drink was indeed delicious before taking another sip to prove her love for the concoction.

Parker once again laughed, followed by a wave, and Ella couldn't stop her heart from racing. She thought about downing the drink in one gulp so she could head back over and become one of the thralls flocking for Parker's attention. Instead, she took Danna's hand and led her out to the dance floor.

∽

After bumping, grinding, laughing, and joking their way through four or five songs that all sounded the same, both Ella and Danna pointed to a side area where a few tables and chairs were catty-cornered to the bar area. Ella dropped down on an overstuffed leather loveseat and patted the area next to her in invitation.

"Oh man, I needed this for sure," she said to Danna. "I think I'm going to come here every Friday night I don't have AJ."

Danna nodded as Ella closed her eyes and nodded slowly to the music. "Anytime you need a dancing buddy, I'm there," she said.

Upon opening her eyes, Danna looked like she was in conversation with someone. Ella turned to look behind her just in time to see Parker still behind the bar but pointing at her watch and making a motion like she was breaking something between her fists.

Confused and addled by the alcohol coursing through her system, she looked back to Danna who looked between her and Parker before shaking her head in defeat.

Ella felt her cheeks turn pink as her eyebrows made a break for her hairline.

Danna continued, "I've told you what I know about her. I'm not going to tell you whether you should talk to her or not. You're a big girl and can make those decisions on your own. I just wanted you to know. Now, what do you want to do?" Danna waited for Ella's response. Thinking seemed to be getting harder as the alcohol continued to take effect.

"Well, I mean, I was thinking I was going to go back for another drink. I don't think saying hello can hurt anything, right?" Ella said.

Danna pressed her lips together and nodded. "All right, let's go get a drink. Just remember to keep your faculties about you. That woman is spellbinding," Danna said, standing up and reaching her hand out for Ella. "Here we go, Odysseus, I'll tie you to the mast to protect you from the siren's song." Ella barked out a laugh at the literary reference but shook her head good-naturedly as they walked back to the bar.

Chapter 3

"Hey, welcome back," Parker said and motioned Ella closer. "I saw you guys headed over here so I went ahead and put something together for you." She pushed a tall glass toward Ella. "I went on what I know: you like vodka and lime, so I am hoping you like other sour fruits as well," she said as she tossed a stemmed cherry into the air. It plopped into the drink, resting on the ice.

"Oh wow, thank you," Ella said, staring into her eyes, enchanted. "It's beautiful."

Parker raised her eyebrows but smiled. "Well, I have never heard someone call a drink beautiful before, but thank you," she said, leaning toward Ella. "It suits you."

Ella lifted the straw to her lips and drank. The flavors were explosive. Multiple tart citrus notes danced on her tongue before the powerful kick of the vodka hit her. This was stronger than her last drink. She knew she was going to have to sip this one. "Oh my God, Parker, this is amazing. It's like a vodka soda on a different level. What do you call it?" Ella said, unable to stop herself from taking another deep drink.

"Sex with the Bartender," she said, folding her arms and grinning. Ella choked on her third sip, and Danna smacked her on the back for good measure.

"You all right there, friend?" she said, smirking.

Ella nodded and felt her face flush from the combination of the alcohol and brief lack of oxygen. "Yes, very good, thank you," she said as she moved out of the line so others could place their orders.

Parker placed a gentle hand on her forearm, stopping her. Ella turned around to find her leaning in again. She felt compelled to do the same. "I'm getting ready to go on break in five minutes. I was going to head outside to the patio to get some air. Would you like to join me?"

Ella didn't have to think about it. "Sure, but I've never been here before. I'm not sure where to go."

Parker leaned in closer. "Just hang out here, and I'll be with you in a minute. You can bring your friend, too, if you want," she said, indicating Danna.

Ella nodded and moved to the side as a girl who couldn't have been drinking legally moved up to the bar and leaned in, whispering to Parker. She couldn't hear what they were talking about from this distance, but Parker was disagreeing as the girl kept trying to grab her hand, on the verge of tears.

"See, this is what I was talking about," Danna said from behind her, placing her hand on the small of Ella's back.

"We don't know what's going on with them, though. There's no reason to judge. Besides, she invited you, too," Ella said while looking back over at Parker, who was trying to keep things from escalating. The girl now had tears streaming down her face as she pulled her hand back and turned to walk away in a huff. Parker lost her trademark smile for a few moments but gathered her resolve as the next young man with glitter all over his shirtless torso came up to place his order.

Danna looked back and forth between the two of them and shook her head. "I'm just going to stay here and dance. Don't drink that too fast. Keep your wits about you and don't fall in love, okay? She's not the sort for a relationship," Danna said and pulled her in for a hug.

"I appreciate your concern. I really do, but we're just going to get some air and chat," Ella said as she felt a warm hand clasp hers. She turned back around to see Parker at her side. The contact was electric as she intertwined her fingers with Ella's and nodded to the back of the club where people appeared to be going in and out of an almost imperceptible door.

Ella couldn't seem to look away from Parker's outfit. A laced-up black leather crop top barely contained her ample chest. Skintight, black-and-white checkered pants and white Doc Martens completed the mouth-watering look. Parker cleared her throat, bringing her out of her daze. Ella looked back at Danna and smiled as if to say "I'm fine, thanks for caring" before allowing Parker to lead her through the throngs on the dance floor swaying to the beat. She never spilled a drop of her drink.

Once they got outside, Parker let go of Ella's hand, and she felt a coldness that wasn't there before, as if they should always hold hands. Many of the patrons called out, waved, hugged, and kissed Parker as they made their way to a porch swing that hung over a reinforced area at the corner of the patio.

"Is this good?" Parker said with a gallant sweep of her arm. When Ella nodded, she braced the swing to allow a tipsy Ella to sit before joining her. "So, you didn't need to tell me you had never been here before. I would have remembered someone as beautiful as you," she said with overt charm.

Ella couldn't stifle a laugh. "Wow, that was cheesy. Do you have a pickup line for me, too? Like, 'is it hot in here or is it just you?'" Ella said as she took another sip of her drink. When she looked up, Parker's smile was fleeting, deflating before her very eyes. *Oh shit.* She was well on her way to being drunk and way too honest. "Oh hey, I'm sorry. I'm more than a little tipsy here and that always results in speaking before thinking. I appreciate the compliment. Really," Ella said, placing her hand on Parker's knee in a gracious gesture.

Parker pursed her lips before smiling again. This one looked more genuine. "No, it's okay. I appreciate people who call me on my bullshit. I have this persona that I do here to try to get tips. You know, the bartender is supposed to be the epitome of sexy and unattainable." She paused and looked down at Ella's hand on her knee before covering it with her own. "Let me try again. You are stunningly beautiful, and from the moment I met you, I knew I wanted to talk to you. How's that?" she said, looking back at Ella with a hopeful expression.

The blush that was threatening took over Ella's face now as she looked down at their joined hands. "That," she said, pausing to let out a slow, calming breath, "was perfect. Thank you."

Parker beamed at her before tracing her thumb over Ella's in a slow, subtle motion.

"I don't understand the bravado. I mean, look at you. You *are* the epitome of sexy. I have to say I prefer the real you. There's no need to try so hard. Just be yourself."

Parker's smile dropped again, but instead of looking upset as she had moments before, she seemed caught off-guard. Without warning, she leaned in and Ella's breath hitched in expectation. Was she going to kiss her? "I don't get to meet a lot of people like you. I mean, have you ever met someone and just knew you want to get to know them better?" Parker looked so honest and vulnerable now.

Ella understood with all her heart. "Yes, I mean, not often, but I was drawn to you immediately. I'm glad you wanted to talk," she said, leaning back as the world started to spin. Parker was oblivious, but she only knew about the few drinks in the bar. Ella was trying to force her addled brain to hold on a little longer to have a meaningful conversation with the stunning person sitting with her.

"Let's play twenty questions," Parker said. "We can do ten questions each. Nothing's off the table. I am an open book, and you can ask me anything."

Ella scoffed but nodded in agreement. Parker scrunched up her face like she was deep in thought before nodding to herself and turning back to face Ella.

"What's your favorite food?"

Well, that was unexpected and tame. "Indian," Ella said in response. "Vindaloo is my favorite. I like spicy food a lot."

Parker nodded. "That's one I haven't tried. Maybe we could go for dinner sometime?"

Ella looked at her, crossing her arms. "I thought we were alternating questions. That was two for you. Not fair," she said, and Parker laughed out loud.

"That wasn't fair, was it? Sorry. You ask me a question," she said as she placed the hand that wasn't holding Ella's over the back of the swing.

Ella was trying to keep things light, but with the alcohol flowing through her system, she wanted to go ahead and shoot her shot. "If you're really interested in dinner, could I get your number?" she said, with a confidence she didn't really feel inside.

Parker clapped her hands together and thrust her fists into the air. "Yes, you can have my number! See, that's where I wanted this whole conversation to go, and you just cut to the chase with your first question," she said, pulling a Sharpie out of her pocket and leaning toward Ella. She took her hand again and pushed up the sleeve of her sweater while looking to her for permission.

Ella sat forward and leaned toward her to give her better access, putting their faces mere inches from each other.

Parker uncapped the marker and started to write, but she couldn't tear her eyes away from Ella's. "I have my next question ready," Parker said as she looked at Ella, who licked her lips nervously.

"Go ahead," she said as Parker finished writing and capped the pen before tracing a feather-light fingertip along her arm all the way up to her jawline.

"Could I kiss you?" she said softly as Ella's eyes went wide.

Yes. Yes! That's the answer! The only answer, right? But she didn't even know Parker. Did she want to move this fast? Suddenly, that last drink kicked in and sent her reeling. "Wow, okay. Let's just take a second here," Ella said as she sat back. The world was full-on spinning now. She looked down to see that the drink was almost gone. How long had they been out here? It couldn't have been long. She put the glass on the table, almost dropping it before righting it again. She put her head in her hands and leaned forward.

"Hey, are you okay?" Parker said, leaning up to place a hand on her forearm. "Do you need some water? Hey, wait, whoa, hang on," she continued as Ella started to freak out.

"So, here's the deal. I've had way too much to drink and very little food. I just want to get home and go to bed, but I need to go say goodbye to my friend. What's her name again?" Ella said as she used Parker's hand to ground herself.

"Wait, hang on. Ella, wait, I'll help you," she said, standing up as Ella struggled to her feet before swaying back and forth. "I've got you. Just hold on to me. You're good," she continued, guiding Ella's arms around her.

"You're pretty. This is nice," Ella said, smiling into her hair.

Parker couldn't suppress a giggle. "Just hang on to me," she said. "Hey, do you need me to go get your friend? You really don't remember her name?"

Ella mumbled, "Nope. First date. But we're friends, so it's okay."

Parker raised an eyebrow, but she knew she wasn't going to get the answers she was looking for. Then, she yelled across the patio. "Robert, do me a favor and go in the back and get my keys. Tell Danny I'm having to cut out early."

Her co-worker eyed her with suspicion. "Oh, you know he's going to be pissed at you, cutting out on a Friday to bed some girl," Robert said.

Parker stared blankly at him and indicated Ella in her arms. "Yeah, that's what I am doing, Rob," she said sarcastically. "Gonna take her back to my apartment and fuck her silly while she tries to maintain consciousness and not throw up on my bed. Just go get my shit, please. I'll call Danny tomorrow myself, but I can't leave her alone. Too many creeps in the world nowadays."

"Oh yeah, you're a regular hero, P. But hang on, I'll get your stuff," Robert said.

"Do you need to sit down?" Parker said as she caressed Ella's back, praying she didn't pass out. Ella sighed against her and began to move slowly to the music.

"No, wanna dance," she said, and Parker couldn't help but laugh again.

"Okay, we'll dance till Rob gets back. Then you have to tell me where you live so I can take you home," she said. Ella hummed into her shoulder.

Despite the less than stellar situation, Parker did notice Ella's perfume: light and airy with notes of sandalwood and something fruity. Was it peach? She couldn't help but realize how well their bodies fit together and how attracted she was to this woman she just met as she fought to keep Ella on her feet and slow dancing to the music. There was nothing more obstinate than a drunk person who didn't want to move. And after additional evaluation, Ella had hit the sloppy phase for sure. There was no way she would let her sit down again.

When Robert returned with Parker's belongings, she was able to shuffle Ella to her side so they could walk. She draped Ella's arm over her shoulder while placing her arm solidly around her waist for support.

"Here we go. Let's get to my car and I'll take you home," she said and encouraged Ella to start walking.

Despite the swaying and drunken pace, they made it to the vehicle. Parker propped her against the rear passenger door, pressing her body to Ella's to stop her from sliding down while she worked on opening the door. Ella threw her arms around her neck and pressed their foreheads together.

"Do you still want that kiss," she drawled, mere millimeters from her mouth. Parker swallowed hard at the proximity, but she wasn't the type of girl who would take advantage of anyone.

"Well sure, but let's do that when we drop you off at your house, all right?" she said, as she disentangled herself from Ella and helped her slide into the passenger seat. She got the door shut and walked over to the driver's side before taking a deep breath to steady herself. This is not at all where she imagined the night would go. She opened her door, sat down, and started the car.

"Where to?" she said to Ella who sat with her eyes shut and a small smile on her lips. On her beautiful lips. But that was for another day. Tonight was just about making sure this woman made it home safe and sound. She did feel at least somewhat responsible for the state she was in now.

Ella opened her eyes and turned to her. "I don't know my address. I just moved, and I've had a lot to drink," she slurred.

Well, what next? "Let's see your phone. Maybe we can get in touch with someone who knows it and can help us," she said as she picked up the iPhone tucked between Ella's legs. It wasn't password protected. That was good. She looked at the most recent text message conversation. *'Love you, sweetheart. Have a good weekend.'* That was to Anna. Was Ella already dating someone? A question for another day.

"Hey, so apparently you and Anna know each other well. Can I ask her for your address?" she said.

That drew Ella out of her stupor as she grabbed the phone, looking panicked. "No, no you can't call her," she said as her eyes welled up with tears. Parker was at a loss. Tears started to stream down her face now, and Ella sobbed into her hands. Maybe this was an ex? Either way, Parker wasn't going to pry tonight.

"How about I just take you back to my place? You can sleep it off, and I'll get you back to yours tomorrow," she said. Ella looked up then, eyes full of gratitude as she calmed. *Good job, Parker, we now have a plan.*

"Put your seatbelt on, darling," she said, shaking her head and smiling to herself. Ella clicked herself in place and Parker started out of the parking lot.

Chapter 4

In all of Parker Chase's life, she would never have expected this situation. First, running into one of the most beautiful, captivating women she had ever met on a random night at the bar. Then, taking said beauty back to her place, but not for any sort of fun-time activities. She knew that Rob probably didn't believe that she was helping Ella and not bedding her. Her glowing reputation and all that. As she looked over at the willowy, alluring blonde sitting in her passenger seat, she felt a sense of diversion from her usual intentions when leaving the bar with a woman. She felt protective.

Ella radiated an energy that seemed to mesh with her own. It was comfortable and enticing in equal parts, like they had known each other for years. But Parker didn't believe in love or romance, not for herself anyway. Still, she couldn't stop herself from sneaking glimpses at Ella during the drive.

"We're here," Parker said, pulling into her assigned parking space at the apartment complex. "How are you feeling? Ella?"

The ride home had been in companionable silence with Parker contemplating the interesting turn of events and Ella drifting in and out of sleep. Ella opened her eyes, turned to her, and smiled. "Yeah, I'm good, thanks," she said.

Parker nodded, got out of the car, and walked over to the passenger side. She opened the door, and Ella clumsily turned herself to get her feet on the ground so Parker could assist with her exit. She laughed as Parker held her up, allowing her to find her balance before they moved toward the apartment. Thank goodness it was a ground-floor garden apartment because she was not sure Ella could make it up a flight of stairs. Parker unlocked the door and helped her over to the couch. Once Ella was settled and comfortable, she secured two ibuprofen tablets from a bottle in the kitchen cabinet and a bottle of water from the fridge before heading back to check to see how Ella was doing.

"Hey, you should take these and drink as much of this as you can," she said, handing her the hangover-prevention accoutrements. Ella placed the small pills in her mouth and drank from the bottle as if on autopilot. That's good. Hopefully, she won't feel like absolute hell tomorrow. "Do you need to eat something? You said you hadn't eaten much today. I have some leftover pizza. It's just from yesterday, so it's still fine. I can also make some noodles if you want?"

Ella looked up confused, before nodding in understanding. "Sure, a piece of pizza would be great. And cold is fine, you don't have to heat it up."

Parker smiled and repeated the cute hand signal from the bar, indicating she should continue drinking the water. Ella smiled and took another large drink before pointing again at her bottle and nodding, just as she had in response to her. Now, that was precious. She retrieved a piece of pizza and put it in a paper towel before bringing it back to Ella, who was resting her head on the back of the sofa and sipping the water. She sat down next to her and handed over the slice. "Here you go. It's pepperoni and mushrooms. You're not a vegetarian, are you?"

Ella took the pizza and hummed into a bite. "Nope. Happily carnivorous." She smiled and winked at Parker, making her heart skip a beat.

"Good to know. That's good info for our second date," Parker said, returning the wink. Ella wrinkled her nose and finished chewing the second bite.

"You don't need to do that overt flirting thing. Your tone changes completely. I prefer real Parker. Nice Parker. The Parker who takes someone home because she's drunk off her ass and she doesn't want to leave her alone. Gallant Parker. A Parker-in-shining-armor," she said, chuckling to herself. Then, she reached out to take Parker's hand. "Thank you so much, by the way. I can't remember if I have said it already. So, just thank you."

Parker looked down at their connected hands, and there was that spark again. It was like tangible light arcing between their fingers. "Oh, no, hey, it's okay. I would hope anyone would do that for someone else. I mean, you hear horror stories about people leaving their friends. I just wanted to make sure you're safe. Do I need to call anyone and let them know you're here?"

Ella frowned as she took another drink of water, exhausting the bottle of its contents. "Look, I did it!" Ella high-fived herself, and Parker couldn't help but laugh as she got up to retrieve a second bottle. Opening the refrigerator door, she made up her mind to press a bit.

"So, are you sure that Anna won't miss you tonight?" Parker took the drink, shut the door, and went back to sit next to Ella who now looked a little pale. "Listen, I'm sorry. I shouldn't be pushy. You just kind of get nervous each time I mention her name, and I want to make sure that your bodybuilder girlfriend isn't going to show up here tomorrow looking for a fight because you stayed at my place," Parker said, nudging her shoulder.

Ella sighed and put down the remainder of the pizza. She turned to face Parker and paused a moment before making her revelation. "Anna is my daughter. She's with her father this weekend so she won't be expecting me home. This is my first time going out after my divorce." Ella searched her face for any sort of reaction.

Parker raised her eyebrows. Now, this was unexpected. She didn't date women with kids. But what she did with the women she brought home wasn't exactly considered dating, either. She was always upfront with women she spent time with, and moms didn't stay over. This could be a wrench in the works. But Parker knew there was something special between them from the first time she looked into Ella's seafoam eyes, and she wasn't ready to write her off just yet. "Oh, that makes sense. Well, I guess it's a good thing I didn't call, huh?" Parker said with a smile, trying to keep the mood light. No reason to try to have any real heavy conversations right now. Ella yawned and set the remains of the pizza down on the coffee table.

"I'm going to change into my pajamas. You can take my room tonight, and I'll sleep out here on the couch. It's super comfy."

Ella smiled in response and mumbled a thank you before stifling another yawn. Parker retreated to her room to locate a simple pair of black cotton sleep pants and a white tank top. She dug out a faded gray T-shirt and a pair of yoga pants for Ella, tucking them under her arm and returning to the living room. "Here you go," she said, handing the comfy clothes over. "I'm going to go to the bathroom and do my nightly routine. The bedroom is just down the hallway on the left." Ella stood and took the clothes while Parker headed to change in the bathroom. It is important to give a lady her privacy.

"A kid?" Parker looked at herself in the mirror, cursing her luck. She wasn't ready to play stepmom to a rugrat, that was for sure. But there was just *something* indescribable about this woman she couldn't put her finger on. Parker was getting ahead of herself and thinking way too many deep thoughts for a first meeting. She would just let things play out and see where things went organically.

Parker opened the bathroom door and headed over to her bedroom to tell Ella good night and see if she needed anything. The room was empty. Perplexed, she turned to go back to the living room. Ella sat asleep on the couch with Parker's clothes draped across her knee. Parker smiled to herself. Ella looked peaceful sitting there, but she wouldn't feel very good in the morning having slept sitting up all night. Parker guided Ella down onto the couch, her body tingling every time their skin came into contact. She placed a pillow under her head and picked up her legs to position them in a more natural position for sleep. Ella mumbled another thank you from Dreamland. Parker smiled and shook her head before taking off Ella's shoes for her and placing them on the floor in front of her. She pulled a comfy sherpa blanket from the back of the sofa and draped it over Ella, who sighed contentedly. Parker then took her phone from the arm of the coach and placed it on the coffee table so she could find it when she woke up. She paused and looked at the moonlight spilling over Ella's forehead. Parker couldn't stop herself from tucking a few errant strands of hair behind Ella's ear or from bending over to kiss her forehead before retreating to her own room, hoping for an easy night's sleep.

Chapter 5

Ella woke up the next morning to some rude sunlight blasting her right in the face. All she was doing was trying to sleep, and Mother Nature just wasn't playing fair. Her neck felt sore, and her joints were stiffer than she was used to. She opened her eyes, looked around, and realized she had no clue where she was.

Ella sat up with a start and looked around, thinking hard. How drunk was she the night before? The good news is she was on someone's couch, so she hadn't had an intoxicated one-night stand. Ella found her phone on a small glass coffee table in front of her, and her shoes were placed under its edge. She also realized she had been tucked in with a nice, warm blanket over her. She leaned her head into her hands and rubbed at her face and head, trying to get her brain to work. That's when she noticed the pizza crust and empty bottle of water, and something clicked.

Parker. She was on Parker's couch. There was a lot she didn't remember, but she did remember that Parker left her job early, taking her back to her own apartment since Ella couldn't remember her new address. She also remembered Danna's damning words about Parker's reputation, but she couldn't be all bad, right? It took a decent person to make sure a perfect stranger had a safe place to crash after getting drunk off her ass.

Ella didn't hear any movement and had no idea where Parker's bedroom was. She checked the time. Ten-fifteen. She wasn't used to sleeping in. She kept teachers' hours on the weekends as well and was used to getting up before the sun rose. But she was also used to getting in bed at a decent hour and not consuming enough vodka to drop a horse, if horses drink vodka, that is. She would have to Google that later when her brain was functioning.

Ella turned her phone on and saw she had multiple texts from her new gay best friend.

Danna, 1:04 a.m.: "Hey, are you good? You and Parker have been gone for a long time and her break was over 15 minutes ago. Maybe you guys rode off into the sunset together. If so, I'm super happy for you. But just check in, okay?"

Danna, 1:16 a.m.: "I checked with Robert, and he said you were sick, and Parker took you home. Hopefully you aren't sick, and you scored! But, just in case, drink lots of water and call me tomorrow to tell me about it. Glad you're safe and I'm so glad we met and hung out!"

Danna had real bestie potential. Ella needed more gay friends, anyway. She decided to shoot her a quick text.

Ella, 10:11 a.m.: "I'm fine, thanks for checking. I don't remember a lot. I woke up on Parker's couch, so I feel fairly assured my lesbian virginity is still intact. It looks like she was a perfect gentlewoman. She even set me up with some food, water, and ibuprofen before I went to sleep."

She checked for a text or message from AJ but found none. Upon placing her phone down, she heard her text notification go off again.

Danna, 10:12 a.m.: "Wow, that's really sweet. Let me know if you need a ride home or if you plan to stay over again…for other reasons."

Ella half-snorted, half-laughed at the suggestion. No one likes to babysit a drunk. She was sure she'd ruined any chance she might have had with Parker with her behavior the previous night.

Ella, 10:14 a.m.: "I'm sure she will want nothing to do with the pile of embarrassment that is me. I'm going to go find her and thank her before I call an Uber to come get me. Thanks for the offer of a ride, though. We must hang out again soon."

Danna responded with a .gif of a cartoon cat humping the air that caught her by surprise, and she barked out a laugh before she could stop herself.

"What's so funny?"

Ella looked up to see a sleep-tousled Parker leaning against the door jamb in the entrance to the living room. She stood up, startled, before thinking the move through. It ended up being a bad decision, and the room took a quick lurch before she could gain her equilibrium. She closed her eyes and put out her hands to steady herself against, well, nothing, but that worked well enough. She opened them again and could not stop herself from staring. Even having just gotten out of bed and still wearing her pajamas, Ella found Parker to be the most beautiful creature she had ever seen. "Hey, so, oh! Nothing, just a funny thing my friend sent me," Ella stumbled.

"Is this the same friend who you had your first date with last night whose name you couldn't remember?" Parker teased, crossing her arms.

Ella chuckled. "That would be her. But I remember her name now. Danna. See, I'm a good first date," she said before looking around, trying to think of something to make the moment less uncomfortable.

"Well, that's good information to have," Parker said, moving toward her small kitchen. "Would you like some breakfast? I've got eggs and toast. Or you can have more cold pizza if you want," she chided.

Ella evaluated her stomach's current state and sensing all systems were go, decided food was a good idea. "Sure, eggs would be great. Can I help?"

Parker already had the fridge open, pulling out an awful lot of ingredients for simple scrambled eggs and toast. "You're welcome to sit at the bar and keep me company if you want, but I figure if I'm trying to earn an actual date here, I need to show you I can cook a mean breakfast for the morning after," she said, standing up with arms full of what looked like fresh herbs and heavy cream.

Ella choked on the water she had been sipping, and Parker giggled, satisfied her words had the desired effect. "Yeah, you have to stop doing that while I am drinking. I'm starting to get back memories from last night, and you need to work on your timing if we're going to continue this friendship. Otherwise, you might cause me to choke to death."

Parker looked at her, confused. "No one said I wanted to be your friend," she said, straight-faced. Ella gulped. Parker broke her grave façade, belly-laughing at her face, which was as red as a stop sign. "It's just too easy to mess with you, even when you're not drinking. I like it," she said, cracking eggs into a mixing bowl before adding the cream. She then grabbed a cutting board and a sharp-looking knife out of the dish drainer and commenced chopping the herbs.

Ella opted to change the subject to something of a slower pace while her brain completed the waking-up process. "That looks wonderful. But I must ask you, is there coffee? See, I'm generally not someone you want to be around until I have had my coffee," she said.

Parker pointed to a cupboard with a knife. "Yeah, I know what you mean. Do you mind setting it up? I'm a little indisposed here," she said, holding up herby fingers.

Ella gave two thumbs-up and headed into the tight space. She pulled down the coffee, expecting something off a grocery store shelf. But this was a single-origin French Roast out of Guatemala. She looked at Parker with confused surprise.

Parker looked up and shrugged. "I like good coffee."

Without thinking about the implications, Ella said the first thing that came to her mind. "I could kiss you right now." She sat the coffee down, placing her hands on the counter in front of her and lowered her head in embarrassment.

Parker didn't laugh this time. "Well, you do still kind of owe me from last night anyway. But we can have breakfast first."

Ella half-exhaled, half-laughed before turning to look at her. Parker was smiling, but it was the real smile she remembered from last night, the one that lit up her eyes with honesty and sincerity. Ella couldn't stop herself from returning the smile, before returning to the coffee situation.

They fell into easy conversation over the next few minutes as Ella mixed their coffee with cream and sugar, and Parker produced some delicious-looking creamy eggs on toast with chives, field garlic, and goat cheese. They each took a plate and moved back to the bar side of the counter, taking up residence on the stools. Parker seemed to be waiting for her to take a bite before eating. Since there was no silverware provided, she picked up a piece of toast and looked at Parker with eyebrows raised in question. She nodded, and Ella dove in. Flavors poured over her palate as the herbaceous notes were forward, but not overpowering. The goat cheese was creamy and tart, and the toast cut the richness of everything in perfect balance.

"Oh my God, Parker, this is amazing," she said with her hand over her mouth.

Parker grinned back at her, and it lit up the room. Ella took another large bite, and a small bit of scrambled egg fell, sticking just under her lower lip. Parker looked contemplatively at her while Ella finished chewing, oblivious. When she noticed the change in Parker's expression, she paused with her mouth open in front of the toast.

"You have a..." Parker reached up as she trailed off. Ella furrowed her brow in confusion as Parker swiped her thumb across her lower lip to remove the bit of food there. Ella's breath hitched at the tender touch, but then she realized what had just happened: Parker had wiped eggs off her face. She lowered the toast and closed her eyes for a moment. When she opened them again, her words caught in her throat as she realized Parker hadn't removed her hand. She now placed her thumb across her lips, shushing her. Ella swallowed hard.

Parker reached to take her hand again, pulling her slowly toward that gorgeous mouth. This was happening, here in the middle of scrambled eggs and toast. Granted, they were amazing scrambled eggs. Fucking Gordon Ramsey-level scrambled eggs. But could eggs be sexy? Ella couldn't wait to find out as she leaned in to meet her.

Parker's pillowy lips were as soft as they looked. She lingered for just a few moments in a chaste brushing of lips before pulling back. Parker looked satisfied while Ella felt lightheaded, and not from the remnants of alcohol this time.

"I just felt like the rest of this morning would be more productive if we just got that out of the way," she offered in simple explanation.

"More productive and less reproductive?" Ella said, blushing. Parker laughed out loud at the quip, shaking her head while looking into her eyes.

"Yes, something like that for sure," she said, before sobering. She pushed her plate back and turned to face Ella fully.

"Listen, I don't know what's going on here," she continued, motioning between them. "But I always go with my intuition about people. When you came through my line last night, you looked up from your phone and I just..." Parker paused, shaking her head, looking for words. "I don't know. You were so charming and beautiful, and I felt this immediate connection to you. I'm sorry if I am scaring you, but I have to say what's on my mind and in my heart," she said, shrugging. "I probably would have left work early if anyone I was spending time with got super drunk. But, I feel like I would have left with you before that if you had just asked. I know this is crazy, but I'm hoping that maybe you feel the same way," she said, the last word sounding more like a question. "I'm sorry. I know we don't know each other well. I'm just saying, I really want to," she said as she blushed and looked down.

  Ella raised Parker's chin with her finger. She looked into those dark brown eyes and found no dishonesty. Parker looked vulnerable and open. "I—yes, I did feel drawn to you from the start. I am all about getting to know you," Ella said, smiling. "I probably know less than you because you were sober last night, and I was less than..." She trailed off. Parker scoffed and nodded. "I do feel something. It's almost like a physical pull. But I don't know if it's just physical because, look at you. You are the most beautiful woman I have ever seen," Ella said. They both blushed at that one. "I'm just so new to this dating thing. I don't feel like I know what I'm doing," Ella said and picked up her breakfast, taking a big bite.

Parker's brow furrowed. "What do you mean you're new to dating? You have a kid, right? Do you mean you're new to dating women?"

Ella nodded as she swallowed more food. "You're right, we really do need to get to know each other," she said, smiling up at Parker who looked genuinely confused.

"We do," Parker said, putting her finger to her lips before taking a bite of her own food and chewing. "You know what's perfect for that?" Ella's eyes widened expectantly. "I think we have about eighteen or so questions left over from last night that will point us in the right direction," Parker said. Ella smiled and nodded.

"Do you want to spend the day with me? I mean, I know that's sudden, but I am free all day. On a normal day, I'd be sleeping off a full night of bartending. But look at me, being all awake and vertical," Parker said with another of those dazzling smiles.

Ella paused to think if she had anything to do and decided, with AJ at her dad's house, she was free. And she did want to see where this could go. "Yeah, that sounds like a lot of fun. Let me just call a taxi and go home and shower and change and then we can hang out for sure," Ella said, taking another bite of breakfast.

Parker's countenance dimmed. "Don't go," she said, barely audible. "I feel like something magical is happening here, and it's almost like you'll break the spell if you go."

Ella swallowed and took a gulp of coffee to wash down the food. "No, don't think like that. I promise I won't be more than a few hours. Besides, I'm feeling kind of grungy in last night's clothes. And my teeth are furry," Ella said, running her tongue over her teeth and grimacing.

Parker looked contemplative before having an obvious *a-ha* moment. "Hey, you could shower here. I have great water pressure and lots of hot water. And then you can borrow something of mine to wear," she said, nodding to herself, having decided.

Ella didn't want to leave, believing there could be something to this magical feeling they were sharing. It was like their pasts didn't matter right now. They were the only two people alive in the bubble of safety that was Parker's apartment. But wearing someone's clothes seemed intimate. Was it too intimate? They had spent less than twelve hours together. Ella made her decision on the fly, going on instinct instead of what would normally seem proper.

"Okay," she said, and Parker executed an overexaggerated fist pump. "Settle down, Jersey Shore," Ella said, and Parker smiled, throwing her arms around her neck, almost knocking her off the stool. Once Ella recovered, she returned the embrace, running the flats of both palms up and down the length of Parker's back. She inhaled and exhaled slowly, enjoying the scent of her hair and not wanting it to leave her lungs.

Parker pulled back with a start. "I didn't even think, but you have a kid, right? Do you need to head home for him? Her? Them? Is there more than one?" she said, not giving Ella time to respond to a question before firing another at her.

"Just the one. Anna Jean. She goes by AJ. Again, she's with her father this weekend, so the short answer is no, I don't need to go home for her."

Parker squealed and jumped off her stool to run to what Ella assumed was her bedroom. Ella shrugged and took the few minutes she was gone to gobble down at the last bit of her breakfast. She returned a few minutes later with a well-worn pair of workout pants, socks, T-shirt, and…underwear? The thought of wearing the panties of a woman she just met was equal parts terrifying and titillating, she had to admit.

Ella saw that the shirt had a band logo and held it up to see it was a picture of Nirvana's final album. Her heart skipped a beat. Parker was a Nirvana fan? "Oh…my…God," she said, pausing between each word. "Please tell me this is not a fluke. Please tell me you like this band," Ella said, looking at Parker expectantly.

Parker looked confused. "Oh wait, is this a band? I just thought the shirt was cool."

Ella's heart dropped. Working with teenagers for a living, it was not unusual to see them wearing Pink Floyd and Metallica shirts because they were fashionable. She closed her eyes and made a broken heart gesture with her hands.

Parker poked her in the ribs, and she opened her eyes. "I'm just kidding. Yes, I love them. I like lots of different music from that time period. Do you like them?" Ella nodded vehemently, and Parker smiled. "Well, that's cool. I'll have to let you listen to some stuff I've been working on. I am a DJ and I have been redoing several popular grunge songs. I layer the original over a dance beat so it's something people can move to at a club. I've put together about an hour-long track, and The Paper Tiger will be debuting it soon."

Ella frowned. "Who is The Paper Tiger, or what is The Paper Tiger?"

"It's another gay bar, maybe an hour from here."

Ella formed her lips into an 'o' in recognition. "I haven't heard of it. I knew Sparkle was our only local gay bar. I just didn't think to look for others."

Parker nodded. "Yeah, I didn't want to debut at Sparkle just because that's where I work. I wanted a fresh crowd so I can get an honest reaction. I mean, it could be total shit. I have a lot of friends at my job, and I worry that people would just tell me what I want to hear rather than hurt my feelings. I didn't want it to be that way."

"That makes sense," Ella said, just picking up on her use of *debut*. "When is it? I'd love to come out and support you, if you want me to. I can get Danna and her friends to come out, too. It will be an event!" Parker nodded, but her eyes belied the sadness she was trying to cover up. "Hey, what's up?" Ella said, tucking a lock of hair behind Parker's ear. She looked up at the touch, and Ella could see there were tears in her eyes. "Talk to me. What's wrong?"

Parker swiped at her eyes before shaking her head and forcing out a laugh. "I would love for my parents to come, but I don't think they would. They don't like what I do. I was supposed to be an amazing athlete like my dad or great with numbers like my mom, but I ended up one of those artsy kids. I tried, though. I guess I'm kind of the black sheep of the family, even though I've never been in any trouble. My younger sister is an amazing athlete and a math whiz, so she ticks their boxes. And it's not like they don't love me. They didn't even care when I came out, but wanting to be a musician or music teacher doesn't sit well with them. They feel like it is all a waste of time and stopped paying for college. That's why I got the job at the bar to support myself while I work on my degree. And they hate that I work at a bar." She stopped and sighed with the weight of parental disapproval on her chest before continuing. "I still talk to them. I go over for dinner sometimes. It just isn't the same." Parker shrugged to show she was finished.

Ella, who had always made sure she supported AJ in whatever she wanted to do as long as she was happy and healthy, felt defensive of Parker. "Wow, that is shitty of them. I just don't get parents who try to impose their lives on their kids. Just because your parents are who they are, doesn't mean you shouldn't get to be who you are, even if that doesn't coincide with what they want for you."

Parker nodded solemnly, picking at a hangnail. Ella picked up her hand and placed a kiss there like it was the most natural thing in the world. Parker looked up to meet her gaze, brightening a bit. "I have a big group of friends, chosen family. It would just be nice to have support from my actual family," she said.

Ella nodded in understanding. "I get that. It was a similar situation with me when I got pregnant with AJ. I was only seventeen, so it took both my and my husband's families working together to make it work. I put in the work, though. I got through with my degree and teaching certificate in four years. How long did it take you to get yours?"

Parker gritted her teeth. "I'm still working on that. I started college right out of high school, but then I went part-time. I've only recently gone back to a full load, and I'm set to graduate this spring. I fit everything around my job at the bar, so a lot of my time goes to my schoolwork or work-work." Parker shifted the subject matter. "So, AJ. Is she in school yet?"

Ella smiled, unable to hide her pride. "Yes, she's a senior this year."

Parker paused and looked confused. "She's a senior—in high school?" Ella nodded again, eyes not leaving Parker's who remained befuddled. "So, if you had her at seventeen, then you're thirty-four?"

Ella considered Parker's face, which was blank. "I'm thirty-five," Ella said, and Parker's eyes widened for the briefest of moments.

Now, it was Ella's turn to be confused. "Why? How old did you think I was?"

Parker looked amused. "I just want you to know it doesn't matter to me. I love older women! I guessed you were a year or two older than me, maybe twenty-six or twenty-seven."

Ella heard those numbers and was flattered before words started to fall into place like puzzle pieces. *Year or two older than me. Twenty-six or twenty-seven.* She felt dumbstruck, looking at Parker in abject horror. She formed the question in her mind, closed her eyes, and steeled herself for the answer. "How old are you, Parker?"

"I'll be twenty-five in two weeks," she said, shrugging. "But, I mean, age doesn't really matter to me..." Her voice faded to an imperceptible whisper as the only thing Ella could hear was the sound of the blood rushing in her ears. The words rang out through her head, echoing. Twenty-four. Twenty-fucking-four years old. How had she missed this? Were there cues? She leaned her head into her hands as she rested her elbows on the counter.

Parker placed a tentative hand on her back. "Is that going to be a problem?"

Ella choked out a sarcastic laugh before turning to look at her. She had former students who were older than Parker.

"Don't you think it should be? You're closer in age to my daughter than you are to me. This is the definition of robbing the cradle. My damn picture would be in the dictionary right next to the words," she said, returning her head to her hands.

"It doesn't have to be a big deal if we don't want it to be," Parker said, and Ella looked at her incredulously.

"Parker, come on. You're six years older than my kid."

Parker cut her off. "Almost seven. Remember, two more weeks?" She held up two fingers, grasping at straws.

Ella scoffed. "That's still a lot of years. I just…" All she could do was continue to shake her head. Parker reached out to take her hand but pulled back at the last moment. It felt different now, like waking up from the sweetest dream and crashing back to reality.

"Just focus on what you feel and not what you think. That's what we have been doing this whole time, right? It's all going to be okay. We'll just spend the day together and talk and—"

Ella shook her head and looked up into Parker's eyes. "I can't. I mean, I need to just evaluate this," she said, pulling her hand away and standing up.

Parker looked distraught. "Just go take your shower and put on clean clothes and you'll feel better. We can just watch a movie together. We don't even have to talk about anything. No pressure. Just, stay, okay? Don't go," Parker said.

But Ella was already gathering her few things together and texting Danna to see if the offer of a ride was still available. She responded with question marks, but said she was willing. She just needed Parker's address. Ella cringed at the thought of having to ask her. "What's your address? Danna is going to come pick me up." Parker looked hurt, but Ella felt like she couldn't breathe. Finding out Parker was eleven years her junior had sucked up all the oxygen in the room.

"Can we talk about this?" she said while staring at her shoes. When Ella looked at her expectantly, she relented. "331 Greenwood Drive, Apartment 3," she said, wrapping her arms around herself. Ella typed the information, and Danna responded that she would be there in ten minutes.

Parker turned to busy herself picking up Ella's discarded water bottle and pizza crust from the night before and straightening the blanket over the back of the couch. Ella moved to help her. "No, I've got it. Thanks," Parker said, not looking at her. Warm energy that had flowed so easily between them just moments ago was gone, replaced with what felt a lot like nothingness.

"Parker, I'm sorry. I need to think. This doesn't mean we can't be friends, I just," she sighed heavily again, "I just need to think."

Parker nodded but didn't look up. "I'm going to go hang out in my room. You have my number. Just let me know when you're finished thinking so we can get back to discovering whatever this," she made an all-encompassing motion between them, "could be." And with that, she left the room. Ella heard her close a door down the hallway while feeling a door close around Parker's heart at the same time.

Chapter 6

"What the actual fuck, Danna?" Ella whined as she got into her friend's car.

Danna stared back, perplexed. "What? What happened?" she said, reversing the car out of the parking space in front of Parker's apartment. "Is everything okay?"

Ella rubbed her face and laughed harshly. Did she give off the vibe that she would enjoy a relationship with someone so much younger than her? What did she wear the night before that screamed 'cougar'? "Well, *okay* may be a stretch. Why wouldn't you tell me she's twenty-four? I have a seventeen-year-old daughter."

Danna's mouth dropped open. "I had no idea how old she was or your age preferences. I'm so sorry. Did you sleep with her?"

Ella looked at her through eyes that were nothing more than slits. "No, of course not. She just…" Ella trailed off before gathering her thoughts. "She just took me back to her house and took care of me."

"Oh yeah, that sounds fucking terrible," Danna said as she pulled out of the complex onto the main road. She was trying to make a joke, but Ella, who wasn't having any of it, continued.

"Then we woke up this morning and she made me breakfast. I felt so…alive for the first time in my life. There is this almost magnetic pull between us. She kissed me and we were going to spend the day together, but I just can't," Ella said, placing her head between her hands.

Danna raised an eyebrow. "It sounds like you guys had a pretty amazing connection, one of those love at first sight things you read about in those romance novels." Danna paused when Ella said nothing but opted to continue. "Is age really that big of a deal to you? Would you throw away a potential connection for a number? Remember what Aaliyah said." Ella turned to look at her, one eyebrow raised. "You know? About age not mattering? Did you not ever hear that song?" she said with a chuckle. When Ella didn't laugh, Danna sighed. "It was funny in my head," she said to lighten the mood.

Ella gave her some more side-eye. "Yeah, that analogy makes me feel like a groomer. Not helpful at all." Ella closed her eyes and sighed again. "She's just a child," Ella began, but Danna knitted her eyebrows together.

"That's not fair, Ella. She made an impression on you before you knew how old she was. She's a perfectly legal adult."

Ella shrugged and nodded. "You're right, that's not fair. But, no, there's no way I can date someone who wasn't even born in the same decade." Ella sighed and sank back into the car seat.

Danna nodded. "You're the one who knows what you want. Just be honest with her. Any girl deserves that," Danna said as they pulled into her driveway.

"Thanks so much for the ride. I owe you one," she said, getting out of the car.

Danna just smiled at her. "Next time we go out, you get to play designated driver!" Ella gave her a thumbs-up as she shut the door and turned around to walk inside her house.

～

Narcissus greeted her, *hangrily*. "Sorry, buddy, but I did put down some extra kibble for you. It's not my fault if you ate it all in the first ten minutes after I left," she said, scooping food into his bowl and scratching him behind the ear.

After showering off the remnants of the previous night, she changed into comfy workout pants and a worn sweatshirt from her high school volleyball days. She sat down on her bed to plug in her phone before resigning to herself that she should speak to Parker. There was no reason for her to run out of her apartment like she did. Well, other than the massive freakout.

What could she say, though? The idea of dating someone so much younger made her so uncomfortable, despite their initial spark. Ella thought about introducing Parker to Alex or AJ, trying to imagine what their reactions might be. All in all, she understood it didn't really matter what other people thought, but she just wasn't ready to deal with that kind of judgment from her family or anyone else. She pulled up the sleeve of her shirt and saw Parker's number from the night before.

Ella, 12:01 p.m.: "I'm sorry to have left like that. Can we talk?"

At this point, she was just hoping for a response, realizing Parker may not be speaking to her again after the way she left. When no notification came, she started to organize laundry into different piles. After sorting the whites and the darks, her phone pinged indicating a message.

Parker, 12:14 p.m.: "Sure. Just text me, though. I can't talk right now."

Ella received the response and nodded to herself. This might be better. Easier. Things were charged when she left and just typing to one another could take the potential for heavy emotions away.

Ella, 12:15 p.m.: "That's fine. I've got a lot to say, and I hate those people who text fifty times to say something instead of typing it all out at once. So, give me a minute to get all this down."

But, before she typed more than a few sentences, Parker sent another message.

Parker, 12:17 p.m.: "Just give me a few and I'll call you if that would be better?"

Oh well, no hiding behind the screen now. Talking to Parker wouldn't be the easiest thing, but if Ella wanted to build this friendship, she needed to be as honest as possible. She put her phone down and walked around the living room practicing what she wanted to make sure that Parker got to hear. Why was this so hard? This is someone she just met. But she couldn't stop thinking about Parker's eyes; so exuberant when Ella agreed to stay for the day and acknowledged she felt the same way and then so emotionless when Ella shut down and fled. She didn't want to think of them so turned off.

When the phone rang about ten minutes later, Ella readied herself for the conversation ahead by taking a deep breath and letting it out slowly before answering.

"Parker, hi."

"Hey," Parker said in a quiet voice. She offered nothing more, so Ella continued.

"So, how are you?" Ella closed her eyes and mouthed *stupid* when Parker didn't immediately respond.

"I've been better." Still flat and toneless, Parker conceded nothing. "What did you want to talk about, Ella?" She didn't sound angry, but low.

"I just, I hope you understand where I'm coming from. I can't just discount our age difference. I could have taught you in school. Wait, I didn't teach you in school, did I?" Horror filled Ella's voice at the idea.

Parker scoffed. "No, my family and I just moved here a little over a year ago. So, there's no chance of that."

Ella's relief was palpable. "Well, okay, good. That would have been uncomfortable, right?" Again, no response from Parker. Ella had to figure out another direction. She sighed deeply before continuing. "I still want to get to know you, and I really want us to be friends. Is that a possibility?" With no immediate response again, she checked the screen to make sure Parker was still on the line.

"Just clarify some things for me," Parker said, letting it hang in the air before Ella consented. "Once you found out my age, did the connection go away for you? Did you start feeling differently about me? Is this a decision you made with your heart or your head?"

Ella opened her mouth to answer, but the words froze in her throat. It would be easy to tell Parker that she felt differently in her heart, but she didn't want to lie. She did nothing to deserve dishonesty. Ella sighed. "Of course, it's a head decision. It's different for me, Parker. I have a daughter. It's a big age difference."

"So, if I was, what? Twenty-nine? Thirty? Would I have a chance?"

Ella thought back to her online dating profile and remembered the age range she chose for her ideal match and winced. "On my online dating profile, I asked to be shown results for women between the ages of twenty-eight and forty-five."

Parker was silent for several long moments. "So basically, you're saying that if I were three years older, you'd give me a chance. But not only that. You're saying you're a hypocrite."

Parker's words stung, but Ella saw what she was getting at and allowed her to continue.

"You're saying you would date someone ten years older than *you*. You must realize it's almost the same amount of time between us. And that's totally hypocritical."

Ella assented in her mind. Parker had her there. There was no real argument that she could present, but that didn't change how she felt.

"All I want is a chance. I can back off the crazy-heavy romantic stuff. We can slow down. I just…just a chance. Can you please come back over? You can drive yourself and you can feel free to leave if you feel uncomfortable in any way. I'm not scared of the fact you have a daughter. I have a sister AJ's age and we get along famously. I'm not scared that you've never been with a woman before. That doesn't bother me at all. I am only scared of you taking yourself away from me and denying what you feel."

Parker's words continued to cut deeply, and in all honesty, Ella fully agreed. On the surface, it was hypocritical. But it didn't change how she felt, what was right in her mind. There was a big difference between twenty-four and thirty-five and thirty-five and forty-five in her mind. She could take a forty-five-year-old to sit next to her at AJ's volleyball games. But what would people say if she brought Parker in her crop tops and tight-fitting pants? Ella knew that's just how she dressed for work. They had already discussed that. Ella would never have guessed she was in her twenties. She just had an air of maturity and worldliness. Parker was an old soul; she was sure of that.

Ella blew out a breath. "Parker…" she said, trailing off. Parker's ensuing huff and reply followed quickly.

"Ella, if you really can't handle this, then just tell me that and I will go. But this is officially the last time I am asking you. I'm not going to beg."

And with that, the ball was totally in her court. She remembered the care that Parker took with her last night, making sure she was comfortable and warm while she slept. She remembered Parker's jokes and the way their senses of humor meshed effortlessly. Most importantly, she remembered the kiss. She remembered how her body felt alive in ways it had never felt before. Could it hurt to just start out as friends and just see where this went? Ella decided to go with her gut. "I'm not going to deny anything I felt. We've already talked about it. I'm not going to lie to you. I wouldn't do that. I honestly do not know how to handle our age difference. But, on the other hand, I have never felt so drawn to anyone before. If you're willing to hang out as friends in a no-pressure environment, I can't think of anything I would rather do." Ella's heart was pounding so hard, she was afraid Parker would hear it through the phone. She heard the immediate shift in Parker's mood in her response.

"Thank you, Ella. All I want is for us to have a chance to get to know each other and hang out. No pressure, though, right? Who can't use more friends?"

"This is true. I'm making all kinds of new friends, apparently," Ella said, remembering the conversation with Danna the night before.

"I'm so glad we talked," Parker said with the utmost sincerity.

"Me too," Ella said. They sat in silence for a beat before saying their goodbyes and moving on with their days.

～

Ella enjoyed her weekends on her own. Of course, she missed AJ, but having her own space for the first time in her life was refreshing. She used the alternate weekends to focus on new and difficult yoga poses and secretly catch up on lesbian movies she had missed over the years. Tonight, she had selected *But, I'm a Cheerleader*, and after tossing together a quick stir-fry over some noodles, she sat down with a beer and put the movie on. It was funny from the start, and she wondered if Danna had seen it. She typed out a text to ask her, but after leaving it unsent, pulled up Parker's number instead.

Ella, 6:31 p.m.: "Have you ever seen But, I'm a Cheerleader?"

Ella, 6:31 p.m.: "Oh, and hi, by the way. I hope your day off has been fun."

She put her phone down, shaking her head, assuming that someone like Parker probably wasn't alone on a Saturday evening. Surprisingly, her phone dinged just a few moments later.

Parker, 6:32 p.m.: "Every real lesbian has seen that movie, Ella. And hi back. My day was very low-key. How about you?"

Ella laughed at Parker's jab.

Ella, 6:33 p.m.: "Just making sure that once I finish the movie, I am an official, card-carrying member of the Lesbian Brigade?"

Parker, 6:34 p.m.: "Well, I think it would be safe to give you a trial membership at that point. But there are several other movies that are must-sees before you become a full-fledged member. And there's a handshake you have to learn. It's kind of a big deal."

Ella laughed again. She realized that she had laughed more in the last twenty-four hours with Parker than she had in as long as she could remember.

Ella, 6:35 p.m.: "Okay Queen Lesbian Guru, send me your list and I'll get on it immediately. I must have that membership. And you can work on teaching me the handshake when we hang out again."

Parker, 6:36 p.m.: "I'll get right on that for you. Gotta go for now, though. I'm getting ready to head out for the night. I hope you have a great one, Ella. I look forward to hanging out again soon. Night-night."

Ella pouted at her phone, actually pouted with her lip out like a petulant child. She could have been the one to hang out with Parker tonight, but *nooooo*, she had to be the logical one. She remembered waking up in her apartment, warm and comfortable because Parker had taken off her shoes, situated her on the couch, and tucked a blanket around her. She remembered Parker making her breakfast and the single, gentle kiss they'd shared. Why did the universe have to send her what seemed to be the perfect woman, just the wrong age? She sighed deeply before typing her response.

Ella, 6:38 p.m.: "I hope you have a great night. Chat soon."

When no response came, she resumed her movie and understood that against her better judgment, their next chat could not come soon enough.

Chapter 7

Parker didn't want to go out tonight, but she was not one to welch on a promise to her friends. After having such an emotionally draining day, she just wanted to work on her music or even just veg out on the couch and catch up on *Wentworth*. Who was she kidding, though? She just wanted to spend this time with Ella.

But that didn't fit the Parker Chase M.O. She didn't fall for women. She didn't desire to spend time with women, outside of the bedroom. She didn't do sleepovers, but Ella had gotten under her skin in basically a matter of minutes, stealing by the walls and towers surrounding her heart and leaving her completely disarmed.

In her almost quarter century on this Earth, Parker had remained detached from people in any sort of romantic context. This is how she liked it. Hooking up. One-night stands. She was a one-and-done kind of girl. She had had multiple opportunities and requests for repeat performances, but she didn't double-dip. It was much easier to keep emotions in check that way.

A few years ago, Parker agreed to a second romp with one of her closest friends. At the time, she thought, why not, because their first encounter was mind-blowing. The second time, however, ended with Amanda begging to reciprocate and making promises of love and affection. Parker was immediately turned off, verging on repulsed, and ended up having to drive the inconsolable girl back to her own place. Their friendship was never the same. It absolutely wasn't happening again.

Parker loved her friends and family, and well, her fans and big tippers at the bar, and had no issues doing so. But something had always felt blocked inside of her at the thought of loving someone amorously. She'd been hurt once, and she planned to make sure it didn't happen again.

Despite all of this, when Ella had texted her to ask her if she had seen a certain movie, her face broke out in an ear-to-ear smile. Ella was stunning, without a doubt. But there was just something warm and inviting about her very aura, comforting and shielding at the same time and so authentic and real.

Ella had no issues with speaking her mind and admitting what she wanted from the first time they met. She called Parker on her front and made her want to be genuine. Ella made Parker feel human, she realized. As someone who had always felt like an outsider, it was like being wrapped up in a blanket on a cold winter's day.

It was things like that which made Parker feel like she was going completely crazy. She didn't even know this woman. And what, she was just totally head over heels? In love?

She shook her head trying to clear a cloud of oppressive thought. Whether she felt like it or not, she needed to get out tonight. She needed lots of alcohol and a pretty, young thing to bring back to her house for some thrills.

Parker messaged Ella back to let her know she would be unavailable for the night, being very clear that she was going out. Hopefully, that would communicate to Ella exactly what type of person she was and maybe she would just go away and take the temptation with her. Yeah, she attempted to convince herself that was what she wanted.

Parker checked her reflection in the mirror, adjusting her outfit and last touches to her makeup. She threw a few punches and a nice, high karate kick, psyching herself up and getting back into her regular mindset.

Come on, P. You've got this. You're going to go out with your friends and meet someone to get your mind off her. She followed with a quick nod as she headed out the door.

"Bitch, you're late!" Rack said, encircling her in his muscular arms and swinging her around outside the club. When she was back on solid ground again, Parker looked around, searching out the rest of their friend group.

Rack's boyfriend Dimitri ran at her full tilt, picking her up and swinging her around as Rack had done just moments ago. This time, when Parker was returned to Earth, she felt a little dizzy.

Rack and Dimitri sported muscle-defining tank tops and jeans and could have been mistaken as brothers if you didn't know any better. They congratulated each other on being able to put Parker on the verge of hurling. It was so fun to have chosen-family big brothers.

Someone kissed and nipped at her neck gently. Parker reached up behind her and grabbed onto Malachi's multicolored dreadlocks before kissing him sweetly on his heavily bearded cheek.

"I was sure you were going to flake out on us tonight," he said, running his hands around her belly and tracing the undersides of her breasts. Parker grabbed his hands and returned them to his sides. She turned around to look into his eyes and found him to already be quite high.

"Hey, Mally, if you're going to take a bunch of E before you come out with us, you still have to maintain enough of your faculties about you to keep your hands to yourself. You're going to grab someone's girlfriend or boyfriend one day and they're gonna kick your ass."

Malachi smiled brightly. "You say that like it's a bad thing," he said, bending over and putting said ass in the air. "Spank me, Daddy! Give it to me, Mommy!" he continued. Parker laughed raucously, but when several passersby scowled at him in his inebriated state, she decided to encourage him to stand up and act right.

"Hey, buddy. Just remember we're still out on the street, not yet in the bar. There's normies out here," Parker said, and he blew a raspberry.

"Has anyone seen Kenna?" Parker said, looking for her friend and the only exception to her one-time only rule. Kenna could sometimes be her part-time lover when both were bored or wanted to share someone new.

Rack and Dimitri pointed across the street. Parker could make out her outline as she stalked toward them.

Makenna was a literal work of art. Her fair skin looked almost translucent in the eerie light along the street. Her long, black hair was braided Viking-style on the sides of her head with the top and the back loose and flowing. She wasn't as tall as Parker, but her thigh-high vinyl stiletto boots evened out the height difference between them. She stalked directly toward

Parker and immediately kissed her fully on the lips. This was often how they greeted one another. Parker kissed her back before Kenna's hand came up to cup her crotch. Parker's eyes shot open, and she jumped back at the unexpected touch.

"You're not packing tonight?" Kenna said with a pouty tone in her voice.

Parker raised one eyebrow in question. "Kenna, when have you ever known me to do that?"

Kenna leaned into her neck and purred. Normally, the kissing and touching were all precursors to the main show, and she loved every moment of it. Tonight, the groping seemed almost intrusive and off-putting. When she took another step back, Kenna looked up at her quizzically. "What's up, P? You know I was just kidding. I know you only strap-on behind closed doors," she said, leaning in close in an attempt to seem alluring.

Parker needed to get out of her own head. There had been many nights when she, Kenna, and sometimes even Malachi would head back to one of their houses with a person or sometimes even a few persons of interest for an entire night of fun. This was how their friend group worked, and Kenna wasn't acting any differently than she had ever done before. She just needed to get over the fact that she found it mildly annoying tonight and get right back on that horse, so to speak. She needed tonight to go smoothly to get back into her groove and stop thinking about Ella.

Parker put her arm around Kenna's shoulders and brought her in for another kiss, pulling back before it could deepen. Kenna almost fell forward at Parker's quick departure. Parker tried not to notice.

"Hey, is everything okay? You seem distracted," Kenna said, and Parker blew out an overly exaggerated breath.

"No, everything's fine. Really," Parker said when Kenna continued to look at her expectantly.

Malachi cleared his throat. "According to sources at the bar, she left her job early last weekend to take home a fucking drop-dead gorgeous blonde who had a little too much to drink," he said, grinning at Parker. "I heard you were plying her with your drinks all night. She was almost too drunk to walk so you happily took her back to your place for a little romp—"

Parker cut him off immediately, feeling the ire rising from her very core. "Hey, that's not fucking funny, dude. I would never take advantage of anyone," she said, shoving her finger in his face.

Malachi put his hands up in an *I give up* gesture. "Hey, I'm sorry," he said, placing one of his huge hands on her shoulders. She initially shrugged him off, but when he touched her again, Parker relaxed into the display of affection.

Kenna looked at Parker, and when she wouldn't return the look, Kenna placed a finger under her chin. Parker did her best to avoid her searching eyes.

"Everything's fine. I promise. Let's just head in and get some drinks and have some fun," Parker said, putting her arms around Kenna's waist and pulling their bodies together. Kenna wrapped her arms around Parker's shoulders as Parker leaned in to gently bite her on the neck. When Kenna moaned into her shoulder, Parker tried to feel turned on. Did she need to try to find Viagra in the sea of drug dealers out here? What is the female version of that? *Effing hell, I need to get out of my own head.*

Kenna's hands came down to cup her ass, and her body began to react a bit. Yes, thank the gods! She had not lost her mojo. Now then, Operation Get-Some commences in three, two, one...

Inside the bar, she bought the first two rounds of shots for everyone, hoping the group was in a tequila mood. As the bartender handed Dimitri the tray with the shots, lemon and lime wedges, and a saltshaker, Parker picked up her two shots and downed them in succession before popping a lime wedge in her mouth. Everyone else looked at her, mouths agape. She just shrugged.

"What are you pussies waiting for?" she said, in challenge. She took one of Kenna's shots and tucked it into her exposed cleavage. Kenna happily followed her lead, licking a path across the expanse of Parker's chest before sprinkling salt on her. She then picked up the shot with her mouth and downed it, licked the salt, and waited for Parker's next instructions.

Parker picked up her second shot and encouraged Kenna to open her mouth by pushing two fingers between her lips. She looked up at her expectantly, as Parker poured the liquid into her mouth. She kissed Kenna again, and this time, let the kiss deepen a bit before grabbing her hand and leading her out to the dance floor.

The boys lined up around them, and the group danced like maenads at a bacchanalia as the alcohol took effect. Rack and Dimitri bought more shots, and the entire group commenced doing body shots off each other as the mood of the evening began to pick up.

Malachi and Kenna had Parker pinned between them as they made out feverishly. She fondled both of them, trying to relax into the music. When she looked up again, someone was watching them with piqued interest. She was tall with a lithe body and icy blue eyes. Her blond hair hit just below her shoulders in waves. Other than the eyes, her appearance was strikingly similar to El…er, that woman she just met whose name she would not even think because it didn't even matter.

Parker waved her over, and the new girl sauntered toward them. She moved with the grace of a ballet dancer.

"Guys, don't look now, but I think we have a nibble," Parker said. Kenna looked up and smiled salaciously at the approaching blonde.

Malachi chuckled. "Well, that's what happens when we chum the water so hard with our sexiness," he said, and Kenna looked at him, open-mouthed, before slapping him gently on the shoulder in admonishment.

"You say it like we're actually trying to attract someone to take home with us," Kenna said innocently, and Parker just shook her head. When the blonde finally reached them, she walked up to Parker directly.

"Hi, I'm Molly," she said before Malachi interrupted her.

"Ooh, I love me some Molly," he said and laughed as Parker rolled her eyes at him before holding her hand out to their new friend.

Molly took her hand and Parker pulled her close into their group. Malachi came up behind her to put his hands on her waist as they moved to the music. Kenna danced on the outside until Parker pulled her between herself and Molly. While she found herself reacting to the touches and all the physicality taking place this evening, her mind and her heart just didn't seem to be in it, at all. She found herself drifting off a lot, thinking about those beautiful green eyes that seemed to be able to look right through her. She couldn't stop herself from wondering what Ella was doing right now, as she went through the motions, letting muscle-memory take over on the dance floor.

When Parker came back to herself, she noticed that Kenna and Molly were in the midst of a full-on groping session while Malachi watched from behind. When he moved to the side of the dancing pair, she saw exactly how much he was enjoying the show from the bulge in his pants. Parker snickered, shaking her head. She took this opportunity to back out of the threesome and move a few spaces down where Rack and Dimitri lovingly slow danced to a song with a thumping beat.

She froze for a moment, looking back at the debauchery that was Malachi, Kenna, and their new friend. Then, she averted her gaze back to Rack and Dimitri. They shared an intimate, loving embrace, conversing about something and laughing with one another. Is that what she wanted now?

Parker had always enjoyed these nights and the trysts they often spawned. She had many memories of Kenna's mouth on her body and Malachi's hands on Kenna as they partook of another lover together. It all seemed so long ago now. She was at war with herself. Did she even want to take them home with her?

"What's up, kitty-cat?" Rack said, looking at her inquisitively.

Parker snapped to attention then and met his eyes. "You know how we were talking about the lady from the bar last weekend?" Parker said tentatively. They stopped dancing and turned to face her, giving her their full attention. "I think…" she said and blew out a breath to steady herself. "I think she might be special," she continued with her eyes closed. When she didn't hear any sort of reaction from the couple, she opened one eye and peeked. They were simply smiling at her.

"Well, well, well," Dimitri said, turning his attention back to Rack. "It sounds like our little girl has gone and grown up on us."

Parker crossed her arms and stuck her lip out in imitation of a small child who has been chastised, but she relented and smiled at them. "It's early, I know. But I finally understand the U-Haul lesbian jokes now. She's pretty much all I think about," Parker said.

"You're serious? About her?" Rack said, raising his eyebrows. Parker just nodded before staring at the floor.

"Hey, I think it's wonderful," Dimitri said. "You know, the first time I met this big lug," he said, indicating Rack, "I said to myself, 'Self, you just met your husband.' And here we are six years later. Although, I'm still waiting for that ring!" he said loudly, directing his statement in his boyfriend's direction. Rack blushed brightly.

"We don't need a ring or a piece of paper to prove that we're in love," he said and kissed Dimitri sweetly on the lips. Dimitri pressed their foreheads together and started into Rack's eyes. They began kissing and thereby ignoring Parker, who moved directly into their space to clear her throat loudly.

"Hey, we were talking about me and my dilemma here," she said, and when the kissing did not relent, she poked them both in the shoulders, hard. "Hey! Guys, come on!" she said. They finally broke apart and glanced sheepishly at her before apologizing.

"Listen, baby girl," Rack said, releasing Dimitri and turning to face her fully. He placed his hands on her shoulders. "I know you don't date or fall in love or anything like that, and I'm sure you have your reasons. But you are one of the kindest and most caring people I have ever met. If you have found someone that makes your heart beat faster, then just go with it. Don't get bogged down with the semantics, thinking it is too soon. Don't think about your past and how it has kept you down for so long. Think about your future."

And with those very words, another picture of Ella entered her mind. This time, it was the one where Ella had just woken up and was checking her phone the night after she slept on her couch. She didn't seem to notice Parker was in the doorway yet, so she took a few moments to commit all the details she could to memory. She loved the line of Ella's jaw and slope of her elegant nose as it met her top lip, which was full and inviting. She loved the way Ella looked relaxed in her environment, even after waking from the previous night's drunken haze. Parker heard an annoyingly loud clicking sound that seemed to be tearing her from the thoughts that had her completely enraptured. She looked up to see Rack literally snapping his fingers in front of her face in an *Earth to Parker* gesture, much to her chagrin.

"Girl, you've got it bad! Were you seriously just thinking of her right now?"

Parker nodded. She wasn't going to lie to Rack and Dimitri. Her soft little underbelly was exposed right now, and strangely enough, it didn't terrify her. She was happy to be truly seen by these two. "She can't handle our age difference, Rack," Parker said sadly. "She's thirty-five and I'm not even twenty-five yet."

Rack looked at her contemplatively before nodding. "Is that a big deal?"

Parker shook her head. "No, not to me. But she's freaking out because she has a seventeen-year-old daughter."

Rack nodded in understanding. "But you're good with teenagers. You and your sister get along well."

Parker nodded vehemently. "That's what I told her, but she says she just wants to be friends," she said, sounding dejected.

"Go home. Right now. Go call her," Dimitri said.

Parker looked back over to Kenna and her grinding partners. Normally, on any given Saturday night, that is where she would want to be: directly in the middle of an undulating pile of bodies and knowing exactly what was going to happen when they finally found a bed together. But, tonight, she wanted something different. She wanted to be sitting next to Ella, watching a movie. Or holding hands and talking. She just wanted to be with her.

"Many amazing relationships start out as friends, Parker," he continued. "The most important thing is just to spend time together and see where things go. You deserve a shot at happiness."

Parker's heart filled with joy at her friend's kind words. She never truly thought settling down with someone would be something she would even contemplate, but now it was all she could think about. With one final look over her shoulder at Kenna and Co., she hugged Rack and Dimitri before finding her way outside. She pulled out her cell phone and saw the missed text from Ella. She said she hoped Parker had fun and that they would chat again soon. Parker began typing furiously, but the first text didn't sound right, so she erased it and tried again. Nothing she typed expressed how she truly felt, so she just stared at her phone.

Parker thought about calling Ella, but it was so late now. Was that a metaphor? Was she too late for a chance at true love? She sighed to herself and put her phone back in her pocket before hailing a taxi to take her back home, completely and utterly alone.

Chapter 8

"Hey, Mom, how was your weekend?" AJ said as she walked in the door Sunday evening. Ella walked over to her daughter and looked up into her big blue eyes before going to her tiptoes up to hug her six-foot-one daughter. She chuckled and put her arms around to pat her mother on the back before stepping out of her arms.

"Geez, did you get laid or something?" AJ said, setting her bag down on the floor before raiding the fridge. Ella paused for a moment, caught off-guard at her daughter's accusatory banter, before deciding now was probably not the time to tell her about Parker.

"Uh, no. Can't a mother just hug her daughter?" This was a good start to AJ's return home. Things had been strained between them since the divorce. Even though neither she nor Alex had discussed the real reason for the split with her, AJ seemed to blame her. Kids just know the darndest things, don't they?

"I guess," AJ said as she shut the door to the fridge with her hip, having acquired everything to make herself the biggest sandwich known to man.

"How was your weekend with your dad? What did you guys get into?"

"It was good. We just stayed home and hung out pretty much. What did you do?"

Ella paused and thought about how to answer that question. Mostly honestly was the correct way. "I actually met up with some new friends and had dinner and did some dancing."

AJ paused what she was doing and looked at her mother with her mouth agape. "You went out? Like, *out* out? Who do you know who would go out dancing with you?"

Ella recoiled a bit. Teenagers could be mean, but this sort of abruptness from AJ was new. "Well, I'm not dead yet. I love to dance. And again, notice the mention of new friends. I've met some people online, and we just hung out. It was a lot of fun."

AJ smirked and resumed making her lunch. "You're meeting people online? That's pretty sketchy, Mom. But, hey, if you need people to go out with, you're surely not going to find them in the teacher's lounge at school. So, dab on 'em," AJ said as she made the referenced gesture.

Ella rolled her eyes at her daughter. She had absolutely no idea what that meant. Why was it necessary to look up phrases online in order to have a conversation with teenagers these days. "Meeting people online is a legitimate way to do it nowadays. You always meet them out in public so if they are *pretty sketchy*, you can just head out with your own vehicle."

"Mom, tell me you didn't drive drunk?" AJ said, looking her squarely in the face again.

"Of course I didn't. I took an Uber," Ella said, sticking with the mostly honest concept. She took an Uber there. She didn't have to tell AJ that she took a Parker home.

AJ returned to her sandwich, shaking her head. "Well thank goodness for that," she said in an exasperated tone.

Ella had had enough. "Hey, what's up with the attitude? You know, I'm allowed to make friends and go out. I'm just trying to live my life."

AJ scoffed, slicing her now assembled sandwich mountain in half. "Yeah, I just hope none of my friends were at the club and got a glimpse of you *living your life*," AJ said before licking a dollop of mayonnaise off her thumb. "You're a teacher, Mom. Please act like it."

Ella was floored. Things had been tense between them, but AJ hadn't said things like this before. "Just because I'm a teacher doesn't make me a nun, AJ. I'm allowed to be an adult

85

and do adult things and activities." Ella left out the fact that she didn't think any of AJ's friends would head into Sparkle anytime soon.

"Why can't you just find somewhere respectable to meet guys? Look at Dad and Rebecca. They met at the church picnic. You're almost forty. You can't just be going out to clubs and getting drunk and going home with a bunch of men!"

AJ had tears in her eyes when she looked up, and Ella realized she probably wasn't as angry as she was still hurt about the divorce. Ella took a step toward her with her arms out, but AJ put her hand up, picked up her sandwich, and walked toward her room.

"Never mind. I'm staying with Dad again next weekend, so you can go clubbing again if you want to." And with that statement, she walked up the stairs and slammed her door.

Ella sighed but decided to let it go for now. She retreated to her own room to call Alex. Hopefully, he could shed some light on AJ's attitude.

"Hey, what's up?" Alex said on the other end of the phone. His friendly voice was always a welcome sound.

"Hey, I just need to talk to you about AJ. Did anything happen this weekend? She has come back in quite a mood."

"Really?" Alex sounded dumbfounded at the idea that his daughter would have come back in a bad frame of mind. "We had a good weekend. I guess she was a little quieter than normal, but I just chalked it up to teenage grumpiness. We did a movie marathon on Saturday during the day, and she took herself back and forth to practice Friday evening and Saturday evening. Rebecca came over, and they were as thick as thieves. She enjoys hanging out with AJ, and I want to tell you again how much I appreciate you being okay with them spending time together."

Ella went over his words, trying to find something in what he said to figure out what exactly was wrong with their daughter. "Of course, I want them to spend time together. She seems like a great person and I'm happy for you. You know that. AJ asked me what I did this weekend, and I told her I met up with some friends for dinner and dancing. She didn't seem to like that at all. Then she made sure to tell me she is staying with you again next weekend, which is fine. It was just very strange."

"We had talked about her staying over next weekend and maybe missing practice. I wanted to take her for an overnight trip to Atlanta to watch a Braves game, but she was supposed to talk to you about it and get back to me. Is that okay?"

Ella never condoned missing practice unless you were on death's door. And since it was AJ's senior year and scouts were frequenting her games, she needed to be playing to the best of her ability. That could only happen if she practiced daily. But Ella was also trying to stay close to her daughter who kept drifting away with every day that went by, it seemed. So, she could relent this one time. "Yes, that's fine," she said grudgingly.

Alex picked up on her tone and laughed heartily. "Wow, that one hurt you, huh?" he joked.

Ella mocked a *ha-ha* at him but couldn't stop smiling. They would always be best friends. The thought warmed her heart. "Something like that. But, yeah, take her to the game. She needs to like one of us, at least."

"Now don't be like that. Tell you what, I'll talk to her next weekend and see if I can find out if there's anything going on. I'm sure she's not mad at you. It probably just took her by surprise that you went out and...*danced*," he said, attempting to put teenage angst in his voice.

Ella laughed again; this time, it was genuine. "Yup, mortal sin and me? Best friends."

"So…" he said expectantly.

"So…?" Ella said right back.

"Did you go on a date?" he said. "You know you can date, right? I want you to be happy, too."

Ella smiled to herself at his kindness. "I did, but it ended up being a big group of friends because we had no romantic chemistry. And then we went to Sparkle—"

"Sparkle? You finally went there? That's great," Alex interrupted.

"Yes, I went to Sparkle with Danna, my date who then became like my best friend, and two of her friends. And…" Ella trailed off. She had to tell someone about the situation, and Alex was always willing to listen.

"And you met someone at the bar, right?"

"I did. It's just—"

Then, Ella told him everything. The entire story. She couldn't stop herself. He laughed in all the right places and didn't seem to be judging her. When Ella got to the age difference, he went quiet.

"See? This is why I can't date her. You go all radio silent on me and that tells me everything I need to know."

"Is it that big of a deal, though, El?" Alex said, using his nickname for her. This broke through her worry and brought her to attention.

"But isn't it? Eleven years, Alex. That's an awful lot to try to rectify, don't you think?"

Alex blew out a breath and took a moment before answering. "It is a lot of years; I'm not trying to say that it isn't. But it sounds like you had instant chemistry. That's hard to find. I'm trying to advise you as if I were in the situation myself. And, I can honestly say that if Rebecca had been ten years younger than me, it wouldn't have stopped me. Love is love, you know?"

Alex had the kindest heart of anyone she had ever known. "I love you, Al. You know that. I appreciate all that you're saying; I just honestly don't know if I can do this."

"Well, then, go with your plan of being friends. Hang out with her, talk with her, get to know her. That kind of stuff. And then, just follow your heart. Always follow your heart, El. You'll know what to do."

"Thanks. I appreciate that. She's so, well, she's very cool. Much cooler than me."

"Naturally," he said, voice full of mirth.

"Asshole," Ella said in retort. "And she's just beautiful."

"Send me a pic?" Alex said, and Ella laughed out loud.

"Ain't happenin', buddy." Getting all of this off her chest to him made her feel a lot better. They ended the phone call, and before Ella could set her phone down, she got a text message notification from Parker. Her anxiety wrenched up a couple of notches.

Parker, 7:35 p.m.: "Hey, what's up, new friend. Hope you had a good day!"

Alex's words rang in her ears. *Hang out, talk, get to know her. Follow your heart.* Well, here goes.

Ella, 7:36 p.m.: "It has been good up until dealing with an order of grumpy teenager, make that extra grumpy, please. How about you? How was your night last night?"

She sent the text without thinking and then wished upon a star that she could just take it back from the ether in which it flew to Parker's phone. When that didn't work, she sighed and waited for the response. Did she want to know how her night had gone? Oh well, an answer was incoming.

Parker, 7:37 p.m.: "Uh-oh. What's up with AJ? Everything okay? And my night was fun, thanks for asking."

Huh. That's an absolute non-answer. Now the question was, did she want to press for more information or just leave it alone?

Ella, 7:38 p.m.: "Yeah, she's been kind of angry with me since the divorce. It's almost like she blames me, which I guess is legitimate. Me=gay, so, no hopes of working it out with her dad."

Parker, 7:41 p.m.: "How did she take it when you told her that you're a lesbian?"

Well, wasn't that the $64,000 question? How *would* she take it? This had always been the worry at the back of her mind.

Ella, 7:42 p.m.: "I haven't exactly told her yet."

Parker, 7:43 p.m.: "Oh. Well, that makes things difficult for you. Do you only date when she is at her dad's? That's got to be hard on your social life."

Ella, 7:45 p.m.: "You got to see me in the remnants of my first date the other night. So, the short answer is yes."

Parker, 7:46 p.m.: "That was your first date since your divorce? Wow, I would never have guessed."

Ella read the last message again, trying to decipher if there was sarcasm in there somewhere. When no additional reply came, she assumed that was just Parker being honest. Good. She liked this version of her.

Ella, 7:48 p.m.: "Thanks, I think. But, anyway, she came home and asked me what I did over the weekend, and I told her that I met up with some new friends and went out dancing. That's when the proverbial shit hit the fan."

Parker, 7:52 p.m.: "I'm guessing if she realizes that her mom is going out dancing that her parents aren't going to get back together again. Maybe that's hard for her to take in?"

Ella, 7:54 p.m.: "I don't think that's the issue. Alex is already with someone else and is head over heels in love. I'm happy for him and we are still very close."

Parker, 7:56 p.m.: "Maybe just the idea of Mom going out, then? She probably wants you to meet someone more organically. Like a church picnic or something."

Was this woman a damn psychic or something? She opted not to text, but to call Parker and interrogate her about her phrasing. The phone only rang once before she heard the line pick up. Before Parker even had a chance to say anything, Ella was already talking.

"Her dad met his new girlfriend at a church picnic, and we were actually just talking, well arguing, about that. Why would you say church picnic? Do you have spy equipment set up here?"

Parker was silent for a few moments before chiming in. "Do you often just call and erupt crazy all over someone you just met?" she said in a teasing tone.

Ella laughed again. "I just did that, didn't I? Sorry, I just had to call to see if I could hear your phone ringing in my closet or something, since you're obviously spying on me."

"Nope, I'm sitting here in my apartment, just texting Mount Crazy before she exploded all over me. Maybe you've heard of her? And now I must sit here covered in the molten insanity while I chat on the phone to her, my new favorite person. So, all in all, a good day," Parker said.

Ella could hear the smile in her voice, and her heart warmed at the thought that she had put it there. Parker's wit could sometimes be the most attractive thing about her. Ella took a moment to think back to her beautiful dark brown eyes and her expressive lips that smiled so freely. She thought about her body dressed up for the club and dressed down for sleep and how much both visions affected her equally.

"I'm honored, I must say. You're very kind."

"No, I'm serious," Parker said. "And on the note of staying serious, is everything okay with you guys?"

Ella closed her eyes and sighed. "Yeah, we'll get there. Apparently, Alex is going to take her to a baseball game this weekend, so that will make her happy."

Parker *hmmed* and Ella questioned the sound.

"Well, if AJ is out of town this weekend, does that mean you're free again?"

Ella bit down on her lip gently, smiling at the idea that not only had Parker remembered her schedule, but that she wanted to see her again. Maybe as much as Ella wanted to see her.

"Uh, yeah, I guess I am. I hadn't really thought about it. You're working though, right?"

"I work Friday night and Sunday night, but I am off Saturday. Can we hang out? We can go get some food, or you can come over and I can cook for you?" Parker's lilt at the end of her last statement sounded like she was bracing for impact, almost as if she was expecting Ella to say no because they had agreed to keep things casual.

"Yeah, we can do that. I was planning on seeing if Danna and the girls wanted to get together and go out to the club Friday night. So, I can always pop by for a drink as well. I've got to get some papers graded right now, so let's chat later in the week and we can make some official plans. Does that work for you?"

Parker exhaled slowly like she had been holding her breath. "Perfect. Text me anytime. Have a good day at school tomorrow, and I hope everything works out with AJ."

After saying their official goodbyes, she messaged Danna to let her know that she was free next weekend and to see if she and the gang wanted to get together at Sparkle on Friday. Danna said she was up for it and messaged back within ten minutes that Val and Wendy would go, too. With weekend plans made, Ella was ready to take on the stack of papers in front of her.

Chapter 9

The first part of the week flew by with most everything remaining the same. AJ was still cold and snappy, but less outwardly angry. On Thursday, her classes began their six-week journey with Edgar Allan Poe, who is the best writer ever, at least in Ella's opinion. They would start the week with "The Cask of Amontillado," which was one of her favorites.

"Raise your hand if you can explain the symbolism and irony in Fortunado's name and manner of dress," Ella said, trying to get the kids excited about gothic horror.

Some classes really responded with enthusiasm to this part of the year, but with this being the last block of the day, most everyone was ready to go home and truly uninterested in what she had to say. She figured she would have to start calling on folks to respond and noticing a young man near the back of the room with his head down, decided to see if he was paying attention.

"Zeke, why don't you tell the class what you think?" At the overly loud mention of his name, the young man raised his head and blinked a few times before wiping his chin. Ella was a very understanding teacher and knew that paying attention for hours on end wasn't the easiest. But there was never to be any actual sleeping in her class. And even though Zeke was homecoming king and one of the captains of the football team, he was not getting a break.

"I'm sorry, Mrs. Gardner. I didn't hear what you said," he said, and the class snickered. Ella stood from where she was perched on the edge of her desk and uncrossed her arms. He was a good kid and always respectful, but he just couldn't seem to stay awake for the advanced placement literature class at the end of the day. She could throw him a bone, though.

"I was asking about Fortunado in the story. Have you read it?" Zeke nodded, then shook his head again trying to clear up the cobwebs. "First of all, tell me about the symbolism in Fortunado's clothing."

"Yes, ma'am. The story took place during a carnival, and he was dressed in a motley costume and a jester's cap. So, he was effectively the fool in the story."

Ella was impressed with his answer. It's always good to find students who do actually read the stories. "Yes, that's right. And can you explain the irony in his name?" she said as she moved across the front of the room.

"Yes, his name sounds like he would be fortunate in the story. He was anything but, with the dying and all…" Zeke trailed off to more titters of laughter from the class. He smiled along with them, but the gesture seemed a bit strained. Zeke was obviously a good student and was trying his best. She had to figure out where this inability to stay awake came from and see how she could help.

"That's right, Zeke. Did everyone get that? Put stars next to that or underline it in your notes. That will be on your test."

Notebooks were opened and much scribbling on pages sounded at that point. They went through more information to be included on the test before the bell rang, signaling the end of class and the end of the day.

Ella raised her voice above the din. "Everyone have a good night. We'll get back to it tomorrow. Zeke, can you hang back for a second?" Several of his athletic friends *oohed* at him, and he smiled sheepishly before walking up to the front of the class. When everyone had left the room, Ella sat at her desk and indicated he should take the student desk across from her.

"I want to make sure everything is okay with you. You're obviously reading the material, but you just can't seem to stay awake in my class. Can I suggest you get to bed earlier at night or is that just ridiculous of me?" she said with an intentionally warm smile on her face.

Zeke smiled back, obviously relieved at her friendly tone. "I probably should. All of my schoolwork is suffering right now.

But I'm picking up extra late shifts at the grocery store. It's almost prom time, you know?"

Ella knew that prom was in the next few weeks as AJ and her friends had already talked about how cool it would be to ditch it. "I understand that, but I don't want your grades to suffer. It's much more important that you keep your GPA up and get into a good school than it is to save up money to rent a stretch limo or whatever extravagant thing you're saving up for."

Zeke blushed a little bit and looked down. "In all honesty, Mrs. Gardner—"

"Miss Gardner," Ella corrected.

"Miss Gardner," he rectified. "My parents can't afford a tux for me. So, if I want to go, I have to save up for one."

Ella withered at her own ignorant assumption. Unfortunately, there were a lot of low-income kids in the area. It sounded like Zeke didn't want anyone else to know. She would protect his secret and do anything she could to help him out with his classwork. "I hate to hear that. I'm actually very impressed with your work ethic. There's not a whole lot of people your age who could work like you do and keep their grades up. I just ask that you not sleep in class. If you need extra time on assignments, I'm flexible. But I'm going to need you to grab a coffee from the caf' and stay awake during class discussions, all right?"

Zeke nodded and visibly relaxed. "I will. I like the story a lot, just don't tell my friends. I have a reputation to uphold, you know?"

Ella shook her head ruefully at him before giving him a thumbs-up. With a self-deprecating grin, he picked up his books and retreated to the halls. Ella pulled out her grade book and started going through it to see which students were missing assignments when she heard a knock on her open door. She looked up to see AJ standing there.

"Hey, love, how was your day?" Ella said, putting her grade book aside and moving to greet her daughter. AJ let herself be hugged, but she was too cool to hug Mom at school.

"It was fine. I'm on my way to practice now. But I wanted to say bye. I'm headed over to Dad's tonight. I already packed my stuff for this weekend and won't be back home," AJ said darkly.

Ella couldn't stop herself from worrying that Sunday's argument was still affecting her mood. "I'm happy for you to head to your father's tonight, but I want to talk first. Please?"

AJ rolled her eyes without looking at her mother. "What's up? I have like five minutes before I have to start moving toward the gym," she said, looking at Ella expectantly.

"I'm worried that you're still mad at me about our disagreement on Sunday," Ella said and waited for a response.

AJ became obviously agitated. "No, Mom, it is literally not a big deal. You can do whatever you want, date whatever guy you want. Do your thing. I just have a lot of sh—er, stuff going on right now," AJ said, and Ella nodded with understanding. They were still at that point where AJ didn't want to swear around her mother, much.

Senior year was tough. She had to worry about keeping her grades up at the same time she was trying to earn a volleyball scholarship. Ella just wanted to be there for her and help her through it. They had always been a team, best buddies. This distance between them was just something Ella wasn't prepared to deal with.

"Hey, you know I'm always here for you. You can always talk to me, and I will help you with anything I can. I love you, Anna-Banana," she said, hoping that using her childhood nickname might resonate.

AJ giggled despite herself and finally met her eyes. "I know, Mom. I love you, too," AJ said and hugged her. When she pulled back, her eyes were filled with tears.

"Hey, what's wrong? Talk to me," she said, but AJ took a step back, wiping her eyes and shaking her head.

"Not right now. But maybe we can hang out after I get back this weekend? Maybe Sunday night?" she said, sounding hopeful.

"Of course. Just text me when you're on your way back, and I'll make whatever you want for dinner. Maybe we can watch a movie or something?" Quality time with your teenage daughter who literally hates you sometimes was a rare commodity these days, and she would relish any time they would have together.

"Yeah, that sounds great. Just order pizza or something and we'll pick a movie. Anyway, I've got to go. Coach Matthews will make me run sprints if I'm late. I hope you have a good weekend, Mom." And with that, she was jogging down the hallway towards the gymnasium. Ella sat back down at her desk, going back to her paperwork. After about an hour composing a list of missing assignments, she decided to pop down to the gym and sneak into volleyball practice.

AJ was the most impressive outside hitter she had ever seen. She deserved the scholarship offers she had already started receiving. She had an intensity when she played, and even when she practiced, that not even Ella had been able to command. Every time she went skyward and smashed a ball to the other side of the net, it almost looked like her teammates on defense stepped out of the way. No one wanted to try to bump one of those spikes.

Ella had always been an assistant coach for the Benton High Lady Dragons until AJ had come up from the junior varsity squad in her freshman year. She had stepped down at that point, preferring the role of mom in the stands as not to blur the lines of their relationship by also trying to coach her directly. She had taught her everything she knew growing up, and at this point, AJ could probably teach her a few things about the game.

She felt her phone vibrate in her pocket, pulling it out to see a new text from Danna.

Danna, 4:16 p.m.: "Hey lady, what are you into tonight? I know it's a weeknight, but I have invited a big group of friends over for an impromptu game night. Are you available?"

Ella thought to herself about AJ's decision to stay at her dad's and pondered the idea of a Thursday night get-together with her new friends.

Ella, 4:17 p.m.: "So, just making sure there's no euphemism. You literally mean a game night, right?"

Danna, 4:18 p.m.: "That's code for a drunken orgy, actually."

She then sent a winky-face emoji to which Ella chucked and rolled her eyes.

Danna, 4:19 p.m.: "It's pretty low-key. Everybody brings a six-pack of beer to share and then we just play board games until around midnight. Nothing crazy. Besides, Wendy, Val and I want you to meet the whole gang."

Midnight. When was the last time she had seen midnight on a weekday when school was on? Oh well, if she wanted to shed her teacher-mom persona, this was probably a good start. It sounded like fun for sure.

Ella, 4:21 p.m.: "Yeah, that sounds great. What time should I stop by? And do I need to bring anything other than beer?"

Danna, 4:22 p.m.: "People usually start trickling in at about six. And no, just the beer. I'll order some Chinese food as well. See you then!"

Ella looked at her phone and realized if she were going to get to Danna's on time, she needed to get back to work. As she stood up to exit, she watched AJ obliterate the second-team libero with a kill that knocked her flat on her rump. She smiled to herself as AJ's teammates high-fived her while the coach walked over to check on the young girl who sat stunned on the gym floor. That was her daughter out there, and she was damn proud.

※

Ella raided AJ's closet again for some hip clothes. She absolutely must go shopping soon and get some more outfits that fit her new, cool self. Well, cool may be a stretch, but new, nonetheless. Tonight, she found super-skinny ripped jeans that were just a little too long thanks to the height difference between her and her daughter. Good news is they looked great with a slight cuff at the bottom. She picked up a faded army green T-shirt with the words *Love is Blind* on the small pocket. She threw on her casual black peacoat and some Chucks, this time, midnight blue with stars on them, and headed out the door.

When she got to Danna's, there were already a couple of cars there. She didn't even get a chance to knock before Val threw open the door and hugged her in greeting. Ella had never been a hugger, but her new friends seemed to do it often. Strangely, she didn't mind. Maybe finally being able to be herself around people had opened her up a bit.

"What's up, girlfriend!" Val exclaimed, pulling her through the door by the hand. "Now you already know Wendy and Danna, of course, but let's introduce you to a few more good people."

Ella smiled at the room and waved at all the new faces.

"Good lord, Val, let her get in the door first," said a lovely black woman with closely buzzed pink hair. "Hi, I'm Teyana, and this," she said, pointing over her shoulder at a petite woman whose platinum-blond hair and bright blue eyes reminded her of an actual porcelain doll, "is my wife, Rose."

At the mention of her name, Rose came over and shook Ella's hand. "Hey, great to meet the woman who Danna can't stop talking about," Rose said, then realizing how it might have sounded, clarified with, "in a platonic way."

The room erupted in laughter as Danna walked over and bear-hugged her to the point she was on her tiptoes.

"Guys, this is the coolest addition to our group. Everyone say hi to Ella," she said, and the group did so. "So, you met Teyana and Rose," she said, indicating them again. Ella waved sheepishly again. "And of course, you know Val and Wendy. This," she said, pointing toward the stunning redhead who danced with Val and Wendy last Friday, "is Aubrey. She's with Val and Wendy. It's some weird throuple thing. I dunno."

At the mention of their supposedly secret arrangement, three pairs of eyes went wide and looked around the room.

"Guys, you're safe here. No one is going to judge. Love is love, right? Do your thing!" Danna said, and with that, a round of applause and lifting of beer bottles in salute accompanied by murmurs of acceptance rained around them. All three looked a little uncomfortable but smiled at each other knowingly.

"Finally," Danna said, and it almost sounded like a weighted statement, "Ella, this is Aubrey's friend Tallulah," she said, indicating a leggy blonde who was moving to shake her hand.

Tallulah was stunning, that was for sure. Her long, straight hair was back in a loose ponytail with strands out and around her face for emphasis. Ella estimated they were about the same height, and Tallulah's slate-gray eyes bored into her own as she gently grasped her hand.

"Tally," she said simply as they stood in the middle of the room, grasping hands and staring into each other's eyes. "I've heard a lot about you. It's nice to finally put a face to the name," she said, smiling and dropping Ella's hand.

At the loss of contact, Ella snapped back into reality. "Oh, yes, hi, nice to meet you, too," she said, breaking eye contact and feeling her cheeks pinken. Danna walked up to her, placing a hand on the small of her back.

"What do you mean, 'put a face to the name'?" she said with an air of good-natured ribbing. "You haven't stopped looking at the picture Aubrey sent you earlier."

Danna apparently had a thing for being bracingly honest at the expense of her friends' comfort. Ella would have to remember not to tell her anything that she didn't want the whole group to know. Tally's head lolled back, and she stared at the ceiling as if to say *Lord, give me strength* before blushing furiously.

"Thanks, Danna," she said without meeting Ella's eyes. "Can I get you a beer? I brought the Michelob Amber Bock. I know most people don't like the darker beers and I usually end up drinking my own, but…"

Her voice trailed off as Ella held up her Newcastle Brown Ales with a smile on her face. Tally smiled brightly, pulled out one of her beers, and gave it to Ella. She then happily received one of Ella's as they moved into the kitchen to find a bottle opener, when the doorbell rang. Danna opened the door to accept the food delivery, and the night was on. Beers were traded and laughs were had as the night approached. Ella had spent most of the evening paired off with Tally, getting to know one another.

Tallulah Calvin was thirty-two and a chiropractor from Thistle Village, a quaint town about an hour away. She and Aubrey met a few months ago and went out on exactly two dates before resolving to be friends. She had never been married and had no kids, one dog, and two cats. On paper, she was kind of perfect so far. But Ella just couldn't shake the excitement of getting to see Parker tomorrow at Sparkle.

"What's your favorite type of music?" Tally said, crossing her fingers and closing her eyes wistfully. She was cute and fun.

"Well, I like a little bit of everything, but my favorite is definitely '90s grunge. I love Nirvana, Pearl Jam, Babes in Toyland, Alice in Chains, most anything from that genre. What about you?"

Tally had uncrossed her fingers, opened her eyes, and looked almost aghast. "Oh, that stuff was always way too angry for me. Life is happy so we should listen to happy music, I think. I like country music. I absolutely love Morgan Wallen."

Ella blinked and must have looked dumbstruck. Country music was at the bottom of her list. "Oh. I don't know who she is. I'm not a huge country fan, personally," she said, and noticing the look on Tally's face, continued. "Not that it's not okay to be a country fan. That's totally okay in my book."

Tally relented and patted Ella's forearm. "Morgan Wallen is a man. And don't worry, I have plenty of time to bring you over to the dark side," she said, lifting her eyebrows to emphasize her point.

Ella laughed gently. *No way, baby. Not happening.* She decided to change the subject. "What about movies? What kinds of movies do you like?" she said, almost dreading the answer. Tally's face went directly into think mode as she tapped her temple.

"I like suspense movies. Anything like a thriller or mystery. And I like horror if it isn't too gory. I like any excuse to cuddle, so horror movies are important," she said, looking at Ella out of the corner of her eye.

Ella smiled gently and returned the flirtation. "Yeah, cuddling is important. I have lots of scary movies memorized, so

I could always warn you when something is getting ready to happen. I could, you know, cover your eyes for you, or something," she said. Wow, she was not good at the flirting. Ella looked back to Tally who was smiling openly and knowingly.

"Maybe we could test that out some time?" Tally said quietly, and Ella guessed her intent was not giving Danna anything else to announce to the room tonight. Ella opened her mouth to accept, when her phone started to ring. She checked the caller ID only to discover the call was from Parker. She held up one finger apologetically before getting up to walk to a quiet area to take the call.

"Hey, what's up?"

"Hey, I was just thinking I hadn't talked to you in several days and wanted to check in. Is this a bad time?"

Ella didn't even have to think. "No, of course not. I'm just over at Danna's house for a game night."

"On a school night?" Parker said and lowered her voice an octave. "Well, well. Miss Gardner likes to misbehave. Good to know."

Ella felt her heart and other, lower parts of her body flutter. Parker was officially going to kill her with the innuendo and flirtatious comments. "Ah, yes, I'm a rebel. I probably should let you go, though, and hang out with these crazy folks," she said, despite wanting their conversation to continue.

"Yeah, you're right. I'm sorry to bother you. But, please come by and let me know when you get there tomorrow night. I'll find you on my breaks and we can hang out a bit," Parker said with a fake commanding tone.

Ella laughed, knowing there was nothing in this world that she wanted to do more than see Parker, even if for just a few minutes. "Yeah, I will. Who else would I let make my drinks?" They both said their goodbyes, and Ella returned to sit with Tally on the loveseat.

"Was that your daughter?" she said, and Ella was frozen for a moment. She didn't want to outright lie, but what was she supposed to say to the woman she just met? *No, it was the twenty-four-year-old bartender who took me home last weekend?* That wasn't going to work.

"Uh, yeah. Everything's fine. So, what are some of your favorite TV series?" she said, and their conversation drifted smoothly until Danna called the games officially on.

The first game they decided to play was a lesbian version of Win, Lose or Draw. Danna had printed out what looked like at least a hundred slips of paper with different television shows and movie titles with lesbian content. Even though Ella was newly out, she had spent a lot of time seeking out queer content on all of the streaming apps. She was ready.

The teams were split with couples and as much of a throuple as possible on opposite teams. The pink team was Danna, Aubrey, Ella, and Teyana, while Val, Wendy, Rose, and Tally made up the purple team. Danna was first up and, upon drawing her paper, rolled her eyes and nodded. Tally started a one-minute timer on her phone and signaled that she should go.

Danna only had to pick up an orange and black magic marker in each hand before Ella and the rest of the team screamed *Orange Is the New Black* as the answer. They were up 1-0.

Next up, Tally drew a slip. Her mouth dropped open, and her face colored a bit, but she put the slip in her back pocket and nodded resolutely. Once Danna started the timer, Tally grasped her breasts and looked expectantly at her team.

"Wait, wait, wait," Aubrey said. Danna paused the timer for the discussion. "This is drawing, not charades. She can't use her own body to give hints."

"Unless she takes her shirt off and draws on her naked body," Teyana chimed in, and everyone laughed again. "But, even then, I think it would be against the rules. Fun, but not legal."

There was much discussion to be had before it was decided she could only use the large pad of paper provided. Once Tally started drawing, she was consistently drawing stick

113

figures with small boobs and stick figures with huge boobs that were crossed out before more arrows were drawn to the A and B cup-sized caricatures. Her team was baffled, and when they didn't get the right answer, Ella was ready with the steal.

"*The Itty Bitty Titty Committee*," she said confidently, and Tally pointed to her before looking at her team in sheer exasperation.

"Seriously, guys? Have you never seen this movie?" she said, and Val and Wendy looked at each other and shrugged.

"I'm not interested in any itty bitty titties. Have you seen my wife?" Rose said and winked at the voluptuous Teyana.

Tally sighed and handed over the marker she had been holding to Ella, who was now caught looking down at the way her breasts were accentuated by the black tank top that showed just a teasing bit of cleavage. Ella snapped out of it, took the marker, and stood. Tally looked back at her knowingly.

"Enjoying the view?" she said as she passed Ella on her way to sit back with her team.

Ella's eyes went wide as she realized she'd been caught. She drew her clue and had to pause and think. She had seen *Bound* before. It was one of the hottest movies she had ever seen, in fact. But she had to think of how to translate that to pictures. Once the time started, Ella drew rolls of tape and ropes. When no one had managed much of a guess about halfway through, she decided to throw handcuffs into the artistic mix.

"Is this porn? Danna, did you put the title of one of your kinky pornos in there?" Rose said.

Val and Wendy both chimed in at the same time with "you wish!" before everyone erupted in laughter again.

"No, it's not porn! But I honestly have no idea what she's drawing," Danna said.

Ella could have screamed in frustration. "Come on, guys, seriously?" she said, pointing repeatedly at the different ways you might bind someone that she had drawn. When the timer ran out, she sighed and pointed to the opposing team. Everyone shrugged. Everyone, that is, but Tally who smiled like the cat who caught the canary.

"*Bound*," she said simply, and everyone groaned at themselves for missing something so obvious. Ella walked over to shake Tally's hand in an exaggerated *thank you*.

"Next time, we're on a team together," Ella said to the room. Tally nodded her agreement, staring up at Ella.

The group played a multitude of games before calling it a night around eleven. Ella, who had been up since around five that morning, couldn't stop yawning. Everyone was hugging each other. Val and Wendy each took one of Aubrey's hands as they went to Wendy's car to probably go home and have a sexy threesome. Kudos to them.

Ella shook hands with Teyana and Rose on their way out the door, leaving just herself, Danna, and Tally. Danna walked over and squeezed Tally in one of her big hugs.

"It was good to see you again, Tally. Thanks for coming by," she said and released her. Tally, who was now a little rumpled, smiled broadly and smoothed out her clothes.

"Yeah, this was great." She looked up at Ella and shied away quickly. "I hope I have a standing invitation now." Ella looked down and smiled at the floor.

"Oh, you definitely do. Hey, by the way, we're going to Sparkle tomorrow if you want to come with us," Danna said. Ella stuttered internally at the invitation, understanding that it might make things difficult if Tally accepted. And she did. Of course, she did.

"Yeah, I'd love to. Just meet up with you guys here and we'll take a taxi van? I'll set it up if you want," Tally said. Well, that's more points on her spreadsheet. She's kind, generous, and considerate of others. Danna clapped her hands together.

"Oh, that would be perfect. We'll all plan to meet here at eight. See you guys then. Lock up on your way out," she said, backing away from Ella and Tally with a huge smile on her face.

Ella guessed this was part of her plan. Well, she couldn't fault Danna. It was a solid plan, and it had potential so far.

"Well," Tally said expectantly.

Ella chuckled nervously. "Well, this is where I get off, I guess." Ella closed her eyes and shook her head. When would she ever be able to say the smooth things?

Tally's eyes went a little darker. "That's definitely good information to have," she said and reached out to take Ella's hand, gently intertwining their fingers together before finally looking back up and into her eyes.

"I had a fun time talking tonight, and I look forward to hanging out tomorrow. Will I be able to get a dance?" she said, continuing to hold Ella's gaze. Tally took her other hand in the same movement, never breaking eye contact.

"Sure, I don't count on being all that busy anyway. I'll have plenty of dances for you," she said.

Tally closed the short distance between them and brought their hands behind Ella's back. Their lips were an inch apart, if that, when Tally said, "Good," and leaned forward to bridge the gap.

Ella realized what was happening only in the moment before their lips touched and was able to turn her head to the side so the kiss landed on her cheek. Smiling apologetically, she took a small step back. Tally looked confused.

"I'm sorry, I'm just a slow mover, I guess. I don't know what the girls have told you, but this is all pretty new to me," Ella said, untangling their hands to emphasize her point.

Tally chewed the inside of her jaw thoughtfully. "I'm sorry. I thought we were in the same place and feeling the same thing. I didn't mean to…" Tally looked truly uncomfortable. Ella raised her chin with her forefinger while attempting to smile reassuringly.

"No, it's okay. I had a great time this evening; I think I'm just a little old-school when it comes to the dating stuff." *Yeah, right. Other than last weekend with Parker. Other than that one other time when I kissed a woman the first time I met her. Good job, Ella. Lying to others and yourself now. Good combo.*

Tally visibly relaxed, placing a hand on her chest and exhaling a laugh. "Thank goodness. I thought I came across all predatory for a second," she said, putting her fingers on her temples and shaking her head gently. "But, I'm patient. I look forward to seeing you tomorrow night. We can do a lot of dancing and talking and not-kissing."

Ella tried to figure out how she felt about the kissing or not-kissing, but just decided to let the chips fall where they may. "Sounds good. I'll lock up here. See you then," she said as Tally waved and walked out the door.

After watching to make sure she made it to her car, Ella closed the door and leaned her head gently against it. Exhaling slowly, she tried to make sense of it all. She heard Danna's bedroom door open, and next thing she knew, her friend's hand was on her shoulder.

"Did you have a good time?" she said, and Ella looked up into eyes that were twinkling with mischief.

"So, that was totally a setup, right?"

Danna shrugged, but never lost the trouble-making expression on her face. "Well, not exactly. I told Wendy and Val about the situation with Parker, and we all decided you needed to meet Tally. The game night is established, and she has been here before. The three of us just made sure she was going to be here this time so you could meet up. We were pretty sure you'd hit it off. What did you think?"

Ella blew out a breath, taking everything in. "She's great. We have some things in common and some not so much, but I'm more than willing to hang out with her and get to know her."

Danna nodded, focusing intently on her face while Ella tried to avoid her eyes. "But, she's not Parker," she stated. It was not a question.

Ella looked up at her with a face full of feigned confusion. "What do you mean by that? Parker and I are not dating," she said, overemphasizing not and trying to prove her point.

Danna smiled even brighter. She was not buying it. "Methinks the lady doth protest too much," she said and nudged Ella with her elbow. "You may not be dating. But you're definitely smitten."

Ella shook her head. "It's not even that. It's just crazy, intense physical chemistry. That's what it is, it's all physical. I mean, have you seen her? You've seen her. You know what I mean," she said, attempting to explain it all away.

Danna pursed her lips and tilted her head left to right in acquiescence. "That is totally possible. You could just be attracted to one another. Maybe there's nothing romantic there," she said, then paused. When Ella glanced at her, she looked to be deep in thought. Danna looked back at her with another broad smile. "Have you thought about just hooking up? One-night stands are her thing after all," she said.

Ella opened her mouth to say what a ridiculous idea that was, and more than once, before closing it and thinking about the suggestion. It might be Parker's thing, but was it hers? Could she do a one-night stand? Would Parker be interested? The idea was actually quite enticing. She must have cracked a smile because Danna started laughing and pointing at her.

"You need to talk to her. I guarantee you, if you do, you get laid. Plain and simple," she said, shrugging.

Ella tapped an index finger against her smiling lips. "I'm honestly not sure what I think about casual sex. Would I want my first time with a woman to just be a random lay?"

Danna shrugged. "Well, only you know that. Maybe this might help you get it out of your system, and then you can move on to actual dating. Tally seems to be smitten with you, and I think you could enjoy getting to know other women who aren't Parker."

Ella eyed her friend, confused. "So, you're telling me to have sex with Parker and date Tally? That doesn't sound like something I would ever do," she said. She had never been involved with cheating on either side of the equation, but she knew deep down that she was not that kind of person.

Danna shook her head. "No, I'm not saying that at all. I'm just saying you're allowed to date instead of going full-on relationship," she said with another good-natured smile on her lips.

Ella visibly relaxed. "How do I go about this? How do I *date?*" she said, making air quotes around the word.

"Just let both parties know that you're keeping things open. You just want to be completely honest with everyone. If there's no promise of commitment and they know that, I don't think you're doing anything wrong. You are allowed to date more than one person at a time," Danna said.

Ella pondered the thought of dating and how weird it was when you spent almost the entirety of your adult life married. "This is all so strange," she said, and Danna wrapped her up in one of her big hugs.

"It just gets weirder, my friend. And you're the new hot commodity. Now, go home and get a good night's sleep. You have a big night ahead of you tomorrow." Ella pulled back to look at her, shocked. Danna just shook her head and walked her to the door.

Chapter 10

After school was over, Ella headed home to stare at her closet again. Could she pull off another sweater/skinny jeans combo? Probably not so much. *To AJ's closet we go.* She wiggled her hips in preparation for the evening of dancing, finding a red poet's shirt with a plunging neckline. It was sheer enough to give a glimpse of everything underneath, so she found a camisole to wear under it. Paired up with some tight black dress pants and strappy sandals, it seemed to be the perfect outfit. She took a selfie and sent it to the group with Danna, Val, and Wendy, and the responses were immediate.

"Oh, my actual goodness. That's hot," Val messaged back. Danna sent a wolf-whistle .gif, and Wendy sent a big thumbs-up from her and Aubrey. This was apparently the outfit. She picked up her purse and keys and closed the door behind her.

Pulling into Danna's driveway, Ella saw that everyone, including Tally, had already arrived. She took a couple of deep breaths to relax before heading in to greet everyone. She hadn't even gotten halfway up the driveway before Danna opened the door and came out to greet her.

"You look so hot tonight. I swear we're going to have to beat them off you with a stick," she said, taking Ella into her arms for a big hug.

Ella chortled. "Well, I don't share your fears. But I am definitely looking forward to this evening. Thank you so much for allowing us to use your place as a hub," she said, entering the foyer and taking off her black leather jacket. Danna took it from her and folded it over her own forearm. Ella noticed she was not following her and turned around to find her with a very strange expression on her face.

Ella looked quizzically at her. "Is everything okay?" she said, as Danna looked down at her jacket before looking back at her.

"Yeah, everything is fine. I've just been thinking," she said, idly playing with the zipper on Ella's coat. "I'm just concerned that I gave you some bad advice last night. I shouldn't have encouraged you to sleep with anyone and I shouldn't have made you feel like you're being a player. I know we've only just met, but I want you to know I don't have that impression of you," Danna said, looking away.

"Hey, no, I didn't think that at all. I appreciate any advice you can give me. I know you don't think badly of me. I wasn't under that impression at all. I honestly feel like I don't know what I'm doing most of the time anyway. You're kind of like, my fairy grand-lesbian. It's nice," Ella said with a wink.

"You do realize you're older than me, right? Fairy grand-lesbian? As if!" Danna looked at her, appalled, then they both shared a giggle.

Danna looked back up at her still looking a bit troubled. Ella placed a hand on her forearm. "Really, it's okay," she said, and Danna took a deep breath and nodded. "Now, shall we get this party started?"

They moved into the kitchen where Wendy and Val were sharing a moment with Aubrey, and Tally was standing off to the side enjoying their witty banter. Ella's eyes went wide, and her mouth fell open at the sight of her. She was leaning against the kitchen counter in a black-and-white patterned mini dress. The spaghetti straps showed off lightly freckled shoulders and an expanse of her exposed, delicious back. The dress just kissed the top of her knees and was accented by pointed-toe black pumps that made her sculpted calves look like they went on forever. Tally noticed her noticing and blushed before setting her drink down and moving over to greet her.

"Hi," she said simply, wrapping her arms around Ella's neck to pull her into a hug. She felt Tally's body heat mingling with her own. She closed her eyes to commit the feeling to memory. When Tally stepped back, they smiled at one another.

"Hey, yourself. How was your day?" she said, and they spoke casually about their workdays before Danna announced that the 'party bus' had arrived. Ella made an *after you* motion with her hand, and Tally sauntered past. She could do this, right? Tally was beautiful, and even though she didn't get that immediate tightening in her chest like she did when Parker was around, Tally was the one she should pursue. Parker who? Right, decision made. The group loaded up in the back of the van and headed out for the evening.

~

Ella was the last one out of the van as she promised to text Parker when they had arrived and didn't want to do it openly in front of everyone. Parker responded with around twenty-seven thousand hearts and a drink emoji with a question mark. She never got the chance to pass along Parker's suggestion as Danna announced that the first thing they were doing when they went inside was drinking. Her mind was drifting when Tally came up behind her and squeezed her hand.

"Hey, is everything okay?" Tally asked.

Ella squeezed back and looked down before dropping her hand intentionally. How long would it take that electric feeling to form with Tally's touch? It would be nice if that could kick in at any moment now. *Do you hear me, Universe?* she said inside her head. This was all very disappointing.

"Yeah, just looking forward to getting in there and shaking my tail feathers," she said, doing the cabbage patch. Everyone stopped mid-conversation to laugh at her, and she shrugged.

"Wow, someone get this woman a drink," Danna said as they all headed into the front door.

Once everyone was inside, Ella followed Danna to get in line at the bar. She could barely see Parker over and around the crowd and bottles in front of her. But what she could see made her insides do flip-flops. When it was finally her turn to order and they were once again face to face, she discovered Parker was just as stunning as she had remembered.

She was wearing a black dress shirt with the sleeves cut off, suspenders, and a bow tie in patterns of black, silver, and bright blue. Her hair was sculpted in billowing near-black waves that spilled down her back and over her bare upper arms. When it was finally her turn to order, Ella couldn't speak over the lump that had formed in her throat. Parker froze for a few seconds as well before visibly shaking herself out of her reverie. Parker smiled brightly and reached across the bar to take her hand. She didn't feel the need to drop it as she had felt compelled to do with Tally's and looked down at their joined hands for a moment. Someone behind her cleared her throat obviously. Ella looked back to see Wendy, who raised her eyebrows into her hairline. She dropped Parker's hand and laughed nervously.

"Hey, good to see you. Let me get a vodka soda with lime, please," she said, staring into those coffee-colored eyes. She could lose herself if she weren't careful.

"Don't tell me. I remember how you like it," Parker said, and while it wasn't full of her bartender persona, the phrase still sounded flirtatious. Ella chuckled again and handed Parker her debit card, making sure that their hands did not touch. She wasn't sure she would survive another touch and could possibly just combust where she stood.

Parker handed her the drink a minute later, and of course, it was just as delicious as last time. Ella started to move out of line, but Parker gently grasped her forearm.

"Hey, my first break is in a few hours. I'll text you just before," she said, ceasing her touch. Ella missed it already. She nodded at Parker before the rest of the group placed their orders and were on their way out to the dance floor.

They spent a good amount of time dancing as a group before Wendy, Val, and Aubrey shuffled to one side and into a more secluded part of the dance floor unofficially reserved for make-out sessions. As Val leaned in to kiss Aubrey, Wendy grabbed her waist from behind and began kissing her neck.

"Are you enjoying the show?" Tally said, leaning in to speak directly into her ear.

Ella startled before turning around to greet her. "Give me a heart attack, why don't you?" she said before wiping her brow in a *whew* motion and placing her hand on her chest. "I was just thinking to myself what a wonderful place this is, you know? People can just come here and dance with who they want or," she paused, nodding at her three friends who were now officially grinding on the dance floor, "dry hump whoever they want and it's all good."

Tally laughed, and it was a musical sound; light, feminine, and full of mirth. "That's true. This is only your second time here, right? You came last weekend with the crew?"

Ella swallowed hard. She hoped Danna's penchant for being overly verbose had not spilled a glass of Parker Chase onto Tally. "Yeah, this is just my second time," she said and left it at that. Tally didn't indicate there was anything to know, like she got so drunk a beautiful stranger had to take her back to her place. With the warm memory of Parker's care on her mind, she decided to finish her drink and acquire reinforcements.

"Hey, look at that," she said, holding up the glass and giving it a brief shake to emphasize its emptiness. "I'm going to go get another. Can I get you something?"

Tally apparently took it as a challenge and opted to drain her white wine spritzer. "Yeah, since you're going, if you don't mind. I'll just take another," she said, handing Ella the glass.

"I'll keep her warm for you, friend," Danna said, sidling up to take Tally in her arms. "Pick me up another long neck while you're there?" she said, and then they were swallowed up by the crowd which moved in unison to the beat.

"Sure, I'll just bring out my third hand to carry that!" she said to the empty space where Danna and Tally were moments ago.

Ella got back in line at the bar, and when she finally made it back to Parker, she found a drink waiting on her. Parker nudged it toward her expectantly with that ever-present smile. Ella returned the smile wordlessly before trying the drink. This was another Sex with the Bartender. And it was good. So good.

"I saw you coming over, so I went ahead and made you one. That one's on me, by the way. I am officially buying you a drink. See how debonair I am?" she said, straightening her bow tie and picking up her suspenders so they snapped down on her shoulders.

Ella gulped, getting lost in her own dirty, dirty thoughts. "You're so kind, thank you. How much longer till your break?" she said, unable to resist trying to get even just a bit of time with Parker.

"You're in luck. I'm just closing out and I have half an hour. Shall we dance?" Parker said, coming around the bar and offering her hand to Ella. She took it and all was right with the world, until she remembered the drinks she was fetching.

"Shit, I forgot to get drinks for my…friends," she said, not knowing how to ambiguously label Tally. Parker raised her eyebrow, and Ella waved her hand dismissively. "Danna and Tally. I know you know Danna, but Tally wasn't here last weekend. Anyway, I need to pick up a white wine spritzer and a Bud Light," she said.

Parker nodded and turned to the shirtless, muscular man who took her place behind the bar. "Hey, Rack, can you do a white wine spritzer and grab a Bud Light for Ella? Just put it on my tab," she said, and Rack nodded.

"You got it, girlfriend!" Rack said in a surprisingly high voice that did not fit his hulking, sculpted frame. He looked at Ella expectantly. "So, you're Ella?" he said as he was sorting out the drinks.

Ella looked at him, bewildered. "That's me," she said, sounding unsure. "Am I in trouble?"

Rack laughed out loud; a hearty sound that did not sound at all forced. "You've got two ladies here tonight? It's brave buying drinks for two women at the same time. I sense a catfight. Oh, tell me there's going to be a catfight," he said, making swiping motions with his hands and hissing.

"Uh, no. Two of my friends asked me to get them refills while I was over here," Ella said, and Parker grabbed up the drinks Rack provided. He pouted.

"Damn. Oh well, enjoy your night!" he said and blew her a kiss. Ella smiled and made the motion to catch it, which just sent Rack into another fit of laughter. He looked pointedly at Parker and nodded approvingly. She grinned back at him, without abandon.

Parker indicated Ella should lead the way, and they made their way back to find Danna and Tally dancing like wild animals. She and Parker looked at each other and shared a smile. Danna was the first to turn and meet them, freezing for a moment before taking the beer Parker offered her. She took a big swig before tapping Tally on the shoulder.

"Hi, I'm Parker," she said, holding out her now-free right hand to Tally, who grasped it before looking at Ella and Danna in succession.

"I'm Tally. Nice to meet you. You're the bartender, right? Is that my special delivery?" she said, pointing at the drink in Parker's hand. When she nodded, Tally took the drink with a curtsey. Parker bowed back, and they both laughed nervously. Ella looked at the floor. Danna looked among all three of them before rolling her eyes and suggesting they all dance so Parker could enjoy her break. She immediately threw her arms around Ella's neck and began a conversation that neither Danna nor Tally could hear over the music.

"It's so good to see you!" she said, enveloping Ella in an all-encompassing hug. When she pulled back, their faces were once again in each other's space. Ella could only stare at her sensuous lips, which made her think about their first kiss. *Eggs. Just think of eggs and get yourself under control. You can make it through this,* she pep-talked in her head. She moved behind Parker where at least she could be in control of the situation and began to dance.

"Yeah, it's great to see you, too," she said. And she meant it. She couldn't deny the fire that burned deep in her core when Parker was close. Touching her, even casually, was almost too much. When the song changed to something with a deeply driving beat, Parker ground backwards against her, reaching up to thread her hand through Ella's hair. The touch made her heart skip a beat, and her nipples hardened as Parker's suspenders ran over them. She closed her eyes and groaned to herself before placing her hands on Parker's hips. When she looked up, she saw

Danna and Tally dancing together, but Tally's eyes were focused on them. Ella decided to make things a lot more casual. With a welcoming smile and a step back, she motioned Tally and Danna over to join them. Tally took the opportunity to interject herself between Parker and Ella's bodies, and Danna moved in behind Parker, who looked momentarily startled, but then found a rhythm between Tally and Danna.

Tally stared up at Ella before grabbing her waist and grinding out her apparent frustrations on her upper thigh. Ella looked back at her before glancing over her shoulder and finding Parker's chocolate eyes. They were heavy-lidded and full of want. Parker then wrapped her arms around Tally's waist and pulled her in to grind out a sexy dance on her backside while reaching for Ella. Tally's eyes went wide, as she came to understand she was losing the battle she and Parker were in.

"I'm going to go to the bathroom," Tally said, removing herself from the foursome. She left without waiting for a reply. Ella looked at Danna, who motioned she was going to go with her. She then looked at Parker, who smiled back wryly and stepped back into her space.

"So, that's your…friend?" she said and crossed her arms.

Ella blew out a breath and shrugged noncommittally. "We met last night at a game night. Danna invited her to come tonight. We're just kind of getting to know each other."

Parker nodded, resigned and seemingly more to herself than in response to Ella's answer. Then, she smiled brightly, and Ella recognized the falseness in its lack of luster. "Well, I guess we can all use more friends, right?" she said and looked at her watch. "My break's almost over, so I'm going to head back. I hope you guys have a good time tonight," she said and started to walk off.

Ella clasped her forearm gently. Parker stopped but didn't look at her. "Parker, I..." she said, trailing off. Parker finally met her eyes. There was a lot of hurt in them and it tore at Ella.

"Look, it's all right. I know where I stand. I don't expect anything. We're good. We're friends, right?" Parker said, but she didn't look like she meant it.

Ella pulled her around to face her. Parker still didn't meet her eyes. Ella lifted her chin to meet her eyes. "Yes, we are friends. But I want you to know, I'm not with Tally. I'm not *with* anyone." Parker smiled again, but it didn't reach her eyes. Ella couldn't stop herself from wrapping her in a comforting embrace. She didn't want Parker to hurt. It was excruciating for Ella to see the pain in her eyes. She felt Parker's arms encircle her waist and lost herself for a moment in whatever magic was between them. It was like the rest of the world fell away when Parker was in her arms.

Parker stepped back first, and Ella immediately missed the feel of their bodies pressed together. Parker smiled up at her again, but her eyes darted away almost immediately. "I do need to get back. Text me sometime?"

"Are we still hanging out tomorrow?" Ella said, and Parker visibly paled at the mention of their previously agreed upon hang-out session. "Hey, I didn't mean to—we don't have to if you don't want to. We had just already talked about it, and I thought I'd check," she said, running a hand through her hair. Damn it. Had she just put Parker into a position to say yes when she no longer wanted to?

"Sure, yeah. Just text me tomorrow afternoon, and we'll figure it out." And with that, Parker gently squeezed her shoulder before returning to the bar area. Ella could only stare after her.

～

"Girl, you've got to deal with this situation," Danna said, as they sat on her porch after everyone had gone home.

The group had returned to Danna's house after an extremely uncomfortable rest of the night at Sparkle. Tally would hardly look at her, instead spending most of the rest of the evening dancing with Danna. With Wendy, Val, and Aubrey off doing God knows what, Ella spent most of the evening dancing on her own or with strangers. She also opted to give Parker her space and didn't see her for the rest of the night.

"What situation? Parker is my friend. I have told her that in no uncertain terms we cannot be together. I was enjoying hanging out with Tally," she said.

Danna stared at her incredulously. "Are you serious right now?" she said, and Ella looked up to meet her withering stare with one of her own, throwing her hands up in the air. She picked up the glass of iced tea Danna had given her and took a long drink.

"You have to be able to feel what everyone else can see," she said and placed a gentle hand on Ella's thigh, who fixated on a spot on the ground while Danna talked. "Ella, there's something there. There's a spark. You guys can't stop yourselves from just staring at each other when you're together. I'm not telling you that you have to explore it, you just have to realize that it is happening and how it might affect other people."

"I know, I know," Ella said with a weary sigh. "I didn't mean for this to happen. I didn't know for sure that there would be that same kind of energy. This is only the second time I've seen her. And now, I've fucked up everything with Tally," she said, slumping down in the rocking chair.

Danna put a comforting arm around her. "It's rough when everyone wants you, huh?" she said, squeezing her shoulder.

Ella flipped her off, then chuckled good-naturedly. "Do you think I still have a chance with Tally?" she said.

Danna's eyebrows knitted together in response. "Are you still interested in her? I mean, I just assumed—" she said, all swagger gone from her posture.

"Of course I am. I still want to see what happens. I think I'll just ask her out and go from there. The worst thing she can say is no," Ella said, pulling her phone out of her pocket and typing out a text. She didn't seem to notice Danna's discomfort. "There," she said after hitting send. "And now we wait."

Danna took a long drink of her iced tea and looked off into the middle distance. When Ella's phone started ringing, she looked at her friend expectantly. Danna still did not meet her eyes.

"Hey, Tally, thanks for calling me back," she said. When Tally didn't immediately respond, she opted to continue. "So, I had a great time tonight, and I was wondering if you would like to have dinner with me sometime?" When there was no response again, she pulled the phone away from her ear to make sure the call was still active.

"It looked like you had a good time tonight," Tally said with acid in her voice. "But it didn't seem to be me you were having a good time with."

Ella mouthed *fuck* under her breath. She regrouped and thought back to what Danna had told her, that dating multiple people is acceptable if you're honest with all parties. "Listen, I'm just getting to know different people. Parker is just a friend," she said.

"I'm not interested in who you are getting to know, biblically or otherwise. She didn't look like just a friend, and I'm not interested in a fling with you," Tally said. Her tone was murderous.

"I'm not looking for a fling either. I'm just not sure how to do this. I just wanted to date after my divorce, you know? You're one of the first people I have met that I have truly been interested in. Ahh! I don't even know if I am doing this right! I got married right after I graduated high school. This is my first foray into the dating world. I'm sorry if I hurt your feelings. It wasn't my intention," she said and sighed deeply. All she could do was wait for Tally's response.

"So, you're not dating her? The bartender? Are you dating anyone else?"

"No! I'm not dating her. And, no, I'm not dating anyone else. I'd just like for us to have dinner and see if there's anything we can build upon. I understand if you're not interested, though. I won't push you any further. Again, I'm really sorry," Ella said. After yet another pause, she heard Tally sigh and follow it up with a chuckle.

"You must be irresistible. Okay, let's have dinner. How about next weekend?"

Ella thought for a moment, remembering AJ would be back then. But she was almost eighteen now and would have to learn how to handle the fact that her mother was trying to build some semblance of a social life.

"That sounds great. Let's chat later in the week and we'll set up a time?" Tally agreed on the other line, and after disconnecting the call, Danna just shook her head with a much smaller grin than normal.

"Damn, Ella. You've just got them falling all over you. Did she agree to dinner?" When Ella nodded, Danna nodded back. "I figured as much. And you're still *hanging out* with Parker tomorrow?" Danna's tone was knowing, but Ella wasn't fazed.

"Yes, of course I am. Why wouldn't I?"

Danna took another swig of iced tea before she looked at Ella directly in the eye. "Because you're playing with fire. You know that, right? If you're sure all you want to do is be friends, then be friends with her. But I'm telling you that going back to her apartment is only going to go one way and I think deep down you know it," she said.

Ella looked at her quizzically. "You're the one who told me to explore this. You even suggested that I consider a one-night stand with her. And now, it seems like a bad idea to hang out with her? What's going on?"

"Nothing. I just…" She trailed off and ran a hand through her hair. "You know you're going to ruin any chance with Tally, and I think it will really hurt her." Danna looked back at Ella imploringly. Ella couldn't hide her confusion. Danna stood and started back inside.

"Danna, nothing is going to happen," she said to her retreating form.

Danna stopped and, without turning around, addressed Ella again. "Famous last words, my new friend. Good luck," she said and walked back inside her house leaving Ella utterly dazed and confused.

Chapter 11

Ella pulled into the parking space in front of Parker's apartment and took a moment to evaluate everything. She again pulled something out of AJ's closet to wear; more super cool shredded jeans to go with a distressed, long-sleeved, charcoal gray Henley and her high-top black Chuck Taylors. She felt much more confident than she would be in her own clothes. She pulled down the car's vanity mirror to run her hand through her wavy, ash-blond curls before concluding she was presentable. Getting out of the car and retrieving the fifth of Grey Goose vodka, she took a deep breath to steady her nerves before walking up to Parker's door and knocking.

It didn't take long for her to answer the door. As soon as she did, all of Ella's senses were immediately engaged. Her eyes were filled with the picture of loveliness in front of her. Parker was in a simple black T-shirt that sat right above her belly button and very sporty looking khaki capris that showed off her ample hips and ass. She could hear Nirvana Unplugged playing through speakers. Her nose was filled with the amazing aromas coming from the kitchen. Suddenly, there was a wooden spoon leveled at her mouth.

"Here, taste this. Is this almost right?" Parker said in greeting.

Ella smiled awkwardly at the gesture, but the smells coming from the food being shoved into her face were too much to deny. She blew on the steaming sauce before taking the spoon and feeding herself. It was absolutely one the best vindaloos she had ever put into her mouth. The umami flavor hit hard with notes of more spices than she could even imagine. The heat followed, and it was powerful, but not debilitating. The finish was slightly tart from what she knew was vinegar with multiple fresh herbs. She couldn't stop the hum of pleasure that escaped her lips as her eyes closed. But then, her eyes popped open in realization of exactly what was going on here.

"You…made me a vindaloo?" Ella asked, honestly surprised.

Parker nodded, smiling. "Lamb vindaloo to be exact. I've always wanted to try to cook lamb, and I need to continue to work on my curry repertoire. This seemed like the perfect opportunity for both." Parker stood expectantly in front of her as Ella looked at the spoon and then back at her.

"You made me lamb vindaloo?"

"Uh, yeah. You said it was your favorite. Did I get something wrong?" Parker looked uncertain.

Ella took her hand and pulled her gently into a one-armed embrace, making sure to hold the spoon away from their clothing so there was no danger of staining. "This is one of the kindest things anyone has ever done for me. I'm just floored," she said, pulling back to look into her eyes and was instantly mesmerized. A lock of hair had escaped her low ponytail, undoubtedly while she was cooking, and Ella couldn't stop herself from tucking it behind her ear. Parker gulped audibly, and Ella stepped back to put some distance between them, breaking the moment.

"Sorry," Ella said, but Parker shushed her by placing the spoon gently on her lips.

"No apologies needed. Friends hug, right?" she said, and Ella inclined her head in agreement. Parker made a sweeping motion with her hand, indicating she should enter.

"So, what kind of movie do you think we should watch?" she said without looking at Parker. "I've got all the streaming apps. We can use any of mine if you don't have them." Ella pulled her phone out of the back pocket of her jeans and pulled up Amazon Prime to peruse options. When Parker didn't respond, Ella met her eyes and she looked slightly dazed. The movie question seemed to snap her out of it.

"Um, yeah. I think I have them all. Do you like horror movies? I'm always up for something scary." Ella just stared again at this woman with whom she continued to find much in common. She just had to remind herself that if Parker was online dating, they would never have met. That filled her with less relief and more sadness than she wanted to admit.

"I love horror movies. I love everything from slasher to paranormal to Hammer horror from the '50s," Ella said and began to look through the online catalog.

Now, it was Parker's turn to stare. "Uh, yeah. I like all that stuff, too. I usually nerd-out at people when they tell me they like scary movies. Have you ever heard of Mario Bava? He was an Italian filmmaker—" She stopped talking as Ella looked at her, mouth open and obviously flabbergasted.

"Mario Bava is one of my favorites." The statement hung in the air as they continued to gawk unbelievingly at each other. Ella looked away first.

"I think a lot of people just don't give older horror movies a chance, but I always loved that kind of stuff. What's your favorite Bava film? Don't tell me. Let's write it down on a piece of paper and swap them. That way we can see if this *is* fate." Parker made the statement with an inflection in her voice and a wink, but she wasn't sure that the Fates weren't spinning their threads tonight in her living room.

Parker got a sheet of paper and two pencils. She ripped it in two and handed Ella one of the halves and one of the pencils. Ella seemed to really be finding the fun in the situation, but Parker was having a hard time stopping her hand from shaking. She quickly wrote down *The Whip and the Body* and pushed the paper over. Ella made her notations and folded her paper over several times before pushing it towards her.

Parker opened Ella's paper, sincerely relieved that it said *Black Sunday*. That almost would have been too much. Being huge Bava fans, they had both seen the other's movies previously, but they agreed to watch them both. She finished up the curry in the next hour so they could have an early dinner before they settled in on the couch for their scare-athon.

Dinner was pretty outstanding, even if Parker did say so herself. Ella continually thanked her for going to all the trouble, and she repeatedly said it wasn't a problem. Because it wasn't. This is what you do for someone you care about. It was going to be hard to just have a friendship with Ella, but she was convinced that, in time, she could make her see that they could be together. She just had to be patient and play the long game.

Ella got the movie set up as Parker began making a digestif. Mixing the vodka Ella brought with some sambuca and ice in a cocktail shaker, she crafted a black licorice martini. She took two glasses out of the freezer and poured the drink. Parker topped everything off with a stick of quality black licorice and headed to where Ella sat watching some movie trailers.

"Hey, this one is new, but I think I'd like to see it with you. I know we've got two movies picked out, but maybe we could watch it next time?" Ella said as she looked up to see Parker standing next to her with their drinks.

Parker still couldn't believe her luck. Sitting here in her apartment was the woman of her dreams. They were hanging out, things were going smoothly, *and* Ella was now alluding to there being a *next time*. Inside, there was much cheering, but she had to play it cool on the surface. "Yeah, sure, that would be great," she said, handing her a glass. "I didn't even think to ask you if you like licorice, but it has a lot of properties that are good to consume after a big meal." Parker took a long drink from her glass.

Ella did the same and hummed with pleasure. "That's absolutely delicious," she said, taking another big drink. Parker sipped hers and giggled, reaching over to gently press the glass away from Ella's attempt at a third drink.

"Slow down there, Tiger."

Ella smiled apologetically. "I have this tendency to drink pretty heavily when I'm nervous," she admitted, biting her bottom lip. "But I am guessing you figured that out after the other night...and morning."

Parker stared at the movement and wanted only to replace Ella's teeth with her own in a tenderly nipping kiss.

"Hang on," Parker said, taking Ella's drink and setting them both down on the coffee table. Ella looked at her incredulously while Parker took her hands, looking her directly in the eye. "We had this discussion earlier, but I know where you're at. You don't have to worry about any pressure or expectations from me. If you want to be best friends, I'm up for that. Most importantly, I don't want to make you nervous."

Ella couldn't stop herself from pressing her lips to Parker's knuckles in a move that was solely relief. "I appreciate that more than you can know," she said, dropping their hands to pick up her drink for another sip. Parker noticed the relaxation in her demeanor now. She was just hopeful that Ella wasn't paying attention to the pink blush she could feel on her cheeks and the fact that she was ultimately not relaxed in the slightest with her in close proximity.

They watched the first movie in relative silence, but Parker couldn't help stealing glances whenever she could. Ella sprawled out in one corner of the couch with her long, slender arms draped over the top and the armrest. For most of the movie, her left knee was tucked up against her body with her right foot on the floor.

Parker sat in the middle of the couch alternating between placing her hands down on either side of her and clasping her hands together on her lap. With Ella's long arms straightened out to their fullest, there was no way she could stretch out for fear of their arms grazing against one another. Ella's fingers tapped and idly played with the junction of her attached-back sofa cushions, probably less than an inch from Parker's shoulder. She had a hard time focusing on anything that wasn't this intense closeness.

Once the credits rolled on the first movie, there were a few uncomfortable beats of silence. Parker moved to pick up their now empty glasses, consumed with nervous energy and unable to sit still. "More to drink?"

Ella pursed her lips and seemed to ponder. "I don't know how I feel about a belly full of licorice," she said, rubbing her tummy for emphasis. "I love the flavor, but I don't know if I would want more than one. It was intense."

Parker nodded in understanding. "Yeah, I agree. We could have some vodka rocks, or I could come up with another concoction. Or..." she said, drawing the last word out suggestively. Ella looked at her and raised her eyebrows. "I can make some mixed drinks and we could play a drinking game while we watch the next movie," Parker said as she put her arms out to the side in a *ta-da* motion.

Ella chortled. "Do you really think we will find a Mario Bava drinking game online?" she said, and Parker furrowed her brow in response.

"We can just use a generic horror movie drinking game," Parker said.

Ella breathed in deeply and closed her eyes before letting it out. "I'm in."

Parker held up her hand for a high five, and Ella chuckled before slapping their hands together. "Friends high five, too, in case you were curious," she said in a playful tone.

"You know, I think I had that part figured out. I have had friends before. You're not my first, Parker Chase," Ella said suggestively.

Parker chose to ignore the double entendre potential and opted against teasing her or flirting back. She then picked up the dirty glasses and headed into the kitchen. Having plenty of orange juice, she decided to make some screwdrivers in tall glasses. She carried the drinks back into the living room and handed one to Ella, who took a sip.

"Nothing wrong with a screwdriver," she said and held her glass out to Parker to cheers. Parker clinked their glasses together and started deeply into Ella's eyes.

"Here's to giving amazing new friendships a chance."

Ella returned her gaze with the same intensity, never breaking the eye contact as both took another long drink. It was Parker who turned away first, laughing nervously.

"Well, let's find this game and get the movie going."

They found several drinking games and chose one of the most ridiculous ones. Some of the rules of the game were hilarious like taking a single sip if there was a scary doll and finishing your drink if someone ran upstairs to get away from the killer. They were forced to refill their glasses a few times before the movie was over, and both had achy stomach muscles from the amount of laughing they did at the game and each other.

"Where's your bathroom?" Ella said between giggles, begging and pleading to get a break so she could catch her breath.

Parker pointed down the hallway. Ella excused herself, and Parker just lay back in the corner where Ella had just been sitting. She was surrounded by Ella's very scent, citrus with light floral undertones. It was almost exactly like what spring evenings smelled like, when the first flowers of the season were starting to bloom. She closed her eyes and took a few deep breaths, wanting to fill her lungs with the essence before she got back. When she heard the bathroom door open, she moved quickly back to her spot in the middle of the couch.

Ella stumbled just slightly as she moved back into the living room, bracing herself against the wall as she went. "I have to get out of the habit of drinking so much. You're going to end up with bad opinions of me," she said as she ambled her way back to the couch. Parker held her hand out to help Ella make it back to the couch safely. She fell more than sat into her previous spot in the corner, unable to stifle a laugh as she sank down. She never let go of Parker's hand.

"I don't think it's possible for me to have a bad opinion of you," she said, making meaningful eye contact with Ella. "I can't imagine how hard things have been for you. You've been a mother since you were seventeen. You never got to have much of a young adulthood. I'm sure there's probably a lot of cutting loose that you're just dying to do. I'm just happy to have you here hanging out with me. I always want to be the person who gets to hang out with you when you're a little more than tipsy. I will always take care of you."

Ella felt her heart skip a beat and the heat rise in her chest until it reached her cheeks in a full blush. Parker was so kind and beautiful and sweet and, God, so sexy. No, wait. Not sexy. Friendly. Parker was friendly. They were going to be the best of friends. She noticed Parker staring at her mouth and then back at her eyes, almost as if she were asking permission. But she didn't move. Parker kept the distance she promised she would keep when they initially found out about their age difference.

And there it was. Mood killer. Perfect. She put it at the forefront of her mind. Ella gently pulled her hand away and sat back into the corner. Parker looked sad for a moment, but quickly masked it.

"So, what do we do now? I'm not sure we should drink more," Parker said.

Ella laughed, a short, barking sound. "No, definitely no more to drink. How about you get us a couple of waters and we can just put on a nice, calm movie and we just kind of wait for the alcohol to wear off?"

Parker nodded and got up to retrieve two bottles from her refrigerator. She returned to the couch to see that Ella had stretched her legs out on the couch and was holding the blanket that had been draped over the back; the same blanket she had tucked around Ella last weekend. Parker surveyed the situation. Did she want the couch all to herself? Or maybe she needed to stretch out and wanted her to sit at the other end? Ella smiled warmly at her confusion and held up the blanket for Parker to, what exactly?

"I've queued up *Fried Green Tomatoes*. I figured I need to get caught up on more lesbian movies so I can go ahead and get my permanent card," Ella said and smiled brightly. When Parker seemed to balk and didn't move, Ella continued, hoping to provide comfort. "Friends share blankets, right?" Ella said, and Parker met her eyes with a deer-in-the-headlights expression. She started to rethink her invitation when Parker finally spoke.

"Right, yes, they do. These are things that friends do," she said in a forced tone with all the words stringing together into one long statement. She opted to move quickly before Ella changed her mind, despite realizing it was probably going to be torturous for her. She moved back to where Ella was sitting, and when she was unable to come up with a proper friend cuddle position in her head, she looked to Ella for ideas.

"So, how do you want to do this? I can sit where I was and you could put your legs on my lap," she said as she hefted Ella's legs and scooted herself underneath. *This is great. I can do this.* She looked at Ella and smiled as she placed her hands on her shins, all friend-like. A gentle smile peaked at the edge of Ella's lips as she never averted her eyes. Again, she raised the blanket, and Parker eyed her inquisitively.

"Come here," she said, barely audible. When Parker didn't immediately move, Ella leaned up and wrapped an arm around her shoulder, pulling her tenderly into her space. Parker's head now rested on Ella's chest and Ella wrapped her arms around her in a warm embrace. She took in a slow deep breath and expelled it slowly at the feeling of being folded up in Ella's arms. She felt sheltered and cherished as Ella placed her chin on top of her head and began to gently stroke her shoulder.

Parker thought her heart might explode with joy at the feeling of just being held by this woman she met only a week ago. She felt the tears stinging her eyes. It had been so long since she felt safe with anyone, but almost from the very moment she met Ella, she would have given her anything, any part of her, even the ones she had shoved so far down so long ago. It seemed like yesterday and a hundred years ago all at once.

Parker had not let herself go with anyone, always keeping her guard altogether in place. Yet, here she was, tucked up with Ella, a fortress around her as she felt naked in her arms. Could this be a safe place? Could Ella be her safe place so she could finally relax and let go?

"Do you want to turn the movie on?" Ella said above her.

Parker loved feeling the vibration and timbre of her voice reverberate through her chest as she spoke. She reached around blindly for the remote before finding it on the back of the couch behind her. There was no way she was moving. Despite the immense comfort she was feeling now, she was on tenterhooks thinking that Ella could change her mind about their situation at any moment.

She leaned up the slightest bit to be able to angle the remote at the television just right to start the movie before returning to her previous position. She chanced putting her arms around Ella, and when the other woman did not complain, Parker exhaled happily.

Ella continued to stroke up and down her shoulder and upper arm, alternating between gentle massage and feather-light caresses. Parker's body shifted between an almost cosmic solace and intense pleasure. She didn't know whether she would end up being exceedingly sexually aroused or fall asleep. But, as her body juggled both sensations in equal amounts, she knew she was happier than she could remember being in a very long time.

The movie was lovely and emotional, and when she sniffled during one of the saddest scenes she had ever watched, she felt Ella hug her even closer, if that was possible. When Ella placed a soft kiss on the top of her head, she shuddered involuntarily. She leaned up to look at Ella and discovered she was also teary.

"That was emotional to say the least," Parker said with a self-deprecating chuckle as she wiped at her eyes. She sat up a bit more while not removing herself from Ella's space. Parker could not stop herself from reaching up and wiping a tear from under the other woman's eye. Ella leaned into the touch, brushing her lips across Parker's palm.

When Ella looked up again, her eyes burned with desire. Parker gulped, wanting to move in and kiss her, but also wanting to respect Ella's decision to remain friends. When Ella took her hand and kissed each of her fingertips in succession, Parker's resolve was all but gone.

"Ella, I—" she said, but Ella slowly leaned in and placed her mouth on Parker's, mimicking their first gentle kiss. Ella leaned back and gazed at her searchingly. Parker closed her eyes and expelled a breath that was meant to calm her arousal. When she opened her eyes again and met Ella's darkened gaze, all hope of that evaporated.

"I'm not sure this is something friends do," Parker said cautiously, giving her one more chance to back out. Ella didn't smile, and when she leaned in and kissed Parker with purpose, all previous determination to keep things on a friendly level was gone.

Ella's lips tasted like the sweetest candy, with remnants of orange from their earlier drinks. When Parker felt Ella's tongue tentatively running along her lower lip, she felt herself quiver with the sensation and willingly opened her mouth to receive her. The slow burn between them had just ignited into a towering inferno of delectation.

Ella made a noise that was a cross between a moan and a whimper and that was all the encouragement Parker needed to take over. She pulled back momentarily to change their position and tug Ella onto her lap. They were both already breathing rapidly and erratically.

"I may not have done this before, but I want you to know, I'm not afraid," Ella said before leaning in and crashing their lips together again. Parker brought her hands around to Ella's back, running them down to cup her ass and pull her closer. Ella wrapped her legs around Parker's middle and their centers were connected despite the clothing in the way. Parker felt the immediate contact and groaned into Ella's mouth at the same time she moaned softly.

Kisses turned more intense then as Parker could not stop herself from nibbling gently at her lower lip. As she filled Ella's mouth with her tongue, Parker gently tugged at the hem of Ella's shirt. Ella deftly removed it in one fell swoop, revealing a lacy black bra. Parker's mouth watered at the sight. She lowered her mouth to gently bite at Ella's taut nipple through the fabric. Ella hissed out her approval at the move, gently rocking and grinding her hips down into Parker, who immediately felt the wetness in her underwear increase exponentially.

Parker pulled back and looked into Ella's eyes for permission. When Ella met her stare and leaned forward to deliver a tantalizing lick to her bottom lip, Parker's hands went around to unhook her bra. Once undone, Ella removed the offending article of clothing, dropping it on the ground.

Ella was anything but shy as she leaned forward, offering her now naked breasts to Parker who happily partook. She tentatively licked a nipple before sucking it into her mouth wholly, applying precise pressure and eliciting a long moan from Ella's lips. She brought up her hand to Ella's other nipple, alternating rolling it between her fingers and gently pinching.

"Parker, God, you're driving me crazy," she said breathlessly, her chest heaving. Parker didn't relent, instead moving her mouth to the other nipple while her hands slipped down and fumbled with the button on Ella's pants.

"Bedroom?" Ella said, putting her hand on Parker's seeking one. Parker temporarily ceased the carnal assault on her breasts. She had been totally lost in the moment, and Ella's voice felt like it was coming from somewhere very far away. This woman was just all-consuming. "If you don't take me there now, we're going to end up fucking on the couch."

Parker looked up into Ella's eyes, which had gone dark with desire. If she was going to do this, she was going to do it right. Ella was different—special, and this needed to be more than just sex on a couch. She was going to make her first time remarkable for her, in every way that she could.

Parker nodded her approval and held her hand out to the side, helping Ella to stand. She then rose from the couch and kissed Ella sweetly before taking her hand and leading her down the hall to the bedroom.

Once inside, Ella leaned back against the door and Parker closed the distance between them. She took Ella's hands and placed them above her head as she attacked her mouth with her own. Then, Parker dropped to her knees, and Ella looked down into her heavily lidded eyes before placing her hand on Parker's cheek. Parker turned her head into the touch and brought one of Ella's fingers to her lips before sucking it fully into her mouth.

Ella gasped at the new sensation and added another finger to join the first in the warmth between her lips. The feeling of having her fingers lavished by Parker's obviously talented tongue was the greatest foreshadowing of what was to come.

Parker tugged her pants down so achingly slowly before helping her step out of them. Ella stood in front of her in nothing but her panties, and Parker could only stare for a moment, taking in the sheer statuesque beauty that was Ella's near-naked body. Her heart swelled in her chest in anticipation of what was about to happen and what it would mean to her. To them both.

Parker rose up on her knees and placed her hands on either side of Ella's hips. She gently stroked up and down her thighs before leaning in to kiss the panel of her lacy black thong. She could feel the heat radiating from Ella's core as it arced across her moist lips. She felt Ella start to breathe heavier and looked up at her. Ella was staring at the ceiling with her palms pressed flat against the door.

"Hey, is this all okay? I just want to make sure you're—"

Ella looked down at her momentarily before tugging down her underwear. "Parker, stop talking and fuck me," she said on a breathy moan. When Parker grinned but still didn't move toward her, Ella thought she would just go completely insane as she felt a fresh wave of wetness threaten to escape down her thighs.

"Parker, please…" she whimpered.

"Oh, I definitely like it when you beg me," she said, ceasing her teasing and placing a soft kiss on her pubic hair before encouraging Ella to lift her leg and placing it securely on her shoulder. Ella was bared to her now and she got to see exactly how ready she was. Parker's own arousal doubled, but she knew tonight would be about this beautiful woman pressed against her bedroom door.

Parker ran a single finger through her folds, and Ella practically jumped at the contact. Parker pulled back, and Ella, breathing heavily, whined again and looked down. When their eyes met, Parker placed the finger in her mouth, sucking Ella's heady essence from it. She saw Ella's eyes go wide at the motion. Ella tasted exquisite like fine wine, salty and sweet and fully intoxicating. Parker couldn't wait any longer and leaned toward Ella.

She gently ran her tongue over Ella's core, light strokes that would not push her over the edge too quickly. Parker tongued her entrance before making long, languid strokes along her lips until she finally ran the flat of her tongue over her clit. Ella moaned again and ground down onto Parker's face, trying to increase the amount of contact. When Parker took her fully into her mouth, Ella's legs began to shake in earnest. Parker knew the first orgasm would come quickly, but she would make sure it would be the first of many tonight. She pushed two fingers inside Ella and matched her strokes in time with the licks on her clit. Ella's legs began to shake fiercely, and Parker heard her name being repeated over and over and louder with each repetition.

"Parker…I…I'm coming!" Ella said, seemingly looking for reprieve from the licentious attention Parker lavished upon her.

But Parker never ceased her efforts. Ella's entire body tensed as she screamed before going slack. She placed one more kiss on her thigh before getting to her feet and taking Ella in her arms. She was breathless and leaned her weight fully on Parker, boneless in her post-release state. Parker encouraged her to wrap her legs around her, and when Ella did, Parker turned her around and carried her the few remaining feet to her bed.

"Wait, Parker, wait..." she said, obviously still flustered from the mind-blowing orgasm she had just had.

But Parker had no intention of waiting on anything. She had to have more. Ella was a drug, and she was now fully addicted. She tugged off her own shirt before retreating backwards off the bed to remove her pants. She had to feel Ella fully against her. In just a bra and a pair of boy shorts, she lay on top of Ella, feeling their bodies press together. Fevered skin melded as they became one being of one mind with just one shared desire.

Parker moaned at the contact. "You feel fucking amazing, Ella," she said before kissing her deeply once again. Ella immediately returned the kiss and wrapped her arms around her neck as their tongues played and searched in each other's mouths. Parker ran her hand down Ella's body, finding her wetness and placed her hand over the heat between her legs.

Ella startled at the contact. "I can't, not again. Not yet," she said, breaking the kiss.

Parker leaned up and smirked. "Do you trust me?"

Ella looked at her, and Parker felt Ella searching her soul before nodding. She kissed Ella again as she entered her slowly. She moved her fingers gently in and out, never removing her gaze from Ella's, who opened her mouth to protest before a long, low moan escaped her lips. When she added a third finger to her controlled strokes, Ella's eyes rolled into the back of her head and her mouth fell open on a silent scream.

Parker let her body weight propel her, moving her hips in rhythm to the thrusts she was bestowing on Ella's center, driving her fingers impossibly deep while never relenting the pressure on her clit. Ella met her eyes again and she looked wild, like an untamed creature. But Parker knew she had everything in her arsenal to break her.

As she continued pumping in and out of Ella, she bent over to take a nipple in her mouth, flicking and biting in turn. Ella bucked under her, panting. Parker knew her climax was close, and she wanted it again. She felt Ella's walls begin to clamp around her fingers so hard she could barely move inside of her.

"Oh God, oh God, no, wait. Wait a second," Ella said.

Parker stopped her movements, scared she may have been unintentionally rough in her desire. She looked down at

Ella with concern. "What's wrong, darling? Have I hurt you?" she said.

Ella shook her head and looked a bit embarrassed. "No, I just need to…" she said, biting her lip and looking sheepish. Parker lifted her eyebrows and waited for her to continue. "I need to use the bathroom," Ella said as she looked away self-consciously. When Parker just beamed at her, Ella blushed.

"There's no need to be embarrassed. Just let it happen," Parker said.

Ella looked at her skeptically. "I don't think you want me to just let that happen, Parker. Just give me a second," she said and struggled underneath her, trying to get up.

Parker didn't let her up and leaned more of her weight onto her to keep her in place. "Please just trust me," Parker said and looked deeply into Ella's eyes. She stopped struggling and nodded, even if looking a little skeptical. Parker nodded and kissed her deeply again. When she resumed her strokes, Ella pulled away from the kiss and began to protest again. "Ella, I've got you. Just let go," Parker said into her ear, and when she began increasing the speed of her thrusts, Ella closed her eyes and moaned repeatedly. This time when Parker felt everything tighten inside of her, she curled her fingers upward in addition to her thrusts. Ella's eyes popped open again and she began to protest again, but Parker shushed her with another kiss.

Ella's moans increased in pitch and frequency. She screamed Parker's name again as her walls clenched down so hard, Parker could barely move her fingers as the orgasm exploded through her core. Parker was rewarded with a familiar flood of wetness which now dripped down her wrist. She smiled knowingly to herself as she gently brought Ella back down. When her breathing returned to normal, Parker pulled her hand away and sidled off Ella to lay beside her, hand propping her head up so she could look down at her.

"Are you okay?" Parker said, moving Ella's sweaty hair off her face. Ella opened her eyes and looked at her questioningly. Parker grinned smugly and looked down as if to instruct Ella to have a look for herself. The wet spot spread over the entire crotch of her underwear.

Ella looked up at her and at first looked very surprised before worry took over. "I'm so sorry, I didn't mean to do that. I told you I had to go," she said, blushing, but Parker shushed her.

"You know you just ejaculated, right?" Parker said. Ella went even redder and turned her head away. She placed a kiss on Ella's shoulder. Did she think this was a bad thing? "So, I don't know the rules in the State of Straight, but, here in Lesbo-land, this is a very good thing and not all that uncommon. At least, not in my bedroom," Parker said with a cocky smile.

Ella glanced back at her and, when finding that Parker wasn't making fun of her, seemed to relax a bit. "My first thought is to apologize to you again, but I won't. I've just…I've never done that before."

Parker nodded in understanding before leaning down to kiss her on the tip of her nose. This was not the first time this had happened to someone she had bedded. "It was amazing. You're—Ella, you're just perfect." Ella looked at her again searching her face for any trace of mocking. Parker wrapped her up in her arms and nuzzled into her hair.

Being tucked up in bed with Ella in a state of sheer bliss was even more breathtaking than Parker ever thought it could be. She just couldn't stop touching her, mapping the planes of her abdomen with light brushes of fingertips, carefully kneading at her hips and bending over to trail kisses across her collarbone.

When Parker felt Ella shiver underneath her, she pulled a blanket up to cover them before pressing their bodies together to help her warm up. "Is that better?" Parker said, and Ella hummed out her response as she drifted in and out of sleep.

She lay her head on Ella's shoulder with every intention of staying awake and watching her sleep for a while. But the drowsiness slammed into her like a boulder and before she knew it, she joined Ella in her slumber.

When Ella awoke, she was completely enveloped as Parker's arms wrapped solidly around her in her slumber. She looked over at Parker. Even disheveled and with sex-mussed hair, she still fully believed there was no one in the world who was more ravishing than her. She wouldn't have wanted her first time with a woman to be with anyone else. Her body had never felt more thoroughly fucked and pleasantly spent ever in her life. Ella just couldn't stop herself from smiling. She looked over at Parker and tranquilizing euphoria completely gave way to scorching desire. There was no way this night was going to end without Ella getting a taste of her.

She leaned over to place a gentle kiss on her temple. Parker's eyes fluttered open then, and Ella was filled with a deep want that she felt low in her stomach. Parker had rocked her world, that was for sure. And she had every intention of returning the favor.

Wordlessly, Ella cupped the back of Parker's neck and pulled her into a searing kiss, voraciously searching Parker's mouth with her tongue. She rolled their bodies so she ended up on top and pressed herself fully between Parker's thighs.

Ella could feel the wet heat between them, a mixture of her spendings and the rapturous beginnings of Parker's arousal.

Tracing one hand down Parker's chest and feeling her nipple harden through the material of her bra sent her to an even higher echelon of craving she could feel in the very core of her being.

She could feel Parker's body tensing beneath her and erroneously assumed her want was multiplying as well. Ella was on another plane of existence and initially didn't hear Parker's request for her to slow down.

"Wait, Ella, it's okay. You don't have to—" Parker said, but Ella shushed her with another burning kiss.

"I'm no pillow princess, Parker. I want to touch you. I want to make you feel the same way you just made me feel. I want you to come for me," she said, trailing kisses down Parker's neck. She could feel Parker's heart beat like a jackhammer when she trailed her lips to her pulse point, then Parker began shaking.

Again, Ella assumed the reactions were Parker giving over to her own desire, until she felt Parker go completely stiff and rigid. When she pulled back, she was looking at someone who was in the grip of sheer terror. Her heart caught in her chest.

"Parker? What's wrong?" Ella immediately shifted to the side to take her weight off Parker who was breathing quickly and shallowly. She placed a hand gently on Parker's shoulder as she could see her body break out in a sheen of sweat. Ella sat up in alarm now as her face went pale.

"Parker, you have to talk to me! Tell me what you need me to do, please!" she said, pleading and trying to stave off the terror that threatened to consume her.

Parker finally looked at her then and held up a finger as if to tell her she needed a moment. She gently placed a hand on Ella's chest and pressed as if encouraging her to move back. Ella complied and sat up, moving to the far edge of the bed. Parker then reached out to her and clasped her hand. Ella placed her other hand on top of Parker's and waited for the panic to subside. It was all she could do.

After what was probably less than a minute, but felt to Ella like an expanse of years, Parker began to breathe normally. Ella felt the relief course through her. She dropped Parker's hand and went into the bathroom for a wet washcloth. When she returned, Parker had closed her eyes, but her color had returned to normal. She gently climbed back on to the bed and placed the cold compress to Parker's forehead, making sure to not invade her space.

"I'm sorry," Parker choked out on a sob.

Ella felt her eyes well up. "Why in the world would you apologize for that?" she said, tentatively picking Parker's hand up again. When she didn't pull back, Ella chanced a tender kiss on her knuckles.

"I just…can't…" Parker said, crying in earnest now. Ella went to her then, wrapping her body around her protectively. Parker was racked with sobs she couldn't seem to stifle. Ella merely rode out the waves of emotion with her, never letting go. It was the easiest thing she had ever done, holding Parker in the throes of a deep, emotional release. She wanted to be there for her in her time of need.

When Parker seemed to be calming down, Ella wiped at her face lovingly with the cloth, attempting to settle her after the tidal wave of feelings that had just crashed out of her. She took another deep breath and opened her red-rimmed eyes to look at Ella.

"I guess we need to talk," she said simply.

"I am happy for us to talk about anything, but please don't feel pressured to talk about something if you're not ready. I'm so sorry I've hurt you. I didn't mean—" Ella said as Parker shook her head, eyes filling with tears again.

"It's not you. It could never be you," she said, stroking a single fingertip down the path a single tear took down Ella's face. Parker took another steadying breath, and when it seemed like she wasn't going to cry again, Ella prepared herself for Parker to continue, not knowing what to expect.

"I…was hurt. When I was younger. An adult—" Parker said, barely above a whisper. That seemed to be all she could get out, but Ella had heard enough. She couldn't stop her own tears from flowing now, placing a hand across her eyes. Parker moved to her now and placed her head on Ella's chest, searching for more of the comfort she had so freely given before.

"It was my music teacher at my old high school. He was always so nice and funny, and he didn't treat me like a kid. I often stayed after school for private music lessons with him, and one day, he offered me a soda. As I drank it, I started feeling weird. Next thing I know, I woke up in my car with my parents banging on my window. I told them what happened, and my dad immediately became suspicious. They took me to the emergency room and called the police. It turns out the guy was sending all kinds of inappropriate messages to students. He was arrested and won't be able to hurt anyone else and I'm thankful for that. But I don't know if I'll ever truly recover. I don't think I'll ever not feel broken."

Ella held her tightly, crying softly into her hair, placing soft kisses on her forehead. She could feel Parker's tears had started anew as her face pressed softly into her. Ella wanted to surround Parker with feelings of warmth and acceptance, for her to know she was safe, treasured. For her to know she was…loved.

"Parker, I'm just so sorry. I would never try to force…" She trailed off, but Parker shook her head vehemently before raising up to look at her.

"No, I know that. It's nothing you did. It's all me. I just can't be touched…that way. By anyone. I'm so sorry," she said, looking embarrassed.

Ella shook her head now. "Don't you dare apologize for that. You've done nothing wrong."

Parker sighed deeply. "I honestly had no idea this was going to happen between us tonight or I would have had this discussion with you ahead of time. And then when it started, I wanted it to be all about you and your first time with a woman," she said, turning over onto her side to face Ella.

"I don't think either of us knew this was going to happen, so don't apologize to me for that. Don't apologize for any of this," Ella said fervently. "There is absolutely nothing for you to feel sorry about."

Parker took a steadying breath and nodded, moving her head to find comfort in the crook of Ella's arm.

Ella just couldn't understand it. Who would look at a child and rationalize such a heinous act to be acceptable?

"Do you want to talk more about what happened? I just want you to know I am open to listening, but only if you want to talk."

Parker was already shaking her head. "I can't," she said, eyes welling up with tears again. "But it has always been like this for me. I enjoy the giving aspect of sex. I'm sure you have already been informed of my reputation at the bar by your friends. It's not a secret, and I am not ashamed. I like pleasing women and I'm good at it, so," she said, shrugging.

Ella couldn't stop herself from giggling. She raised her hand as Parker eyed her suspiciously. "Yes, I can attest to that. I will vouch for you. You are very, very good at it," she said, placing a sweet, understanding kiss on her lips. She pulled back quickly, realizing her possible error at taking liberties when Parker was so vulnerable. "I'm sorry. I shouldn't have," she said, but Parker just smiled brightly at her before leaning in to kiss her. It was just as sweet, but her lips lingered a little longer to get her point across.

"It's all right. I can kiss. I'm hoping you remember that, at least," she said salaciously.

Ella felt her cheeks color furiously before burying her face in the pillow. It didn't help, though. She could feel the blush extend over her entire upper body. "Oh, I remember," she said at a normal volume before finishing with "I seriously doubt I could ever forget it" in sotto voce.

When Ella raised her head again, Parker was looking at her searchingly.

"You're the first person that I've wanted to make the effort with in a very long time," she said. "I feel so comfortable around you, I thought I could go through with it." Parker sighed heavily, but apparently had more to say and soldiered on. Ella didn't dare move as not to derail her.

"This is why I don't do relationships. Most girls are just happy to get off and go, you know? And there's not a lot of questions. I don't have to worry about having to explain myself to them," she continued. "I tried to date a girl my senior year of high school, but we weren't together very long. When I seemed disinterested in sex, she was quick to move on. I just decided at that point that one-night stands were the way to go. I've never wanted anything else," she said. When she opened her mouth to say more, she closed it quickly and smiled sadly.

Ella's eyes went wide as she realized what she was saying. "Are you saying no one has ever touched you?" she said, trying to keep the surprise out of her voice, filling it instead with understanding. Parker averted her eyes and chewed nervously at her bottom lip before shaking her head.

Ella did her best to hide the utter shock she felt, but then, she was overcome with a feeling of pure exultation. Everyone at Sparkle thought they knew Parker. They thought she was a player who cared only about herself. It turns out she was the most selfless person there. No one knew the real Parker Chase but her.

She had chosen to share something so intimate, so personal. She trusted Ella, and her heart warmed at the sentiment. She was the only one who truly understood Parker. Ella felt tears well up in her eyes again.

"Parker, I want you to know that your secret is safe with me. I would never tell anyone what you've told me tonight. I am honored that you have even chosen to talk to me about it. I—" She stopped before uttering what she had begun to say. It almost came out without thinking. I love you? That would just be too confusing for them both. "I'll protect you," she finished, and Parker smiled brightly.

"I know. I trust you. I really do," she said, then taking on a sheepish expression, she continued. "Honestly, I'd like to try again sometime if you're willing," she said. Before Ella could answer, she spoke again in a rush. "I mean, I don't know if this was supposed to be a one-time thing. So, if that's the case, then that's fine, too. I just, I don't know how long it would take me to get there and it might not be something you're interested in and that's okay, too—" Parker cut herself off when she saw Ella's eyes alight with laughter.

"I'm more than happy to do this again. I'll be as patient with you as you need. Friends with benefits sounds good to me."

Parker did her best to mirror Ella's elation, but she felt her heart break a bit on the inside. *Friends with benefits. Well, that's as good a place as any to start.*

Chapter 12

Ella woke up Sunday morning with a lightness she had never experienced. She felt like a person reborn. And she couldn't stop smiling.

She returned home after leaving Parker's house in the wee hours of the morning. Following Parker's confession, they stayed up all night talking. They discussed their families, hopes and dreams, music, movies… anything that came to mind. They laughed a lot and hugged even more. Even though they remained in the earlier state of undress, there was no additional sexual activity. Instead, as she lay naked in Parker's arms, there was pure intimacy and affinity for one another. Parker had made a home for herself, directly in Ella's heart.

Ella picked up her phone to check the time. Eleven? She couldn't remember the last time she slept in this late. She had to get up and get the house cleaned and chores done before AJ got back in the evening.

Ella noticed she had some missed text messages and was unsurprised to see they were from Parker. Before she even looked at her words, she could feel her heart skip a beat.

Parker, 4:34 a.m.: "Thanks for texting me to let me know you got home safely. But I want you to know I miss you. I miss you being here with me. I hope that's not too forward and out of the range of 'what friends do,' but it's true."

Parker, 4:36 a.m.: "And thank you for tonight. I've never felt so close to another person in my life. Let me know how everything goes with AJ today. I'm sending good energy."

Ella sat up with a start. In her post-coital reverie, she had forgotten AJ wanted to have some big talk tonight. She sighed, knowing the whole situation with her daughter could go sideways quickly. Teenagers were hard. Did she keep the receipt? Is it too late to send her back?

Ella knew her day would not actually progress until she sent Parker a message, letting her know—what exactly? That she missed her, too? That she was pretty sure no one else would ever be able to live up to the experience they just shared? There was no doubt in her mind that she had already developed deep feelings for Parker, but there was still something there, blocking her from letting go completely.

The age difference was a large part of it. She could just imagine AJ's sullen expression when she eventually told her that not only was she a lesbian, but her girlfriend was closer to her age than Ella's. Girlfriend. Wow, that was a new concept. Was Parker even girlfriend material?

But wasn't that just the extent of what she needed to worry about? She had come out to Alex, her parents, and all her close friends, and not experienced any sort of judgment. But AJ's opinion mattered most to her. She missed their closeness and was afraid that this would only drive a bigger wedge between them.

Was she intentionally keeping herself walled off from her daughter, and maybe she was giving off a distant vibe that AJ was picking up? Maybe Ella's behavior was contributing to the distance between them? She rubbed at her temple. *This is an awful lot of poignancy before coffee*, she thought as she headed downstairs. AJ was sitting on the couch with her bags at her feet and her head in her hands.

Ella could hear her sniffling as she walked into the room. "AJ?" she said as she sat next to her on the sofa and gingerly placed an arm around her shoulders.

AJ looked up and the pain Ella saw in her eyes made her own heart hurt. "Why are you still asleep? You're always up early. I came over to talk to you. I told you I would be here. Why weren't you down here?" AJ said in a condemnatory tone.

Ella's words were robbed from her throat by the look of betrayal in her daughter's eyes. "Honey, I wasn't expecting you until tonight. I…was out late last night," she admitted. AJ's face screwed up even more.

"My God, did you go out again?" she said, accusation burning in her eyes.

"Yes, I did. You know, I'm an adult, AJ. I am allowed to do adult things," she said, but AJ interrupted her.

"If you're so desperate to meet new guys, you don't need to be doing it out in bars, Mom. I'm expecting to see some video of you drunk and doing something horrible on Snapchat," she said.

Ella looked at her incredulously. "What have I done to make you have such a low opinion of me, AJ? I know you're upset that I have been out all of twice now. But you've been angry with me for months. I want to know why," she said, rubbing AJ's shoulder.

She shrugged out of the touch. "Why do you think everything has to be about you?" AJ shot back and began crying anew. "Don't you think I can be going through my own shit?" She put her head in her hands once again, and her body shook with quiet sobs. Ella reached out her hand, cautiously placing it on her daughter's knee. AJ didn't shake her off.

"I don't think everything is about me. And I want to know what's wrong with you. I've been asking you to talk to me, and I respected your wishes when you didn't want to. But now I need to know. I'm worried about you," Ella said, a tremble in her own voice now. AJ must have heard the emotion because she looked up again. For the first time, Ella could see there was no anger in her eyes, just unadulterated pain. And her heart ached to take it away.

Ella reached up to caress her face, and AJ launched into her, wrapping her arms around her. Ella held her as she cried, stroking her back and hair. The weeping completely overtook her for a few minutes, but Ella welcomed the show of real emotion. This weird and unprovoked vexation had been hard to bear, but if that is what she had to endure to get through to the real issues lying underneath the surface, she accepted it. Seeing her daughter completely wrecked was heart-wrenching and all she could was hold on tight for both their sakes.

After a few minutes, AJ's sobs softened into sniffles. Ella reached toward the coffee table and came up with a handful of tissues for her. AJ chuckled as she took them and cleaned herself up. "How about you tell me where this is all coming from? I'm a cool mom now, remember?" she said, winking at AJ, who eyed her inquisitively. They giggled together.

She had never really been a 'cool' mom, though. Alex got to do all the fun things. Ella was the disciplinarian, the coach. AJ would always have gone to Alex with her issues first, and eventually, she would have come to her mother, probably at his instruction.

AJ sighed deeply, before turning to face her on the couch. Ella sensed the divulgence was forthcoming and waited patiently. AJ opened her mouth to start but looked down again. Ella reached out to take her hand as a sign of encouragement.

"Mom, I—" she started again, before faltering.

Ella lifted her chin to look fully into her eyes. "Anna Jean Gardner," she said, using her full name to get her attention. "There is nothing you can tell me that will make me stop loving you. Kids your age make mistakes and bad choices. Whatever has happened, your dad and I will help you fix it. Just tell me so we can get started."

Flashbacks of herself at seventeen filled her mind. She remembered telling Alex she was pregnant and then the two of them telling their parents together. She remembered the initial tears, but most importantly, she remembered the love that everyone had for the life growing inside of her. Then, it crossed her mind for the first time. Was AJ getting ready to tell her she was pregnant? Ella's heart palpitated in her chest. She couldn't stop herself from asking.

"AJ, you're not pregnant, are you?" she said, barely above a whisper. AJ looked up at her sharply with a look of utter disgust. But then, that look morphed into a smile and the laughter that rushed out of her completely confused her mother.

When AJ caught sight of Ella's screwed up face, she broke out into another fit of unabashed laughter.

"Okay, well, that's obviously one crisis averted. Glad that was funny to you. Now, can we please get down to the issue at hand. You're kind of freaking me out here," Ella said, eyeing her suspiciously.

AJ laughed hard one more time before wiping the tears out of the corners of her eyes. "No, it's just so funny because you went in the exact opposite direction from what I'm going to tell you," she said. Ella's brows knitted together in utter confusion.

AJ opened her mouth, but no sound came out and she shrugged. She took another deep, steadying breath and exhaled slowly. She took Ella's hands and looked directly into her eyes. "Mom, I'm gay and I just didn't know how to tell you," she said and braced for impact.

Ella felt her heart that had been beating so erratically just moments before slow down from the relief that had just washed over her.

"I didn't know how you would react. I'm sorry to have kept this from you. I shouldn't have, I know. But your opinion matters so much to me. I was just afraid of your reaction," she continued.

Ella was suddenly overwhelmed. Here was her seventeen-year-old daughter being even braver than she had been. She was able to come out and confess her truth even though she was terrified of the potential reaction. Ella could only stare off into space as the feelings welled up inside of her.

AJ reached out and grabbed her hand. "Mom? Even if you're angry or disgusted with me, I still need you to say something," AJ said. Her voice had gone watery again.

Ella turned back to her, eyes welling up with tears of her own. "AJ, I—" she said, and the words caught in her throat. AJ deserved to know she wasn't alone, and they would face their battles together because they were the same. And they were a team. "The reason that your father and I got a divorce is because I'm gay, too," she said and let the words hang between them.

AJ's sharp intake of breath made her look up again. Her daughter looked absolutely shocked, and Ella prepared to receive a lecture. But AJ squealed out a high-pitched noise and jump-tackle-hugged her on the couch. She plastered Ella's face with kisses, and Ella couldn't stop herself from laughing.

"If you don't get off me, I'm going to have to tickle you!" she said, reaching up AJ's sides. It had been a very long time since they had a tickle fight. She had momentarily forgotten that AJ was now taller and stronger than she was. She quickly lost the upper hand, but it was worth it.

Once they had both settled down, neither spoke for a long moment. Ella took AJ's hand and kissed it reverently. AJ looked up at her, and she could see the palpable relief in her eyes. "Mom, why didn't you tell me? We've always been close."

Ella's thoughts mirrored her daughter's. "Probably the same reason you are just now telling me. I was scared, AJ. I was afraid that you would be upset with me or even not want to be around me," Ella said, and the confession made her feel small and worried.

AJ picked up her mother's hand and kissed it just as Ella had done for her moments before. "That's fair. I'm not upset with you," she said and looked away. They sat in silence for a few moments until AJ spoke again. "Have you always known?" she said.

Ella tongued the inside of her cheek thoughtfully before nodding. "Yeah, ever since I was your age. I wasn't at all ready to accept myself and kind of tried to be extremely straight. Your dad and I were very good friends, so I thought if I started dating him, I wouldn't constantly be thinking about girls, you know?" Ella stared at the floor, thinking about how much her life had changed all those years ago. At the time, and in her teenage angst, she was sure her life was over. Now, with hindsight at 20/20, she knew she would never have chosen to take any other path.

"Mom, do you wish your life was different? Do you wish you would have come out in high school?" she said cautiously.

Ella didn't even have to think about her response. She shook her head. She was so impressed by AJ's courage. Where would she be now if she had come out at seventeen? But Ella wouldn't have changed a thing. Everything she went through brought her the wonderful, fearless person sitting next to her, who possessed the mettle to live her absolute truth at such a young age. What other job do parents have to do that is more important than to send their children out into the world being better people than they are?

"My love, anything that gets us to this point right here, right now is the path that I was supposed to take. I have no doubt about that. I am so happy in my life right now and that's largely because you're in it. You're amazing, and I am so proud of you," she said, just before rubbing her hands together. "But, let's get to the good conversation," Ella said, lifting and lowering her eyebrows suggestively. AJ eyed her suspiciously. "Do you have a girlfriend?"

With the question uttered, AJ began to blush furiously. But she also couldn't stop herself from smiling. "Yeah, actually I do. You haven't met her. We met this summer at volleyball camp. She goes to a different high school. Havenwood High, actually."

Ella *ooohed* at her daughter's catch-22. "They're your biggest competition when it comes to the regional tournament next week. That's a tough one. What position does she play?"

AJ rolled her eyes at her mother. Of course, she would want to know about her as a volleyball player before asking about her as a girlfriend. "She's a setter. She's up to be Setter of the Year in the region this year. She's so good," AJ said, and Ella couldn't stifle her retort.

"Oh, I bet she is. Good hands, right? I mean you must have really nimble hands as a setter…" she said, letting the dirty joke hang between them. AJ looked at her, mouth agape, before Ella clapped her roughly on the shoulder and laughed at her own joke. She was funny, dammit.

"*Mom*! Oh, my God, I can't believe you just said that."

Ella just beamed at her. "So, tell me about her outside of volleyball. What's her name, what's she like. That kind of stuff."

AJ thought for a moment. "Well, her name is Kathryn, but she goes by Kat. She's a senior, too." She paused, pursing her lips as if deciding exactly how much to tell her right away. "She's amazing, Mom," AJ said with a look of such sincerity that Ella felt it in her own heart. She nodded at her to continue.

"She's so funny. And kind. She's always doing these nice things for me like messaging me just to ask me how my day is," she said wistfully. "You know, just the small stuff. I know that it's not been very long, just a few months, but I think I love her," AJ confessed, again looking like she expected Ella to reprimand her for being childish.

Ella pondered AJ's situation in comparison to her own. She would have never thought it was possible to fall in love with someone after only a few months, but here sat her daughter, confessing her innermost secrets. She understood AJ's predicament now because wasn't she in a similar situation with an even shorter period of time having elapsed? She knew her feelings for Parker were something she had never experienced before, but...love? It was almost too much to ponder. She snapped back into reality with AJ's hand on her arm. Ella placed her own hand on top of her daughter's.

"Anna, only you know for sure how you feel about this girl. If you just met her this summer, it does seem pretty soon, yes. But I am not going to tell you what you are feeling."

AJ chuckled ruefully. "Well, you and Dad reacted exactly the opposite of how I thought you were going to act. He was freaking out, telling me there was no way I was in love after only a few months. I pointed out that he and Rebecca have only been together for a few months. He didn't have much to say after that," she said. They shared a laugh, and when Ella raised her hand to high-five her, AJ looked at her knowingly. She formed her mother's hand into a fist and fist bumped her. Oh, yeah. Ella was *definitely* cool now.

"Have you told her you love her?" Ella said. AJ's brightness dimmed a bit as she shook her head. "Hey, you can't be afraid. If you know in your heart that you love this girl, you've got to let her know," she said. AJ just nodded.

"When did you know?" AJ looked quizzically at her mother. "That you were in love?" Ella clarified. AJ blushed deeply and lowered her eyes as she sucked on her lower lip, a nervous habit she had carried over from childhood.

"Mom, I honestly knew the first time we met. We just clicked, you know? And it's complicated, I know. We go to different schools, we are huge rivals in volleyball, we don't get to see each other as often as we want, but we decided we weren't going to let that stop us. If you've got something worthwhile, then I think it's worth fighting for, even if it doesn't look great on paper."

Ella gulped audibly and attempted to hide it with a cough. It was almost like AJ was speaking directly to her and she didn't even know it. AJ was wise beyond her years, and she was overcome with the pride swelling in her chest. Something inside her just knew that this kid was going to be okay. "Well, that sounds like confirmation to me. When are you going to tell her?"

"If everything goes as planned, we should be playing Havenwood for the regional title a week from Tuesday. I'm going to tell her then, after the game. I'm going to do a promposal right there, in the gym and in front of everyone. I figure that should prove how much I love her," she said.

Ella was again astounded at the level of valor her daughter possessed. "That's an amazing choice for a grand gesture. I would think that would be proof for sure. I'm so impressed with you," she said, again emotion clouded her voice. "You're so brave, going out on a limb like this. I don't even have the words to say how proud I am," she said, eyes shining.

AJ smiled wholeheartedly as her eyes welled up again. "So, next Tuesday, her parents will be at the game and we want you guys to meet. They know about us. Kat has been out a lot longer than I have, so we hang out there most of the time. Her parents are so cool. I think you'll like them. And I want you to get to know Kat. I think you'll love her, plus I want us to hang out here sometimes, too," she said.

"Of course, you know I will be there. I am happy to meet her and her family. I want you to bring Kat here and to your dad's. But we need to have many more discussions before we talk about sleepovers, little one." Ella slapped her own knee in overexaggerated emphasis of the amazing joke she just made. But she noticed AJ wasn't laughing. She looked very guilty.

"You've already had sleepovers at her house. You're sleeping with her," she said, understanding AJ's expression.

She nodded at her mother without looking at her. "Are you mad? I know it's been a while since we had any sort of sex talk."

Ella felt lightheaded for a moment but worked on grounding herself. Her daughter was a teenager and sex was pretty much inevitable for kids these days. The important part was keeping lines of communication open, and making AJ feel comfortable was step one. "I'm not mad. You're practically an adult. I can't make these decisions for you," she said, shrugging, before pushing forward with the uncomfortable but necessary conversation. "Was she your first?" Ella said and held her breath, waiting for her daughter's reply. When AJ nodded slowly, Ella was able to breathe again.

"I didn't want my first time to be with just anybody. I have always pretty much known that I wasn't interested in boys, so I just didn't date much. After I met Kat, I knew, you know? We were actually each other's firsts…" She paused, but did not appear to be finished speaking. Ella remained silent and still, allowing her to continue at her own pace. "It happened a few weeks ago and that's the reason I wanted to talk to you and Dad. It's serious between us, and I want both of you to be a part of that with me."

She looked at her mother expectantly, but Ella had nothing to say. AJ was so far ahead of where she was at the same age, what advice could she give her? 'The student becomes the master' adage was coming true before her very eyes in her daughter, and not just in volleyball, apparently. Ella put her arms around her and hugged her within an inch of her life. AJ squeaked out her protest before Ella let go, and they both laughed.

"I trust your judgment. I appreciate that you want to introduce her to us."

"Well, Dad introduced me to Rebecca when he felt like he knew, and I assume you will do the same when you meet someone. Some *woman*," she corrected and nudged Ella's shoulder playfully.

Ella nudged her back, but her heart wasn't in it. Was she doing her relationship with AJ an injustice by not talking to her about Parker? Was Parker that person in her life? Did she know like AJ knew? She also worried that talking about Parker now when AJ was most vulnerable might feel like she was trying to one-up her. She wanted this to be her time to shine.

"So," AJ said, eyes twinkling with mischief.

"So?" Ella mirrored the word, but with a question in her voice.

"Have you met anyone on any of these nights that you've been going out clubbing?"

Ella froze, not knowing exactly how much she wanted to divulge to her daughter. "Uh, yeah. I've met some people. Some new friends," she said, emphasizing the word friends. AJ winked knowingly and mimed 'friends' in air quotes. Ella hit her with a couch cushion.

"I met Danna for a drink last weekend, but we ended up having no chemistry. We're friends, though. I've hung out with her and her friend group several times. I do have a date next weekend with a woman they introduced me to at a game night," she said.

AJ perked up immediately, scooting to the edge of her seat. "Is it serious?"

Ella frowned and shook her head. "No, not really. I don't think it will be either, but you've got to kiss a lot of frogs before you find your prince...ess? Princess?"

"You, uh, kissing a lot of lesbian frogs, Mom? Is that what you're trying to tell me?" AJ said, absolutely grinning from ear to ear. Now it was Ella's turn to blush.

"Yeah, no, I have not."

"Have you not met anyone who just kind of makes your heart beat a little faster whenever you're around her?" AJ said, holding up her thumb and forefinger close together and squinting.

Ella looked at her, frowning. "Calm down, Shakespeare. No need to start waxing poetic at me," she said.

AJ harrumphed. "Mom, you're an English teacher. You should know Shakespeare wasn't a romance writer."

Well, AJ had her there. "If I find someone special who I am a hundred percent sure about, I will introduce her to you. I promise. You will be the first to know, my love," Ella said, crossing her heart and placing her hand on her chest in assurance to her daughter. AJ seemed to accept her words as she stood up and picked up her bags.

"I've got some homework to do, but maybe we can watch a movie later?" she said.

Ella clapped her hands together excitedly. "Oh, we can watch a lesbian movie together! Have you seen *Kissing Jessica Stein*? The trailer looked good."

AJ rolled her eyes but aimed a good-natured smile at her. "I haven't. Sounds good," she said, putting her bag on her shoulder and walking toward her room. She stopped and turned around.

"Thank you, Mom. Thank you for being so understanding. And thank you for telling me about you. I love you," she said.

"I love you, too," Ella said, and with that, AJ went into her room and shut the door.

∽

It had been an emotional day so far for Ella and before coffee even happened. She walked into her kitchen to start an entire pot for herself. After grabbing a cup and heading back to her room, she felt her phone go off in her pocket.

Parker, 12:05 p.m.: "I'm just worried I've said too much and now you're not talking to me. If you're not, could you at least tell me that? I'm freaking out here with this no response stuff."

Ella smiled down at the phone, gently running her finger across Parker's profile picture.

Ella, 12:06 p.m.: "I'm sorry and no, that's not it at all. It has been a morning to say the least."

Parker, 12:08 p.m.: "Everything okay?"

Ella, 12:11 p.m.: "Yes, everything is fine now. AJ came home early and we had our talk."

Parker, 12:11 p.m.: "AND? Don't leave me hanging."

Ella, 12:12 p.m.: "She came out to me."

Ella was in the middle of typing out another text when Parker video called her. She answered on the first ring.

"Are you fucking serious? That's crazy! Is she okay? Are you okay? Did you tell her about you?" Parker rattled off questions like an excited child.

Ella chuckled at her and held up her hand. "One at a time. Yes, I am serious. Fucking serious even. She is fine. I'm fine, and yes, I told her about me. It's been quite a release," she said.

Parker was uncharacteristically quiet for a moment. "Ella, I'm so happy for you," she said, and Ella could feel the honesty in her words. It warmed her heart.

"Thank you, Parker. I'm quite happy, as well," she said, before remembering Kat. "Oh, and she has a girlfriend. She thinks she's in love and they're having sex, but I am still totally good." Ella did her best wide-eyed, pained smile for emphasis, and Parker laughed loudly.

"Uh-oh. That's a hard one to swallow, huh? It's cute that she's in love, though. When my sister came out, my parents were cool with it, too. Of course, I came out way before her, so I was happy to set the stage."

"Sounds like your little sister has quite the role model to look up to," she said, unable to hide the affection in her voice.

She was overtaken with a picture of Parker lingering in her mind from last night. When she had said she was going home, Parker wrapped her body around her, playfully trying to persuade her to stay. Ella was finally able to break her hold and got dressed. When she looked back over her shoulder to say goodbye, the air was gone from her lungs. Parker had her head propped up on one fist. She was still in her underwear and had the sheet pulled up to just below her hip. Ella could still see all of Parker's feminine curves as well as the top of a tattoo poking out of her waistband. She started to ask her about it, but after her earlier reaction, opted against it. Maybe one day.

"Well, I wouldn't go that far," she said with a self-deprecating laugh. "I'm just…glad you're okay."

Ella knew that statement had a double meaning and that Parker had put it out there with the intent of talking about last night. She was ready, though. AJ had inspired her. "I am okay, Parker. About everything. I need you to know that. Last night was…amazing, wonderful, sexy and everything a girl hopes her first time will be. I am glad it was with you." She thought she could hear Parker's sharp intake of breath as she pulled the phone away from her face for a moment. Ella gave her time to compose herself as she knew last night was very emotional for her, as well.

"Me too, I'm glad, too. I mean. And I just want to say, I'm so—" she started, but Ella cut her off immediately.

"Don't you dare apologize to me," she said emphatically. "You have nothing to apologize for. We can take things as slowly as you need."

"Am I still allowed to go down on you in the meantime with this benefits arrangement?" Parker said boldly. Ella scoffed at the same time she tried to breathe in, making some sort of feral noise, and felt her cheeks heat up at the brashness of her words. Parker just winked at her.

"Uh, yeah, you know whatever works for you. I'm a people pleaser," she said, nonchalantly before meeting Parker's eyes on the screen and repaying the wink. "We'll go at your pace. Whatever you want," Ella said.

"Yeah, I for sure want to please you as often as you'll let me. This can be a very beneficial friendship. See what I did there?" she said, laughing at her own play on words. Ella mocked out a *ha-ha* before relenting with another beaming smile. Parker's expression changed to one of utter seriousness.

"I really do appreciate you. No one has ever made me feel safe in that environment before." She looked down as if gathering her strength before looking back up and directly into the camera. "I did mean it when I said I want to try again. I can't tell you how long it will take, but if you're willing to be patient, I want to make the effort with you. Because, well, you're worth it." She looked down again, toying with a loose thread on her jeans.

Ella decided to go big or go home. If AJ can have the courage to say 'I love you' to her girlfriend for the first time in a gym full of people, then she can have the courage to continue to explore her own feelings with this woman who had constantly occupied her thoughts. But she also wanted to heed Danna's advice to be totally up front, emphasizing her need to move slowly. "Parker, I want to see you again, but I don't want to make any promises right now. I'm sorting through a lot in my head, and I don't want to mislead you." Ella paused to look directly into the camera, making sure Parker was listening and processing her words. She stared back in rapt attention, seemingly frozen to the spot. Ella wasn't even sure she was actively breathing as she stared back at her. "I want to explore our new arrangement. I want us to spend some time together without any pressure or without feeling like we have to put a label on our relationship. Let's just see what happens organically," she continued. Parker blinked and gave the slightest nod.

"And whenever you're ready, I want you to know I am more than happy to reciprocate. But, again, no pressure on you at all. No pressure on either of us. We're just going to go on instinct. Does that all sound good to you? I understand if you want to back out—" Ella started, but Parker quickly interrupted.

"No. That's what I want. What you're describing to me is all I have wanted from the first time I met you," she said.

Ella couldn't stop the heat rising inside her body and curling in her chest in that way only Parker had inspired. She knew she was blushing, but she didn't care. "When can I see you again?" she said, no longer concerned about seeming overly eager.

It was Parker's turn to blush. She couldn't hide an excited giggle. "When do you want to see me? Unless I'm working, seeing you becomes my top priority," she said with uncensored elation.

"You're such a fucking charmer," Ella said. When she realized she had said it out loud, she covered her mouth. The smile that overtook Parker's face was riveting. "Uh, well, when are you off? I have AJ, but she has practice till late and she can tend to herself. I can make it work."

"I am working tomorrow, but I'm off Tuesday. Do you want to come over? I can make us dinner again, anything you want. We can watch that movie you talked about last time you were here…" she said, obvious uncertainty in her voice.

Ella realized she hadn't been looking into the camera, lost in her own thoughts. She didn't want to have dinner with

Parker. She would be pressed for time on a school night. Wouldn't their time be better used for more risqué activities?

"If Tuesday doesn't work for you—" Parker started before Ella cut her off.

"Do you want to waste time having dinner together when we could be doing other things together?" she said, now looking directly into Parker's eyes, hoping she could see the sheer lust she felt in every fiber of her being.

Parker gulped audibly, but regained her composure quickly, not willing to lose the upper hand when it came to who would be on top in two night's time. "No, of course I don't," she said as her voice dropped an octave and became gravelly, eyes darkening with lust. "Do you have a few minutes for me to tell you all of the things I want to do to you when you get here?" Parker said, biting her lip and leaning back against her headboard. Ella immediately felt the wetness in her panties, unable to stop herself from groaning at the thought of Parker between her legs again. Then, she heard AJ's door slam upstairs and it startled her from her memories.

"As much as I would love to, I don't. AJ's here and could come looking for me at any time," she said. Parker pouted, and it was easily one of the sexiest things she had ever seen. "But, if you want to call me back later on tonight, maybe we could chat some more?" she said, sounding hopeful.

Parker's answering grin was almost evil. "That sounds wonderful. Just text me when you're ready for bed and I'll try to give you something to dream about," she said. Ella squeezed her thighs together, searching for some sort of relief from the way Parker's scorching looks were affecting her body. She heard a knock on her door and a soft *Mom?* before looking at Parker regretfully. She had obviously heard AJ's voice and winked before making a motion signifying she should go with her hand.

"We'll talk later," she whispered into the phone, before ending the call and checking on her daughter.

※

Ella sat next to AJ on the couch, both tucked up with plates of spaghetti Bolognese and salad, both enraptured with the movie. AJ was pleased with the punchy humor and a plot device that wasn't overused. Ella was just happy there weren't any explicit sex scenes to sit through with her daughter.

When the credits rolled, they both decided that the two main characters should have gotten together in the end, but *c'est la vie*. AJ collected the plates and took them into the kitchen to load the dishwasher. Ella wondered where her teenager went, as doing the dishes was one thing in their household that was a constant battle, with her often relenting just to prevent an argument. Ella picked up the salad bowls and brought them in to AJ, who happily hummed as she loaded.

"Thanks for doing the dishes," she said. AJ smiled at her before bending down to put the remainder of the plates in. Ella handed her the bowls, but when AJ tried to pull them from her grasp, she held fast. AJ looked at her, obviously confused. "I just want to make doubly sure that you're good," she said, now relinquishing her hold.

AJ put the bowls on the top rack, closed the door, and pressed the button to start the cycle. "I really am fine. I'm just glad we talked. And I can't wait for you to meet Kat," she said, blushing again. Ella reached over and ruffled her hair like she did when she was little. Suddenly, she just wanted time to stop so her heart could catch up.

"I want to meet her, too, my love. I'm looking forward to it, and not just for the volleyball game," she said, chucking her under the chin. AJ giggled and nodded. Ella's heart skipped a beat again, and, against her own better judgment, she decided to spill her truth.

"I, uh—" she started, but the words got stuck in her throat. AJ raised her eyebrows, and Ella coughed, trying to swallow the only bit of saliva she could muster. Why was this so hard? They were open and honest with each other now. She wanted to bridge that gap in their relationship, hoping they could be there for each other. Ella got a glass out of the cabinet and took a sip of water before she could continue. "I may have met someone special," she said quietly and looked at AJ to gauge her reaction, who looked thoughtful for a moment before placing her hand on Ella's.

"It's scary, isn't it?" she said, and Ella could only stare at her daughter.

She couldn't stop the tears from filling her eyes as she nodded in resignation. When the first tear snaked down her cheek, she lowered her head onto her forearm. It had been so long since she had felt this sort of all-consuming emotion. She cried softly as AJ lay gently on top of her and put her arms around her. The more she thought about Parker, the more she quietly sobbed. Never had anyone touched her heart in the way the younger woman had. It had only been a week, but Parker occupied her thoughts and haunted her dreams.

AJ interrupted her thoughts. "You're in love, Mom. And it's okay. There's no rule you have to follow, you know?"

Ella just cried harder as AJ continued to hug her, much as her mother had held her earlier. She finally looked up at AJ, whose face was so full of adoration and understanding. It almost set her off anew, but she just laughed softly. AJ smiled back as a single tear made its way down her cheek. Ella reached up to wipe it off and pulled her into a full embrace.

"You're so wise beyond your years, my heart. Thank you for this," she said, letting her go and holding her out at arm's length to really look at her, taking in the beautiful, intelligent, strong, and loving woman she was becoming. "I honestly don't know if it's, you know, that," she said, making a swirling gesture in the air with her fingers, unable to say the word.

"Love? You can say it. It's not your average four-letter word," AJ said with a wink.

Ella closed her eyes and nodded again before reaching over to pull a paper towel off the roll and wipe her face. "I don't know for sure, AJ. But I'm affected, for sure. What is it you kids say? I'm 'catching feelings' pretty hard?" she said, and AJ barked out a laugh at Ella's continual attempts to be hip.

"Yeah, that's right," she said. "Tell me about her?"

Ella thought about stopping the discussion now, eschewing any more information about Parker. But, in the end, she decided to share her truth, or at least some of it. "Well, it is very new, but yeah. I care about her very much. She's amazing and she makes my heart beat faster, just like you said," she said, looking directly at AJ who was nodding and sporting a knowing smile. "Yeah, you know how that feels, don't you?" she said, chuckling. "I just don't want to move too quickly."

"Well, you have a date next weekend, right?" AJ said.

Ella paled at the mention of Tally, who did not have her heart. But she had agreed to the date. Ella would still go. "No, that's actually another woman I met," she said, and AJ's eyes widened.

"Mom, you're a ho!" she said, poking Ella in the ribs.

Ella sniffled and grinned. "Everything happened so fast, you know? I met Pahhh—er, I met the woman I really like my first time at the bar." AJ gave her a look that said *come on!* at the obvious omission of the woman's name. Even though Ella was talking to her about what was going on in her life, she still didn't want to get her daughter unnecessarily involved if nothing were to pan out with them. "Listen, I know we're talking here, but you're still my daughter. I don't want to pull you into my love life in a direct way until I know for sure. I don't want to just introduce women to you if it isn't going to mean anything."

AJ tilted her head left to right considering her words before nodding in concession. "If you met this woman that you *really like*, why are you going on a date with anyone else?" she said.

Wow, this kid was smart beyond her years. "Well, I like her, too. Her name is Tally and she's a chiropractor. The group introduced us at a game night, and we hit it off." Ella stopped speaking when AJ crossed her arms and looked at her sternly.

"That's your answer right there," she said, and Ella looked at her contemplatively. "You're willing to tell me about Tally, including her name and occupation, but can't bring yourself to talk to me about this 'Pahhh' woman?"

Ella laughed out loud at AJ's spot-on impersonation of her stutter step from moments ago. "You've got a point," she said and sighed, her mind and body worn out from the day's deep conversations. "I promise that it's not something I'm trying to keep from you. When it gets serious, you'll be the first one to meet her."

AJ embraced her mother again and placed a sweet kiss on her forehead. "I'm ready when you are. Just promise me that you'll listen to your heart."

Ella smiled against her cheek. This kid was quite phenomenal, but would she feel the same way when she actually met Parker? Only time would tell.

Chapter 13

When Ella disconnected their video call, Parker could do nothing but stare at her screen. She hadn't moved from where she was stationed in her bed after last night's encounter with Ella and wasn't ready to leave.

Ella made her feel safe. Truly safe. It had never been like this with anyone else. When Ella first started touching her and her body responded immediately, she thought the curse was broken. But the ever-present feeling of horror that seemed to always be lurking under the surface started to take over. The gripping panic set in, and it was just like any time she tried before.

Parker could do nothing but just keep wiping the tears that fell unchecked. What would it take? She had tried all the medications recommended by the doctors. She had tried talking to a therapist. All these options helped in the general day-to-day aspects of her life but this one.

She wondered what it would feel like to have hands roaming her body, over her most sensitive areas. She wondered what it would be like to have a sensual tongue languidly travel up the expanse of her neck to land with a gentle bite on her earlobe; to have fingertips skim her collarbone on the way to tracing the valley between her breasts. Parker's arousal bloomed deep within her at the thought of Ella's tongue, Ella's fingertips.

At the torturous thoughts, she could feel her body come alive. She traced her own hand across her right breast to gently stroke her nipple between her thumb and forefinger, gasping at the contact and imagining that the hands touching her were not her own.

Her other hand swirled languorous circles over her hip before dipping casually inside the waistband of her underwear. Her breathing was becoming more ragged now as her heartbeat increased to a fevered pace.

Parker closed her eyes and focused on memories of Ella's eyes and the way they stared seemingly into her soul. She concentrated on recollections of Ella's hair as it tickled her naked skin and her fingers as they were placed gently into her mouth to suck, the taste of her skin intoxicating and bringing her to greater levels of desire.

Parker remembered being between Ella's legs as she shamelessly hitched her leg over her shoulder to give herself better access. She remembered the thrilling scent of Ella's arousal as she buried her face into the neatly trimmed patch of hair at the apex of her thighs. She didn't think she would ever be able to get enough.

Parker was dripping in earnest now, hand tracing circles around her clit, feeling the level of her arousal skyrocket. She wanted it to be Ella's fingers on her, in her. She wanted to feel Ella lick her from the bottom of her slit to the very top; wanted to feel her tongue deep inside her wet heat as she used her fingers to bring her gently to the very edge of the cliff before guiding her gently over and carrying her back home.

Home. That's what Ella felt like to her. Home is not a building or a place where you return to at the end of the day, Parker now realized. It was a physical space in which you could completely let your guard down and not have to be vigilant or fearful. She was bound and determined to find her way back.

Parker could feel her knees begin to shake as her hips undulated of their own accord, rhythmically and responsively. She recalled the feeling of Ella swelling in her mouth and tasting her release as it dripped down her chin. She remembered Ella clenching and squeezing so hard around her fingers as she came that it became impossible to move them and she was forced to simply curl and move as best she could. Her arousal began to peak around her own fingers as she thrust them in and out of herself.

Her climax came hard, and she called out Ella's name as her body lifted off the bed in ecstasy. The tremors followed, and she imagined Ella's fingers slipping out of her instead of her own, imagined her lying next to her murmuring comforting words and delivering gentle kisses to her shoulder, her chest, her face.

Parker opened her eyes and stared at her bedroom ceiling, waiting patiently for the world to come back into focus, hazy eyes attempting to regain their equilibrium. She wiped the sweat from her brow as her breathing returned to a more normal cadence and her heart ceased to sound like a marching band inside her chest. She couldn't stop herself from giggling as such release gives other emotions free passage to escape.

Parker had another appointment with her therapist tomorrow, and she had every intention of utilizing the time to try to push past her panic. Because she wanted this, more than anything she had ever known. She wanted Ella who made her feel whole and undamaged by life, and who, without even trying, gave her the confidence to just be.

Parker was resolute in her determination, nodding to herself as she rose to shower and go about her day. She had always hoped she could pick up the pieces and put herself back together, but now, and for the first time in her life, she honestly believed it was possible.

Chapter 14

Mundane Monday came faster than Ella expected. After the highs and lows of the weekend, her mind was full to the brim of information she was still trying to process. AJ was gay and had a girlfriend. And they were having sex. Well, she didn't need to think about that. The important thing is that her daughter seemed happy for the first time in a long time.

She looked back on AJ's childhood to see if there were signs she might have missed. She had always been a quiet and introspective child, so there was no sense of any change as she got older that would signify any inner tumult. AJ was always focused and an extremely hard worker. From the time Ella started her on ball control drills before she entered elementary school, she never complained. Instead, she chose to continue practicing even after her mom called an end to their session.

She had never been an angry child, until after the divorce. Ella realized now that the timeframe coincided almost directly with her meeting Kat and what she could imagine would be some confusing and possibly scary feelings for her. She also understood that AJ probably wasn't nearly as angry with her as she had previously thought. A lot happened to her in a short period of time, and she had been overwhelmed. Ella wanted to make sure that she and AJ stayed connected now.

After AJ grabbed a quick breakfast of toast and a cup of coffee, despite the eggs, bacon and freshly squeezed orange juice, mumbling some excuse about a before-school practice session with the team, Ella called Alex to discuss the previous day.

"Good morning, El," he said with what she could imagine would be a knowing smile in his voice. "AJ tells me things went well between you yesterday?"

"Yeah, definitely. She said we each reacted the exact opposite of how she thought we would," Ella said congenially.

Alex chuckled. "Yeah, I did kind of freak out a little bit. I mean, not about her dating a girl, but she told me she's having sex. And I guess these are things you want to know as a father, but also, as a father, these are things you don't want to know," he said.

It was Ella's turn to laugh. "Oh, I get that completely. Will you be at the regional game next week? I think she wants us to meet her family." Ella was stressed about meeting her daughter's girlfriend's parents, but it would be easier if Alex were there. She hoped they would be as down to earth and accepting as AJ felt they were.

"Yeah, I'll be there. Would you be okay if I brought Rebecca?" he said. While it was very considerate that he would ask, Ella did not want Alex to worry about asking her permission in the future. After all, if he planned to marry this woman, she would be a stepmother to their daughter. It was important to put Alex's mind at ease.

"Yes, of course. Al, you don't even have to ask. Besides, she and I need to get to know each other better, don't you think?"

Alex's retort came almost immediately. "Oh, hell no," he said. "I do not need the two of you conspiring against me and sharing funny Alex stories. Negative," he said.

At that moment, she was overcome with love for this man. Alex was kind, loving, warm, and absolutely hilarious. One of her biggest fears when she divulged her sexuality and the need for a divorce was that she would lose him completely. When he instead chose to support her and love her, it was half of what she needed in order to be able to live comfortably in her own skin. Now that she also had AJ's reassurance that everything was okay with them and she was fully accepted, everything clicked into place. She had all of the acceptance she needed in order to move forward and live her life.

"Aw, what's-a-matter," she said in her best baby-talk voice. "Is wittwe Awex afwaid of stowies I could tell?" she said, cackling wildly.

Alex let out one simple, skeptical laugh. "Yeah, something like that," he said. Neither of them spoke for a few moments. When he did, his voice was caring. "You're okay, El? I know you told her about yourself, too. I think that meant the world to her. Not that you're gay, but that you chose to share that with her. When she talked to me on our trip, she was almost inconsolable at the idea that you might not accept her."

Ella's heart hurt at the thought. Not just because it was not something her daughter needed to worry about, but specifically that she had done or said something that gave her the impression that she would not be accepted however she chose to live her life. "Alex, I don't understand why she would think that. You and I didn't raise her in a hateful household; instead, we always taught her to accept people for who they are, no matter their race, sexual preference, or anything else. Why would she think that I wouldn't just welcome her with open arms?"

He didn't speak for a moment. "I honestly don't know. I just know you're tough. I've always been the softie, and you've always doled out the discipline. She looks up to you so much, not just as a mother, but as a coach. I think she just always wants to impress you, and even though it's unfounded, the fear was there. I thought you might be able to identify with her."

Ella screwed up her face even though he couldn't see it. "What do you mean?"

He sighed heavily. "Well, you know…you had the same feelings at her age. In the beginning of our divorce, you told me you had pretty much always been this way. But you couldn't even accept it yourself, let alone tell your parents. They never gave you any indication that they wouldn't accept you for who you are, but that didn't change your fears," he said.

Ella didn't, couldn't, speak for a long moment. There was no need for any self-flagellation. What AJ was going through was the same as all teenagers who were coming-of-age. She remembered the crippling fear she had of her feelings. Even though it took AJ a few months to rationalize her emotions, she had told her everything in the end. And now they were ready to move on in their relationship. "That's true. I just want her to know that we're always going to be there for her, you know?" she said.

"She knows that, Ella. This is why she has told us about everything now. Including the sex stuff," he said and shuddered audibly.

Ella laughed and nodded in agreement. "Yeah, glad we got that out of the way, and we don't have to go through that part again," she said.

After disconnecting the call, Ella retired to her room to get ready for another day teaching high schoolers about the wonders of the written word. She sighed heavily. Tuesday night could not possibly get here soon enough.

Ella suffered through a completely uneventful couple of days at school before Tuesday evening rolled around. She dropped a quick message in her group chat with Danna, Val, and Wendy before sneaking into AJ's room humming the *Mission: Impossible* theme. Thank goodness she wasn't home from volleyball practice yet.

Looking through AJ's clothes for something to wear yet again, she was determined to find something sexy. No wait, did she really want to find something sexy in her daughter's clothes? Learning that AJ was having sex with her girlfriend had been enough of a shock.

Stepping to one side, Ella's foot bumped one of AJ's shoeboxes. When she heard a light buzzing noise coming from the box, she stared it, horrified, but decided to put her head in the sand. *It's her spare electric toothbrush, nothing more.* After doing her best ostrich impression, she began looking through the hangers with AJ's belts. A nice, chunky belt could be really sexy. She saw something pushed behind everything else that looked perfect; it was leather with several buckles and rivets. When Ella started to take it off the hanger, she noticed it was not just a belt. It was also adorned with two more straps that hung in loops from the main piece. Not understanding, she held the belt against herself and noticed the additional loops were positioned to fit around someone's thighs. The buzzing sound came back into focus and putting two and two together, Ella dropped the contraption and grabbed the first thing she saw. She was getting the hell out of Dodge, sexy be damned.

Ella engaged in a thorough production of getting ready for her evening with Parker. She combed her naked body for any imperfections and spots missed while shaving before dressing in what ended up being a cute outfit. More skinny jeans, this time paired with a form-fitting dark purple button-up with three-quarter sleeves. She dried her hair so that her loose waves bounced carefully at the top of her shoulders. Just the slightest touch of makeup completed the look. Instead of her signature Chucks, she picked a pair of casual loafers and, with one last look in the mirror, she was ready.

She texted AJ to let her know she was going out and that she would leave pizza money on the kitchen counter. AJ responded to have a nice date and that she looked forward to meeting 'Pahhh' soon. Ella responded with some laughing emojis. She checked the chat with her friends to see that Val and Wendy had checked in, but there was still no response from Danna.

Even though she was still technically a new friend, Ella had felt an immediate bond with Danna, and the lack of conversation now felt weird, especially the way things were left after the extremely uncomfortable night at the bar. She decided to send her a separate direct message, asking if they could talk soon. When she put her phone back in her pocket, she immediately heard a notification. Smiling, she took her phone back out and saw that the text was from Tally.

Tally, 6:37 p.m.: "Hey, I hadn't heard from you in a few days and wanted to check in. How are you doing?"

Simple and to the point. Ella was caught between the proverbial rock and a hard place. She wanted to do the right thing by Tally, but what was correct? Should she keep their date as promised? It was obvious to her that if she flaked out on Tally this time after what happened at the bar, she wouldn't have another chance. But did she want to see her in that way? She had tried, that's for sure, but the only spark she felt was when she was with Parker, whether she wanted it to be that way or not. The more she thought about it, the more she started to realize it didn't seem to matter what her head wanted. The heart wants what it wants.

She still decided to take things slowly on the romantic front with Parker. She wasn't jumping into any sort of relationship with her, and she felt pretty sure Parker understood that. Well, she hoped so, anyway. There was no doubt there were feelings there, but that was for another day.

Ella nodded to herself, having decided the most honorable thing to do would be to go on the date with Tally, as she had asked for it. They would go out, have dinner and drinks, and at the end of the night, she would just be honest and tell her there was more of a friend vibe going.

Ella, 6:40 p.m.: "Hey, yeah, it's been a busy few days. Hope all is well with you. Are we still on for Saturday?"

Tally, 6:42 p.m.: "Yeah, can't wait. If you're busy, I'll leave you to it. See you then!"

Perfect. Even Tally seemed casual about the situation. She checked her phone once more and saw that despite the text being successfully delivered to Danna, she still had not opened it. Ella couldn't stop herself from frowning, but this was for another time as she was due at Parker's by seven. She picked up her keys and hurried out the door.

Parker had been cleaning and re-cleaning things all day. She went back and forth on whether or not she should actually make something for them to eat, but this wasn't about dinner and she knew it. Ella was hungry, but not for sustenance. Parker felt her heart skip yet another beat as she checked her appearance for what was probably the hundredth time in her full-length mirror.

She had opted for a solid black tank paired with black-and-green plaid, skintight pants. She had left her hair down and flowing and her makeup was smudge-free.

Parker had every intention of trying to give everything to Ella tonight. She wanted to make an offering of her body to this woman who she felt more deeply for than she ever thought would be possible. When she heard knocking on her front door, she closed her eyes tightly for a moment as the anxiety began to creep down her spine like icy drops of water. She physically tried to shake off the feeling as she walked toward the door.

Parker wasn't quite prepared for the vision of loveliness that was standing in her doorway, and she couldn't stop the sharp inhalation that showed her hand. Ella was always beautiful, but this evening, there was something different. She was smiling openly and honestly, much like she had during their first day together. That knowing look was back in her eyes, and it was spellbinding.

She must have been standing there staring stupidly for a while, because Ella's facial expression changed into one of curiosity.

"Can I come in?" she said, and Parker was drawn out of her daze.

"Oh, God, yes, I'm sorry. I just..." She trailed off as she closed the door behind her, securely locking it. Ella turned back to her expectantly waiting on her to finish. "You're beautiful," Parker said in a small voice. She couldn't stop the furious blush from overtaking her face as Ella looked back at her with wide eyes.

"Uh, well..." Ella said in a self-deprecating tone, looking down at the simple outfit.

Parker strode over to where she stood and placed her thumbs through the belt loops of Ella's jeans just above her hips and pulled her gently to her, their bodies only inches apart now, before leaning forward to place a sweet kiss on her lips. "You're beautiful," she repeated, pulling Ella the last few inches to her to place soft kisses on the side of her neck. Ella closed her eyes at the sensation and placed her own hands on the small of Parker's back. When she reached under the shirt to feel the soft, warm skin underneath, Ella perceived what she thought was a shudder. A flashback to their last time together came to the forefront of her mind, and she stopped immediately and stepped back. Parker looked at her, confused.

"Is everything okay?" Parker said.

Ella sighed heavily, grasped her hand, and led her to the couch. She directed Parker to sit down on one end while she sat on the opposite end. "I just feel like we need to talk," she said, and Parker now looked terrified. Ella placed a reassuring hand on Parker's thigh before continuing. "After last time, I just want to make sure you feel safe. I'm scared of hurting you," she said.

Parker rolled her lips inward before blowing out a breath and tucking a leg under herself in preparation for this conversation she hadn't been expecting. "You don't have to be scared of hurting me, Ella. I've told you I want to try. I don't know that it will happen tonight, but I want to pursue this with you, with us," she said, running her fingertips gently over Ella's hand.

"I was so scared I had hurt you and now I feel like I'm going to do something wrong and cause you to have another…I guess that was a panic attack?"

Parker nodded and sighed. "Yeah, that was a panic attack. But I honestly think it could have been because everything happened so quickly. Let's just go slowly and see what happens?"

Now it was Ella's turn to bite her lips contemplatively. "You know I want to," she said, meeting Parker's eyes and finding her desire mirrored. "But just promise me that if anything moves too quickly, you'll tell me. Even if we are in the middle of having sex and you start feeling uncomfortable, please tell me immediately," she said. Parker looked down, clearly distraught at the unexpected turn the night had taken.

Ella hated to cause Parker any stress, but she couldn't shake her memory of Parker on Saturday night, sweat-soaked, pale, and trembling, and whether it was intentional or not, she had been the cause of it. She didn't ever want that to happen again. And she did not want Parker to be embarrassed. Ella took her hand and placed a soft kiss on her palm. "Maybe we could have a safe word?" Ella said, and Parker looked up at her, a completely blank expression on her face. "Does that sound corny? I just thought if I were, you know, doing something in which I couldn't see your face, I wouldn't have to guess if the movements you were making were because you were panicked or pleasured," she said, now looking down at their joined hands as she returned them to Parker's leg and blushing furiously.

Was this a stupid idea? Was she literally the biggest loser in the world? She felt movement on the couch and felt Parker shift back into her space. She prepared herself for another passionate kiss, but Parker wrapped her arms around her neck and squeezed. Ella returned the hug with all her might.

"That is probably the kindest thing anyone has ever said to me," she said. Ella smiled in her hair, never wanting to release her. When Parker did sit back, she took both of Ella's hands in hers and smiled graciously "That sounds like a very good idea. How about 'purple' because this shirt looks fucking amazing on you," she said, winking.

Ella chuckled and nodded.

"Fine, there we go. We have our safe word," Parker said and stood, holding out her hand. "Now, shall we?" she said, inclining her head toward the bedroom. Ella felt her pulse quicken as the blood started to make its way south. She stood up and took Parker's hand.

∽∾

Parker was a phenomenal lover and her orgasm—no, wait, three orgasms—were just as amazing as the first time they were together. Ella's world was fully rocked. As she lay on the bed fully spent but hardly sated, waiting for her heart to settle down and her breathing return to some semblance of normalcy, she felt Parker moving around next to her. When she looked over, Parker was removing her bra while still under the covers. Ella lifted an eyebrow at her as she dropped both bra and underwear onto the floor. Parker looked up at her shyly, and Ella turned her entire body to face her, smiling brightly but making no effort to touch her yet.

"How are you feeling with that?" Ella said, indicating Parker's new state of undress. Parker took a very deep breath, attempting to overcome the building anxiety. When she didn't immediately speak, Ella continued. "Listen, you know you don't have to—" she said as Parker quickly shifted to press her body directly against Ella's. At the delicious, direct skin-on-skin contact, Ella could not stop a moan from leaving her body. Parker's nipples were rock hard against her own chest, and she felt her arousal climb back to a fever pitch. Still, she made no attempt to physically connect despite her desire.

Parker looked into her eyes. "Please," she said, breathless. Although Ella still couldn't trust herself to discern if it was from panic or arousal. "Please touch me," Parker said in a low, sensual voice as she grasped her hand under the cover and placed it on her own shoulder. Ella obeyed by wrapping her arms around her and gently stroking her back. She felt Parker's breath catch before she exhaled in a soft moan that almost drove Ella mad with the longing in it.

"Is this all okay?" she said, not wanting to chance moving too fast. Parker nodded against her shoulder and placed her hand on Ella's hip, gently massaging.

"Do you want me to keep going?" she said, and when Parker nodded again, Ella slowly shifted their bodies so that she was on top, resting gently against her body. When she felt herself slip between Parker's naked thighs and their centers pressed together, her sex throbbed in anticipation. They fit together like pieces of a puzzle, like they were made for each other. She looked down at Parker who had her eyes closed tightly. "Are you okay?" she said, and when Parker didn't respond, she was drawn out of her lust-filled haze. Ella shifted up onto her elbows to look down at her, now very concerned. "Hey, Parker, look at me." Parker still didn't open her eyes.

"Purple," she said in a choked whisper. Ella shifted off her immediately. At the loss of contact, Parker put her hands over her face and began to sniffle. Ella scooped her into her arms and held her as she began to sob in earnest. Years of pain flooded out of Parker and spilled down her cheeks.

"Let it go. I've got you. I'm not going anywhere," she said, and Parker sobbed harder, feeling all of those trauma-tinged thoughts and nightmares rush away like a raging river. It was a release like nothing she had ever felt. She was determined to get rid of it all, right here in the solace of Ella's arms.

Ella cooed and comforted, murmuring words of encouragement as Parker tried to let go of all the memories that were poisoning her. With every tear that spilled down her cheek, she felt a purge in her very soul. When Ella felt her calm somewhat, she gently wiped under her eyes and moved stray strands of hair behind her ear.

"God, my makeup probably looks terrible," Parker said in a sob that was part crying and part laughter.

Ella placed a gentle, lingering kiss on her forehead. "You're beautiful," she said. Parker snuggled into her neck, waiting for the terror to recede and the peace to return. "Are you comfortable, though? Do you want us to put clothes on?" Ella said, continuing to be overly cautious. She felt the panic continue to roll off Parker in waves, although fewer and further between as she seemed to be settling. She felt Parker shake her head against her.

"No, I like feeling your body against me," Parker said, reveling in the feeling of coming back down. She leaned up to place a soft kiss on Ella's lips.

"You know this is totally okay, right? We don't have to move any faster than you're ready to move. I love feeling this close to you," Ella said, leaning down to place soft kisses on her face and neck.

Parker looked up, and her eyes were those of a prisoner in bonds. Ella hoped against hope that she would one day be able to set her completely free.

Parker just shook her head and smiled, almost unbelievingly at Ella's words, before tucking her head under her chin and sighing contentedly.

"When can I see you again? I'm off work on Saturday nights, remember. You may have heard me mention that before," she said with feigned nonchalance as she leaned up to peer at Ella.

Ella froze, her eyes going comically wide. Why would she have made her date with Tally on the night she knew Parker would be available? She would literally be kicking herself if she were able. In her heart of hearts, she knew they had both agreed on friends-with-benefits for the time being. But she also knew that her heart was quickly being taken from her by the mocha eyes that were currently staring directly into hers, expectantly. She decided to be completely honest with Parker. Although she did not want to hurt her, she knew that if they were setting any sort of foundation for anything in the future, it should not be tainted with any sort of dishonesty on her part.

"I would. You know I would," she said, smiling brightly at Parker whose smile had diminished somewhat as she was obviously waiting on the *but*. "But I have a date with Tally

Saturday night." Parker's face remained expressionless as she started to sit up and cover herself with the bedsheet. Ella reached out to her, and Parker looked almost startled by the touch, like she was miles away. Then, Parker nodded and smiled the inauthentic smile she knew so well.

"Right. Well, uh, why don't you come over beforehand and I'll help you get ready. You can even borrow something to wear if you want," she said.

Ella raised an eyebrow skeptically. "You want to help me get ready for a date with someone else?" she said.

Parker nodded with way too much enthusiasm. "Sure. This is what friends do. They help each other get ready for dates and let them borrow clothes." Her voice had taken on a mechanical quality.

Ella pursed her lips but decided it would be better to not discuss it now. "Yeah, sure. I can do that. Thanks. I'm always looking for something cool to wear and you have the coolest style of anyone that I know," she said.

Parker wouldn't meet her eyes but nodded emphatically. "Yeah, sounds great. Listen, I have an early day tomorrow so I will probably just want to get to bed soon if that works for you," she said, getting up out of bed and gathering her discarded clothes. She began dressing, and Ella, although confused, took the hint and went to obtain her own clothing.

"Okay? Well, I'll let you know what time on Saturday," she said, and Parker nodded again on her way to the bathroom.

"You can just let yourself out. I'm going to shower. See you Saturday," Parker said. She didn't even turn around. Ella heard her shut the bathroom door, and it felt just like it did the first time Parker slammed a door on her. Very final.

Chapter 15

The next morning, Ella sat contemplating the previous night over a cup of coffee. Should she reach out to Parker and try to talk it out? Should she just allow her to process the situation? Ella texted her to let her know she had made it home, to thank her for the evening, and to say good night. Parker's response was a very unusually clipped, *"Have a good night."*

Ella pulled up the conversation with Danna to see she had left her on read. She took one more sip of her coffee before lowering her forehead to the table. She was pondering going back to sleep for the day when she heard AJ descending the stairs.

"Rough night?" she said as Ella did not lift her head at her approach. Ella groaned loudly before giving her a thumbs-up. AJ giggled.

"You wanna talk about it?" she said, pouring some coffee and sitting across from her mother at the table.

Ella lifted her head, knowing there would be a crazy indention on her forehead, but not caring. "AJ, I don't even know where to start."

"Well, you can tell me how your date went," she said, smiling wryly.

Ella sighed, not wanting to get into any gory details with her daughter, but also desperate for a sounding board since Danna wasn't around. "The date itself was great. I really, really like her, but…" she said, trailing off. She hadn't mentioned Parker's age previously and AJ eyed her suspiciously, waiting for her to continue. "There's an age difference," she said, shrugging. There. Now it was out in the open for discussion. Maybe Ella could gauge her reaction.

AJ tilted her head slowly to one side, eyeing her. "So, let me get this straight," she said. Ella looked up and gave AJ her full attention. "You like this woman, right?" Ella nodded. "It's that whole *love at first sight* kind of thing?" Ella sighed and nodded again. AJ raised her hands in a questioning gesture. "Mom, what the hell is your problem?" she said but softened the harsh statement with a bright smile as Ella's eyes boggled. "What does it matter if she's a few years younger or older than you?"

A few, Ella repeated in her mind. Should she just come out and tell her? *AJ, she was born in a different decade—the same decade as you, actually*. She shook her head violently to shake herself back into the conversation at hand.

"Well, it's more than just a couple, sweetie. It's quite a few years," she continued, but AJ shook her head and held up a hand for her to stop.

"Mom, you have spent your entire life without real love. Why would it matter? Why would you resist this? Just let go and feel."

Ella thought back to Parker saying something like that to her the first time they made love. She was so kind and gentle and nurturing. Wait, hang on. *Made love?* Not 'fucked.' Not 'had sex.' Her mind immediately titled their encounter 'made love' without even consulting her. Rude!

"Mom?"

Ella started, drawn back to the present again by AJ's voice. "Huh, what?" she said, knowing she had to look certifiably insane right now.

"Are you okay?"

Ella's answering chuckle sounded forced even to her. "Oh yeah, fine, thanks. I just need to get ready for school," she said, standing up so quickly that she knocked her chair over. She bent over to right the chair and when she stood back up, bumped her head on the underside of the table with an *oof* sound.

"Mom, do you need some help?" AJ said as Ella rubbed the back of her head.

"No, no, I'm good, thanks. Just gonna go get ready," she said, tripping over Narcissus's food bowl, spilling the contents everywhere. She bent over to start scooping the food back into the bowl as the cat came over to check to see if he would now be getting new food since the food in his bowl was never enough. AJ got up to go help her.

"I've got this. You go get ready before you fall and break a hip," she said, gently chiding her mother.

"Hey, is that an old people joke?" she said. AJ just shook her head as Ella retreated upstairs, overhearing her daughter mumble something about "psychiatric help" as she went.

∼

She still had no additional messages from Parker but opted to let that go for now. She only had enough intestinal fortitude to deal with one crisis at a time, and right now, she wanted to try to reach out to Danna and see what was going on.

As the phone was ringing, she ran through everything in her mind to try to figure out what she was going to say. She didn't get much time, as Danna picked up on the second ring.

"Hey, I miss you already" was how she answered the phone.

Ella was so thrown off that nothing came out of her open mouth. Who in the world did she think she was talking to? "Uh, if you miss me so much, why aren't you responding to my messages?" she said in a put-on castigating tone.

"Ella?" she said.

Ella responded with a simple 'yes' in that same questioning tone and waited for her to continue.

"Oh, I…hey," Danna said flatly and offered no more.

"So, is everything okay with us? I feel like you're blowing me off. If I've done something to upset you, can we talk?" Ella said.

"I've just been busy," she said and, again, stopped at the simple response.

"Well, so have I, but I have taken the time to message you and check in. I know we're new friends and maybe I'm feeling more of a 'new bestie' connection than you are. If so, that's okay. Just tell me and I will go away," she said.

Danna sighed heavily on the other line. "I've just got some personal stuff going on, you know. I've been talking to someone, and I just haven't had a lot of extra time."

Ella did not have to fake the excitement that crept into her voice at the idea that Danna had met someone she was interested in. "Wow, that's great! I'm so happy for you. We should go on a double date sometime! Hey, what about Saturday?"

"What about Saturday?" Danna replied.

"Well, Tally and I are going on our first date. Would you want to invite your mystery woman to go, and we can make it a foursome? Well, not an actual foursome of course," she said and trailed off laughing, knowing this was right down Danna's lane for humor. When she didn't respond in kind, Ella stopped laughing.

"Yeah, that's probably not a good idea. So, you're still planning on going out with Tally Saturday night?" she said with obvious ire in her voice.

"Yeah, we made those plans last weekend when I was at your house, remember?"

"What about Parker?" Danna said.

Ella tried to hold back her offense. "What *about* Parker?"

Danna scoffed. "Seriously? Are you still trying to deny whatever is between you?"

"Danna, I am not committed to anyone. I am just dating. It is just dinner with Tally. We are only getting to know one another. What's the problem? You do remember originally that you told me to date them both, right?" Ella could not figure out where in the world this attitude was coming from. She and

Danna had hit it off from the very beginning and Ella had foreseen a close friendship in their future. But now?

"Listen, Ella, I have to go to work. Enjoy your date Saturday," she said and disconnected the call. Ella could only stare at the screen. She shook her head slowly as she blinked at the screen.

Well, that's that. She then reached out to Parker to check in. She typed out a quick good morning message before retreating to the bathroom for a shower. When she returned, there was no response from Parker. Great, she thought, 0-for-2 on the day. She was a real lady-killer.

Ella checked her phone during her lunch break hoping for a text from Parker, but there was only a voicemail indicator from an unknown, toll-free number. She was not interested in hearing about potential extended car warranties or lowering her student loan interest rate right now and hit delete without listening.

After a mostly disastrous class on Poe's "Masque of the Red Death," the school day came to a close and Ella could try to relax. She began to grade papers and decided she needed to set aside an entire class period on homophones. Too many of her students were talking about 'prostating' themselves and discussing 'menstruations' when they could just say assistance. Ella closed her eyes slowly and debated banging her head on her desk when she heard a text message come through.

Parker, 3:47 p.m.: "Hey, I'm sorry for being weird. You've been more than clear on the realm of our relationship. This whole situation has just brought up a lot for me and sometimes it puts me in a bad headspace. It is nothing you have done. This is all me. I hope I haven't pissed you off to the point you don't want to talk to me anymore."

Ella was so elated just to get a message from Parker that she immediately tried to call her. When the call was sent directly to voicemail, Ella frowned at her phone. She was typing out a text to Parker when she received an incoming message.

Parker, 3:48 p.m.: "I'm sorry. I just don't feel like talking right now. Can I call you later tonight?"

Ella, 3:49 p.m.: "Of course. Sorry to jump the gun. AJ has a game tonight, but I'll text you when we get back."

Ella typed out 'I miss you' three separate times before opting to leave it off completely.

Parker sniffed and wiped her eyes again. When she saw that Ella was trying to call her again, she knew she would not be able to hide the emotion in her voice. After turning down the call, she apologized and offered to speak later. Ella would be later than normal tonight as she was going to watch AJ's volleyball team. She wondered what it would be like to go with Ella to one of her games and cheer AJ on. Would she ever get that chance? She agreed without bias to enter into this arrangement with Ella but jumping in headfirst had always been a character flaw.

Parker didn't know if she could only be friends, benefits or no. She wanted Ella in every way: physically, mentally, and spiritually. She wanted Ella's face to be the first thing she saw when she woke up in the morning and the last thing she saw before she closed her eyes at night. She was head over heels in love with this woman; there was no longer any doubt. She would have to tell her very soon because trying to hold back this flood of emotions felt like it was going to drown her completely.

Parker looked over at the leather-bound journal she bought at the beginning of her journey in therapy. She had dug it out from the bottom of her nightstand earlier today. Taking a moment to reverently wipe dust from its cover, she resolved to try again. Nothing that her therapist had told her to try had worked previously, but wasn't she a different person now? She had to push through her issues and devote blood, sweat, and tears to repairing herself.

Parker had to give everything another chance to work, to heal her broken psyche. Meeting Ella had refilled her reserves, and she was going to tap into them, hoping to push past everything that held her back from being a whole person. She wanted a chance with Ella, that was for sure. But, most importantly, she wanted to do it for herself. Enough was enough and she was bound and determined to put her past directly behind her.

She typed out the words 'I miss you' to Ella several times before erasing them and putting her phone back on her nightstand. Then, she picked up the book and a pen and began to write down her feelings.

Chapter 16

The rest of the week passed without much change. Danna was still being weird. Parker was still being distant and returning her texts with the bare minimum response. The Lady Dragons had blasted through the competition and made it to the regional playoff next Tuesday. As expected, they would face off against the Havenwood Lady Wildcats and the infamous Kat.

In all honesty, Ella was very excited to meet her daughter's girlfriend and her family. She wanted to finally spend some quality time with the young lady who had stolen AJ's heart. But there was no time to relax this weekend. In just a very short time, she would be heading over to Parker's house to get ready for her date with Tally. This…was weird. But it was Parker's suggestion, so she was simply going to go with it.

It was very important that she have this time with Tally to see if there was an actual spark there. If not, wouldn't that be the sign she was looking for to move forward with Parker? Did she need a sign? Why was she still stuck on this age thing? AJ didn't care and called her out for being a dumbass instead of just moving in the direction she wanted to go. That whole following her heart business? She should probably get on that. But tonight was for a date with the chiropractor. Ella chuckled to herself. *If it doesn't work out, maybe I could still get an adjustment out of the deal.*

Ella, 6:31 p.m.: "Hey, so, do you still want me to come over? You haven't been overly talkative this week and I understand why this would be weird. I will totally understand if you want to cancel."

Ella had tried to check in with Parker to make sure she was okay (probably not) and didn't hate her for going out with someone else (yeah, probably this). It would be totally understandable if she did, but this was her idea to dress Ella for her date. And what did that even mean? Was she going to put her in one of those sexy outfits from the bar? One of those damn fucking sexy outfits that made Ella's heart do triple-time in her chest. The skintight pants and—dammit, what was she thinking about? Oh right. Dressing at Parker's. She tried to focus. That was not something that Ella could ever wear. She wasn't seriously thinking of that, was she? Well, it would help to know for sure what she was thinking if she would text her back. Ella picked up her phone like she could just say 'Siri, make Parker Chase read and then respond to my text.' When nothing happened, she put her phone down, figuring Parker had changed her mind, and started toward AJ's closet when her phone went off.

Parker, 6:39 p.m.: "Yup. Let's do this. You're meeting at the restaurant at eight?"

When Ella replied to confirm she had the correct time, Parker encouraged her to come over anytime. She asked her what she should bring, like makeup or clothes or toiletries. When Parker responded that she should just bring her 'gorgeous self,' a bit of the stress left of her body. She seemed to be acting somewhat normal, thank the gods. No longer feeling like a rubber band stretched to the point of breaking, she headed out the door.

~

Upon arrival at Parker's house, there was an obvious cloud surrounding them. Ella was as overjoyed as always to see her while Parker seemed a little standoffish.

Ella had missed Parker. It had been Tuesday night they were last together, but it seemed much longer to her. She went in for an embrace because, as they had established previously, friends hug. Parker pulled a ninja-like sidestep that turned the potential full-body squeeze into a weird side hug given to acquaintances and relatives who constantly get on your nerves. Ella studied her face, but as always, Parker brandished that mask-smile that tried to tell her everything was all right. She wasn't going to press the situation.

"So…" Parker said, grabbing Ella's hand and dragging her to the bedroom. Ella was immediately overcome with thoughts about the last two times Parker brought her here and what they had done together. She couldn't hold back a shiver. Parker didn't seem to notice.

"I've picked out a few outfits that, one, are very cool and, two, will actually be long enough for you as you have a few inches on me there," she said. When Parker swept her hand out in a voila-type movement, Ella surveyed the display before her.

There were three outfits Parker chose and all three displayed her wide array of styles that she employed. Choice one was club wear: tight red leather pants with a black-and-red, punkish, ripped tank top. At the foot of the bed, under the outfit, was a pair of red-and-black checkered Vans. Parker would look completely edible in it, but it probably was not going to be up Ella's alley…pretty much at all. She was overcome for a moment thinking of Parker wearing this outfit, how much fun it would be to take her out in it and how much more fun it would be to take it off her for a night of delicious pleasure before realizing her mind had drifted and getting back to the task at hand. She mentally slapped a ruler across her hand in punishment. Tonight, Parker was being a friend. No benefits tonight.

The second option was a perfect little black dress. Parker had picked a pair of black-and-silver stilettos to complete the outfit that would be accented by silver jewelry, laid out on the bed beside it. She couldn't stop her mouth from dropping open a bit at the thought of Parker in such an elegant display. Again, her mind wandered, thinking about taking Parker out for a night on the town. But, of course, came back to imagining what the dress would look like casually strewn on the floor with underwear and heels next to it. She had to stop doing this to herself.

The third outfit was the closest to her style. Well, not teacher-mom her, but the style she was going for if she ever had a chance to add to her wardrobe. Fitted, black, stinger jeans with buckles running down the outsides of the legs with a pair of six-eye, black patent leather Doc Martens; a skintight, supple, black T-shirt and a men's style single-breasted vest that was obviously tailored to fit womanly curves. In other words, this was Sex-on-a-Stick Parker. Ella was pretty sure she wouldn't be able to pull this off, but she was surely going to try.

"I'm guessing you're probably going to pick option three?" Parker said with a knowing grin.

Ella chuckled and nodded. "This porridge is juuuuuust right," she said and winked.

Parker nodded and moved the other two outfits to the side. Ella ran her hands over the soft fabric of the vest and guessed it to be silk. There was also an array of ties placed to the side. Ella truly had her pick of some beautiful pieces of craftsmanship. She was drawn to a black tie with patterns of dark purples and reds swirling together.

"That's actually the one I would have wanted you to pick," Parker said, appearing behind her and startling her.

Ella almost dropped the tie, but instead placed it back down on the bed, straightening it to make sure there would be no wrinkles. "I'm going to try my best to pull this outfit off, Parker, but I don't have high hopes to be completely honest with you," Ella said, looking down at her mom-bod.

Parker shook her head dolefully. "I hope one day you can see what I see when I look at you," she said. Ella looked deeply into her eyes, but Parker broke the intimate gaze, instead turning to pick the clothes up off the bed. "Let's get you dressed," she said.

What Ella had forgotten is that she had to remove her clothes to be able to put on Parker's clothes. Her mouth formed into a small 'o.' When she stuttered on the button of her jeans, Parker scoffed and shook her head before placing the clothes back on the bed. She walked over to Ella and placed her fingers gently inside the waistband of Ella's jeans before using her other hand to unfasten the top button. When her hand moved down to the zipper, Ella drew in a stuttered breath. She looked up to meet Ella's eyes and stopped. When she looked down and realized she was getting ready to disrobe Ella, she drew her hands back like they had been burned.

"Oh, God, I'm sorry, I wasn't thinking," she said, stepping back.

Despite sharing her shock, Ella gently grasped Parker's hands to get her to calm down. "No, it's okay. I know you were just trying to help."

Parker nodded, unsure of herself, and turned her back to Ella who finished removing her jeans. They were quickly followed by her shirt, and Ella stood in her underwear in Parker's bedroom. Immediately, she felt the familiar swooping in her stomach and a tingle between her legs.

"I'm ready for you to dress me," she said, going for a light, airy tone. When Parker turned back around, she looked a lot like those vampires that haven't fed for a while in just about any token, creature of the night movie. She was trying to disguise the way she was feeling, but anytime Parker's eyes met Ella's, she couldn't hide it. She was hungry. And she was looking at Ella like she was an off-limits buffet.

Parker let out a sound that was part cough and part nervous chuckle. She handed Ella the pants and stepped back as Ella struggled into them. It was obvious she hadn't tried to wear something like this before, and after watching her struggle in vain for a few seconds, Parker stepped forward to help.

"You can't just pull them on like you do regular pants. You have to kind of shimmy them up a little at a time." When Ella still didn't seem to get it, Parker tried in vain to show her the almost dance-like movements she used to get the extremely tight jeans up over her own full hips. Ella finally got them up and somewhat arranged before drawing up the zipper and buttoning the waist. Parker surveyed Ella's handiwork before seeing several places that the pants were gathered in an unflattering way. Before she knew what she was doing, she dropped to her knees in front of Ella and began tugging the pants down from the knee to draw out the wrinkles around her upper calf. She pulled and smoothed until she had sorted the right leg out. When she moved over to the left leg, she heard Ella make a small, choked sound. Fearful she had pinched her skin somewhere, she looked up to find Ella staring down at her with parted lips.

Parker looked away from her. She gulped, stared at the floor, and returned to her work on sorting out Ella's left leg. "Well, there you go," she said, clearing her throat before looking up at Ella again. Her expression hadn't changed, and she reached out to gently caress Parker's cheek. Parker leaned into the touch momentarily before remembering herself again and standing up. With an apologetic smile, she retrieved the vest and the simple fitted black T-shirt and handed it to Ella. When she put the vest on and began buttoning its length, Parker couldn't stop herself from stepping forward and taking over for her.

Ella looked at Parker, now standing inches away, as she placed her fingertips on Ella's, guiding her as she placed each button in its respective hole with painstaking care. Parker never met her eyes, even when the outsides of her hands brushed the undersides of Ella's breasts with a whisper-light touch. When she heard Ella draw in an audible breath, Parker closed her eyes against the thrill that ran through her. She licked her lips as her heartbeat picked up its cadence.

When she finished closing the final button, she chanced a glance at Ella. She was somewhere else. Her eyes were unfocused, and she looked to be within moments of dropping her head back and letting out a moan. How did Parker instinctively know that? They had made love only twice, but she knew in her very core exactly what Ella wanted her to do. She knew that Ella was on the verge of shedding her false calm like an obstructive outer skin and exposing her inner sex goddess. She had spent so much of her life buttoned up just like the vest Parker had dressed her in. But now? She was just on the verge of some beautiful release. Parker felt her body go taut like a bow string, ready to be plucked. It would only take just…one…touch.

She inserted one finger between the two buttons on the vest just over Ella's belly button and ran it up and down slowly as she reached behind her and pulled out the tie Ella had chosen. Parker imagined wrapping Ella's hands around behind her and tying them together before having her way with her. How delicious it would be to have Ella completely restrained, moaning and bucking under her as Parker pleasured every inch of her body. She retracted her fingers from the vest in order to gently loosen the tie's Windsor knot and began to move the loop slowly down over Ella's head. She wondered if she should stop where she was, as the loop sat directly over Ella's eyes. She could easily tug on the knot to blindfold Ella, allowing delectable games to ensue. Parker stepped back out of the moment, feeling like she had been under some sort of spell.

The gentle landing of the tie on her chest snapped Ella back to attention. She looked down to see it traveling down between her breasts with the very tip resting against her stomach. She ran her hand down its silken length and looked back up at Parker, who had retreated back to the bed and was picking up the rejected outfits.

"Well, there you go," she repeated without turning around. Parker was attempting to busy herself with hanging up the clothes. This woman was captivating. Parker realized she would have to keep her wits about her, or else get pulled into Ella's atmosphere. She was pretty sure she would not survive the impending collision.

~

Ella was surrounded by Parker's very essence, her perfume and the scent that was just Parker. She couldn't get enough. As Parker kneeled on the ground to sort out the extremely tight jeans, Ella happened to look down. Seeing Parker on her knees before her brought her right back to their first night together; the night that had inexorably changed her life as she'd known it.

Ella remembered Parker lifting her leg for her and resting it on her own surprisingly strong shoulder. She remembered Parker's first simple touch and watching her suck every bit of wetness off her fingers afterwards, before nearly bringing her to her knees with her fingers and tongue. She was overcome with the moment and couldn't stop herself from drawing in a breath as the moisture grew between her thighs and the drum line thundered in her chest. Parker met her eyes and she knew. She knew what Ella was thinking and what she wanted, but she didn't react and simply continued to help Ella sort out the bottom half of her outfit.

When it came time to place the tie around her neck, Parker stepped in close. In this proximity, Ella could feel the heat radiating off Parker in waves like lava. She had to be doing everything in her power to hold back; Ella knew she was. In her heart, she knew that she was only fighting the inevitable, or, at best, delaying it.

When Parker's fingers delicately stroked Ella's stomach through the vest, she felt the skin from the top of her head to the tips of her curled toes come over in gooseflesh. When Parker placed the tie around her neck and looked at her with that smoldering gaze, she thought she might just evaporate then and there. All too soon, they both seemed to come to their senses and Parker took a giant leap back. But Ella wasn't ready for the moment to end. As Parker turned around to start hanging up the other clothes, Ella dared a step forward.

"Aren't you going to do my makeup, too?" she said in a register much lower than her regular voice. Parker visibly tensed but didn't turn around.

"Your makeup looks great already. It always does. I think you're ready to go," she said, hanging up the last article of clothing and continuing to stare into the closet. Ella stepped forward again, lifting her hand with the intention of placing it on her shoulder. Then…what? What would she do when Parker turned to her with eyes filled with lust or, worse, pain? She knew the answer immediately. She would take Parker into her arms and kiss away all the torment. Ella would hold her while it all trickled away like a blood-letting of the soul. Then the uncontrollable passion between them would erupt and ignite and nothing would stop them from progressing directly to the bed only a few feet from where they stood now. Ella let her hand drop back down to her side before retreating backwards to the doorway.

"Well…" she said, swallowing with an audible click in her throat. "I guess I'll head out. Thank you for everything, Parker. I hope you have a great evening."

"Yup, will do. Have fun," she said, doing her absolute best to choke back the mix of emotions filling her throat. She didn't dare breathe or turn around as she heard Ella's footsteps recede and her front door open and close. It was in that very moment that she knew she couldn't continue this arrangement. It had to be all or nothing with Ella. She couldn't handle the push and pull of their current situation and the way it tugged on her heartstrings when they were together. She resolved to tell Ella the next time they spoke, and she would deal with the consequences as they fell.

Parker allowed a single tear to trickle down her cheek before scrubbing her face violently and heading to the living room for an evening in front of the television.

Wrong. Everything about this felt wrong. Why was she on the way to meet up with Tally for a date when that is not what she wanted at all?

As she pulled into the restaurant's parking lot, she was overcome with a feeling of what could only be described as a debilitating ache, like she had left something important behind. Or someone. Phantom pain ran through her body. She wanted to be back at Parker's house for whatever. Dinner, a movie, a make-out session, mind-blowing sex, or cuddling and talking until the sun came up. She had to be honest with Tally, first and foremost. But, dammit, Universe, she was looking for a sign that what she wanted with Parker was indeed where she should be.

When Ella walked toward the entrance, she spotted Tally waiting outside. She was beautiful in a cornflower-blue wrap dress that accentuated every aspect of her flawless figure. Ella waved and caught Tally's attention. She waved back with a bright smile, but as Ella approached, she noticed the tightness around her eyes that accompanied it.

"Hi, it's so great to see you again," Tally said, leaning in for a hug, albeit much more tentative than her previous embraces. Ella initially intended to wrap her arms around her waist for a full-on hug, but at Tally's obvious attempt to keep their bodies from pressing together in any way, she could only awkwardly pat her on the shoulder blade before she had drawn away. *What's up with love interests and their weird hugs today?*

"Hey, it's good to see you, too. But is everything okay?"

Tally smiled and looked away before nodding. "Yeah, I'm good. Can we sit down for a moment?"

Ella's brows furrowed of their own accord before she could process what Tally was saying. She looked around at the wrought iron benches in the courtyard waiting area before spotting an empty one and gesturing they should sit. Once they did, Tally stared off into space and seemed to be preparing herself for something difficult. Ella could only wait in uncomfortable silence, steepling her hands on her knees. After a few moments, Tally finally turned to her and took one of her hands.

"I just…" she said, staring into the middle distance for a moment. "I think I've met someone. Well, we've known each other for a while, but only recently have we started to see each other in a romantic light." Tally paused and looked into Ella's expressionless face before continuing. "I just wouldn't feel right going on this date with you. I would like to be friends if you would like that, but I think I am ready to pursue something serious with her. I'm sorry, I should have said something earlier, I know. I've just felt so bad about it, and I wanted to wait until I could talk with you in person. I hope you understand where I am coming from and I haven't ruined any potential for friendship. I just didn't want you to feel like you should continue to chase me," she said.

She did look apologetic despite sounding a little presumptuous and full of herself. She used Parker's last name. Was that just coincidence? Ella was honestly not at all sure how to react to the situation presented to her. She bent over to place her elbows on her thighs and looked down at her shoes. But they were not her shoes. They were Parker's shoes. And her arms were resting on Parker's pants. She couldn't help but chuckle. The signs were right here in front of her, and Tally's words had sealed the deal. Ella Gardner wanted Parker Chase. She wasn't going to fight it any longer. Tally cleared her throat drawing Ella back into the present.

"Oh sorry. Yeah, I'd love to be friends. And I totally understand where you're coming from. I'm not angry," she said and stood up.

Tally mirrored the movement, and Ella leaned over to place a kiss on her cheek. Tally breathed out a sigh of relief. "Oh, thank goodness. I have been so worried you were going to be angry with me." She motioned over her shoulder. "Shall we get some food? As friends, of course."

But Ella had other plans and other places to be. She couldn't stop the smile from blossoming on her face as she slowly shook her head. "Thank you, but I have somewhere I need to be right now. I wish you all the happiness in the world," she said, slowly walking backwards before turning around and heading swiftly to her car.

Chapter 17

Parker decided that ordering enough Thai food for four people was the proper way to wallow in her pit of depression. There was nothing like a big bowl of drunken noodles she could cry into followed by some mango sticky rice. But a text message brought her back to the present. It was her sister. Parker hadn't heard from her in a few weeks and was truly excited to hear what was going on in her life.

Keeka, 8:15 p.m.: "Peeka! I miss you. How are you?"

Her heart lit up with excitement at the use of her childhood nickname. When her sister was little, she couldn't quite get 'Parker' out properly, so Peeka was born. The moniker Keeka quickly followed and, unless they were angry at one another, that is how they referred to each other to this day.

Parker, 8:16 p.m.: "Hey Keeka! I miss you, too. How's school and what not?"

After discussing light topics back and forth for a while, her sister seemed to get down to the real reason for reaching out.

Keeka, 8:23 p.m.: "Can you come over Tuesday? And can you clear your schedule for the whole evening? I've been talking to Mom and Dad a lot and I think I have finally gotten through to them. I want us all to sit down after school and talk."

Parker pursed her lips, wondering what her sister had been saying to their parents. Things were fine as they stood as far as she was concerned. Parker went to the family home for all major holidays and birthdays. She and her parents were civil enough with one another, but they kept discussions on shallow, casual topics. She and her sister could spend as much time together as they wanted, although lately that had been limited by school and extracurricular activities and Parker's work. It was a perfectly comfortable situation, even if not ideal. Parker was happy taking care of herself and living her life exactly how she wanted to do it. There was no reason to change anything.

Parker, 8:25 p.m.: "Kee, what have you been doing or saying to them? Everything is fine exactly how it is now."

Keeka, 8:26 p.m.: "But it's not though. I know they miss having you around more often. I have overheard them talking about it a lot. And I think you miss hanging around here. I just want everyone to be happy."

This was not a good idea. Parker and her parents did not see eye to eye on her career path. They thought it was 'unsavory' to have a daughter who worked in a nightclub and was working toward something musical or artistic as a future career. They didn't see the merit in such an unreliable occupation. But Parker knew she had to be true to herself, and if that meant supporting herself financially, then so be it.

Parker, 8:29 p.m.: "Listen I appreciate it and I love you more than you'll ever know. But this is a lost cause. I'm not going to change. I'm not going to be a number cruncher or a doctor or a lawyer. I'm going to do my own thing and they can't deal with that. We have an arrangement that works out for everyone, and I think that's just what we should stick to."

Keeka, 8:30 p.m.: "But I miss you."

Her heart filled with love at her sister's declaration. She would have to set up some time for them to hang out. Maybe this weekend if she was free and didn't have a lot of schoolwork. But what harm could it do to have dinner with the family? If things got too heavy, she could just leave. She had that option. She could simply tell them that she was going to do things her way, like she always had, and depart before things got ugly. With a deep sigh, she agreed to her little sister's request.

Parker, 8:32 p.m.: "I'll come. What time? And do you want to come over next weekend?"

Kee's excitement radiated through the phone, and Parker giggled to herself. She would be happy to see her sister and, if she were honest with herself, her parents, too. They made plans for a rendezvous at Chez Chase around four.

She then queued up the next episode of *Wentworth* on Netflix when she heard a knock at the door. She checked her watch versus the time she had placed her order and did the math. Wow, only twenty minutes to make and deliver that load of food? Whoever happened to be on the other side of the door would be getting a huge tip.

"Wow, that was fa—" she said, cutting herself off when she saw it was not her food delivery, but Ella who stood before her. "What?" was all she could manage as Ella smiled warmly at her.

"Can I come in?" she said, and Parker nodded, still so flabbergasted the words were not happening. Ella stepped quickly into the apartment and began shifting her weight from one foot to the other almost immediately. "You're not busy, are you?"

"No, I was just texting with my sister," Parker said, holding up her phone as evidence.

Ella looked at her with some confusion. "Your sister's name is Keeka? That's interesting. I've never heard of that before." She was starting to lose her nerve and ramble.

"Yeah, it's a childhood nickname. I'll tell you the story later," Parker said, putting her phone in her pocket and moving cautiously toward Ella who had the energy of a deer during hunting season. Parker did not want Ella to bolt before they'd had a chance to really talk.

"Is everything okay? What happened to your dinner?" Parker said as Ella continued her nervous marching around the entryway. When Ella didn't immediately respond, Parker reached out and took her elbow. "Hey, look at me. What's going on?"

Ella turned to face her and saw nothing but concern in her eyes. She got caught up in her feelings in the moment and took Parker's hand before stepping directly into her orbit. Parker's breath caught as Ella leaned in and kissed her tentatively before pulling back, waiting for a response.

Parker was immediately drawn in as the magnetic pull between them took control. Her arms encircled Ella's waist and drew their bodies and mouths together so there was no space left between them. Parker moaned when she felt Ella's tongue on her lips, but the surprise also brought her back to the moment and she pulled out of Ella's arms. "Wait, no, I can't, Ella. I can't do this with you," Parker said. Ella looked startled but backed off at her request.

Parker sighed heavily as she pulled Ella over to the sofa. When they sat down together, Ella ran her fingers through her hair and placed her head in her hands. Parker paused for a moment to give both of them time to find their bearings.

"I went to meet Tally at the restaurant," Ella began, still not looking at Parker who sat huddled against the arm on the opposite side of the couch. She didn't stop to let Parker speak. She had to get it all out before she lost her nerve. "It just felt wrong. Everything felt wrong tonight. I was on my way over, and I just couldn't shake the feeling that I shouldn't be going to meet another woman," she said and dared a look at Parker, who remained completely stone-faced. She scooted toward Parker and reached out to cup her cheek. This broke Parker from her impassivity, but she shied away from the touch.

"Ella, I just can't. I can't do this with you. I know I said I could, but I'm sorry. I can't just put my feelings aside and try desperately to hold on to the concept that it's better to have you as a friend who I have sex with than not at all. It's not true. This is killing me," she said, placing her hand over her heart.

Ella saw her eyes were frightened and full of hurt. This was self-preservation on Parker's part, she knew that. But Ella had a lot more to say to her tonight. "Parker, look at me," she said, and those dark, soulful eyes looked up to meet hers again. "I shouldn't be going to meet anyone else for dinner because I should be here with you. Whether it's making food together or ordering out or watching a movie or just hanging out or whatever, you're the one I want to do it all with." Ella paused allowing her time to respond.

When she didn't say anything, Ella continued but lowered her voice to emphasize the sentiment behind her words. "Parker, I want to be the one you trust with all of you, however long that takes. Can we go back to our first day together and forget my freak out and just give in to the magic?" When Ella didn't get an immediate response, she retreated back to her side of the couch and reclined with her hands behind her head. She stared at the ceiling as if the answers were up there somewhere.

"You want us to be together?" Parker said.

Ella sat forward and took Parker's hand between both of hers. "Yes, I do. Parker, I want you to meet my daughter."

Parker boggled at this new information but pressed forward. She just had to make sure. "You aren't going to run again? I don't know if I can survive a second time. I can't just let you in and get hurt like that again, Ella. I just can't. I'm not strong enough," she said on a breathy sob.

Ella looked back at her and saw the pure anguish in Parker's eyes. Not just from everything that had transpired between them, but from years of hurt she had endured. Ella wanted nothing more than to erase it. "I'm not. I want to do this. I don't care what anyone else thinks about us. I care about you, and I just don't want to question it anymore. I just want you. Can we try?" Parker met her eyes, and she saw the despair in them begin to dissipate like smoke in a strong wind.

Ella held her hand out to Parker, afraid her touch might be unwelcome. She wanted to give her the opportunity to make the first move. Parker entwined their fingers before shifting her position next to Ella.

"I want to try. Just promise me you won't hold back. Promise me that there are real emotions there. Promise me you feel something, too," she said. Ella moved even closer, nodding vehemently.

"Yes, there is, and I do, very much. You tore my walls down already. I've tried to keep them up, but everything about you just destroys my defenses. I'm tired of fighting this, what we have now and everything it could be in the future," she said, leaning forward, gently skimming her lips across Parker's cheek until she placed a firm kiss on the corner of her mouth.

"That's what I needed to hear," Parker said before leaning in to devour Ella's mouth with a searing kiss.

~

They made their way back to Parker's bedroom shedding clothes and shoes along the way. By the time they ducked inside, they were both in nothing but their underwear. Parker closed the door before placing a hand in the center of Ella's chest and walking her backward toward the bed. Ella felt her knees hit the edge of the frame before she dropped down onto the edge. Parker then backed up out of reach before reaching behind herself and unclasping her bra. Ella couldn't hide her surprise at this version of Parker. At the sight of her naked breasts for the first time, she felt a fire start deep within her core that she knew she would never be able to fully smother. The best news was she didn't want to.

Parker's breath was coming in heavy waves, and Ella could only hope that it was the excitement of the moment and not the start of another panic attack. She stood up and started to go to her, but Parker shook her head, and she sat back down. "I want to do this for you. I'm ready," she said before bending over to remove her black lacy thong. As Parker stood completely naked before her, Ella couldn't stop her breath catching in her chest.

Parker was an absolute work of art. Every feminine curve and swell were perfection personified. Her full breasts were tipped with pink nipples, erect from the excitement of the moment. Her hips were voluptuous, and Ella finally got to see the tattoo that she was so curious about. A phoenix rising from the ashes was blazoned from the edge of her left hip across her abdomen up to her belly button. As attractive as the artwork was, she couldn't stop her stare from landing upon the neatly-trimmed patch of hair between her thighs. She glanced up to meet Parker's gaze, looking for any hesitation in her posture.

"Parker, you're absolutely the most beautiful woman I have ever seen," Ella said with the utmost sincerity. Parker blushed brightly, and it reached all the way down her chest, kissing the very tops of her ample breasts.

"But I don't want you to feel any pressure. We can move as slowly as you want and take as long as you need—" was as far as she got before Parker began stalking toward the bed. The movement stole her words. She placed a knee on either side of Ella's legs before lowering herself onto her lap.

Ella felt Parker's wetness pressed into her lower abdomen and couldn't stifle a groan. She had every intention of moving slowly but was forced to knot her hands in the bed sheets when Parker rolled her hips gently before grasping her shoulders. Ella did her best to maintain her control as Parker tipped her head back and released a long, low moan as she ground languidly into her.

"Hey, look at me," Ella said, and Parker picked her head up to look at her lover. Ella chanced releasing her hold on the bedding and cupped Parker's cheek reverently. "Is this okay? Are you okay?" Parker bit her lip and nodded.

"So far, so good," she said and giggled before a particularly wild thrust hit the perfect spot, causing her to groan out her pleasure. Parker tipped her head back again and increased her rhythm as Ella kept her hands at her side and allowing her to take the lead. But she wanted Parker to be present in the moment. She wanted to stare into her eyes so that Parker could see the depth of the emotion Ella held for her. She wanted Parker to feel safe.

"Look at me," she said again, with a bit more command this time. When Parker focused on her, mouth open and breath ragged, she couldn't help herself from chancing a touch. She placed her hand on Parker's chest directly over her heart. Parker leaned forward to place her head against Ella's.

Ella moved her hands to Parker's back and stroked gently up and down her shoulder blades as she leaned forward to take her mouth again. She was fighting a losing battle. Parker wrapped her arms around her shoulders and pulled Ella into her. She stopped moving suddenly, and Ella was worried something had gone wrong.

"I can put my hands back down if that's what you need. I shouldn't have just—" Parker cut her off with another kiss that rocked her absolute foundation. She pulled away for just a moment to once again try to ensure Parker was in a state of pleasure. Memories of the first two times she tried to touch Parker and the disasters that followed made her want to be extremely careful.

"I want your hands. I want you to touch me," Parker said, taking Ella's left hand and placing it on her breast. Ella licked her lips as she kneaded lightly, feeling her nipple grow ever harder under her palm. Parker leaned in for another kiss, moaning into her mouth as their tongues searched and probed. Without breaking the kiss, Parker picked up Ella's right hand and began to trail it between her breasts and down her stomach to her belly button. Ella resisted at the feel of Parker's pubic hair on the back of her knuckles.

"Parker, are you sure?" she said.

Parker stared back into her eyes and smiled. "I think all I really needed to know is that you care about me like I care about you. You've broken down my walls, too," she said and resumed pushing Ella's hand down. "I need you inside of me."

When the tips of her fingers encountered Parker's slit, she was absolutely dripping. Ella shuddered at the feel of her soft, silky folds covered in the evidence of her arousal. She tentatively ran a single finger up and down while Parker moaned and quavered above her. Ella encircled her waist to support her as she moved while she began to move her hand in earnest, drawing tender, lazy circles around Parker's most sensitive areas. When she gently rolled her clit between her thumb and forefinger, Parker rose up and away from the touch. Ella withdrew her hand and wrapped Parker up in a tight hug.

"You're safe. I've got you," she said into her neck. Parker looked at her again, and she saw only a tinge of anxiety. She rubbed her hands up and down the length of her back before leaning in to kiss her sweetly on the lips.

"Do you want to stop? We can stop all of this and go watch a movie right now. It's all your call. You have the control," she said. Parker looked at her, awestruck, before smiling brightly and kissing her again.

"No, this is what I want. You are who I want. I promise," she said, moving Ella's hand between her legs again. Ella began slowly caressing her again until Parker's movements became more erratic.

"Oh, Ella, I'm close. Don't stop," she said on a breathy moan.

"I won't stop. I'll never stop," Ella said, placing a single finger at her entrance. Parker, feeling the contact, lifted up on her knees to give her better access. They looked at each other meaningfully one more time before Parker sank down, her mouth open on a silent scream at the feeling of Ella entering her for the first time. She began to move in and out, pausing only to curl her finger pressing against the spot inside Parker that would send her pleasure to new, uncharted territory. Parker placed her hands on Ella's shoulders and leaned back to give her better access as she bounced her hips in time with Ella's strokes.

"I'm going to come, Ella, please don't stop. Please just, keep doing that." Ella raised her thumb to gently bump Parker's clit as she thrust downward and that was all it took. Parker shook and quaked on top of her, and Ella coaxed her through her orgasm with gentle movements of her fingers and soft murmurs of comfort until she stopped moving.

Ella was prepared for the tears, but when Parker looked at her, her eyes were full of unbridled desire. She kissed Ella with an intense passion as she pushed her down on the bed. When she pulled back to breathe, Ella could see she looked far from satisfied.

Ella brought her hand to her mouth and licked every bit of Parker's moisture from them. Parker moaned at the display.

"Oh my fucking God, that was so amazing. But, watching you suck me off your fingers like that makes me just want so much more. That was so sexy."

"Oh baby, you can have more. I want to give you everything you have always wanted," Ella said, licking into her mouth again, allowing Parker to taste herself. They both whimpered at the contact.

"You know," Ella said, tracing a finger across Parker's brow. "Technically, I owe you because we've had sex twice and I was the only one who got off," she teased.

Parker grinned. "What did you have in mind?"

"I want you to come in my mouth," Ella said. Parker gasped and nodded.

"Please promise me you will let me know if we need to stop," Ella said, but Parker laid a finger across her lips and nodded in agreement. Ella ran her hands down the length of Parker's back before cupping her ass. Parker grinned but looked at her questioningly. Ella pulled at Parker again before she got the idea. She smiled and bit her lip before nodding and bending over to kiss Ella again.

They moved up to the head of the bed to give Parker something to hold onto. She then maneuvered herself on all fours until she was directly above Ella's mouth. Ella reached up with her hands and placed them on Parker's hips, encouraging her down. She was intoxicated by her smell and taste and was having a hard time moving slowly.

When she couldn't wait any longer, she leaned up and swiped her tongue from Parker's entrance to the very top of her sex. Parker moaned loudly as she completed her descent. Ella licked her in earnest now, intending to draw every bit of pleasure from Parker. She lapped around her entrance, pushing her tongue inside before moving back up to swirl her tongue around her clit.

Parker bucked and writhed but could do nothing but hold on as Ella devoured every inch of her. She licked and sucked and kissed every fold, every inch of Parker's lips before sucking her into her mouth completely.

"Oh...Ella...that's it. Right there. Don't stop, please, oh my God—" Parker's commands were getting progressively louder, passion unbounded. And that's exactly how Ella wanted it to be. Parker kept rising up on her knees away from the intense sensation, but there was no way Ella was going to continue to let that happen. She wrapped her arms up, around, and over Parker's hips and clasped her hands together, practically locking her in place. Now Parker's cries came in earnest.

"Ella, Ella...I can't hold on. You're going to make me come...Ella—" Ella groaned and that vibration was all it took to send Parker flying over the edge. She was screaming her name over and over, and Ella felt Parker flood her face and mouth. When she stopped moving, Ella let her go and Parker flopped down on the bed beside her, gasping for air. Ella rolled over to just check on her again. When Parker opened her eyes and began to giggle, Ella's anxiety fell back to an almost imperceptible level. She couldn't stop herself from reaching out and wrapping her up in an embrace.

"I don't want to annoy you, but I just have to make sure you're okay," Ella said into the crook of Parker's neck.

Parker hummed satisfactorily. "Thank you, love. I appreciate you asking, but I'm okay. I'm more than okay. I'm...happy," she said before kissing Ella gently on the forehead.

Ella picked up on the term of endearment, but it didn't scare her. It just warmed her heart. "I'm here if you need to talk. I just want you to know that." Ella leaned back out of Parker's arms to look into her eyes. Parker only smiled and nodded before kissing her again.

It didn't take long for the kiss to return to earth-shattering magnitudes as Parker moved her body back on top of her lover and covered her body with kisses that trailed from her neck all the way down. When her tongue finally made contact with Ella's very core, it didn't take long for Ella to explode with a fervor she had never experienced before. The orgasm rocked her entire body, and she couldn't stop herself from shaking. The tears came to her eyes then, and her heart swelled to bursting in her chest. The word 'love' reverberated around her head as she felt her spirit slowly return to her body. She looked down at Parker, who rested her head between her legs. Her eyes were closed and she looked content. She could almost imagine she heard a cheshire-like purring coming from those full lips. Ella leaned her head back and wiped her eyes quickly, not quite ready to have the heavy discussion, fearful to push the newly confident

Parker away by saying too much. Then, she reached down and took Parker's hand, pulling her up for another passionate kiss.

⁂

They found each other again in the night. Both seemed to wake at the same time and when their eyes met, no words were spoken. None were needed. They felt their mirrored desire on a spiritual level. Ella lavished Parker's neck with kisses and gentle bites as her hand worked her to a fever pitch. When Parker reached her crescendo, she couldn't hold herself back.

As her walls contracted and convulsed around her fingers inside her, Ella thought she heard Parker say 'I love you' into the crook of her neck. Then, she went completely still. Sensing her discomfort, she kissed her again and curled up into her, pretending not to have heard. She felt Parker relax in her arms and sleep overtook them once again.

Chapter 18

When Ella woke up the next morning, she couldn't stop herself from smiling as she rolled over intending to find Parker's warm body next to her. When all she found was a cold pillow, she sat up with a start, fearing the worst.

Worried that Parker might be upset or overcome about what had happened between them last night, she immediately threw the covers off and sat up at the edge of the bed. She then noticed a lovely smell in the air. Bacon? Was that bacon? Oh yes, that was indeed bacon! Her stomach growled loudly as she had skipped dinner the night before.

She looked around for her clothes and remembered the outfit she wore to Parker's was in her car. And everything she had worn the previous night was lying discarded somewhere between the front door and the bedroom. Then, she noticed something on the nightstand on her side of the bed. A T-shirt and a comfy pair of blue cotton pajama pants were topped with a small bundle of wildflowers tied with a ribbon. Ella picked them up and sniffed them, smiling to herself at the wonderfully sweet romantic gesture, before dressing in the clothes Parker had obviously left for her.

As she started down the hallway toward the kitchen, she heard utensils clanging on pots and pans and soft music playing in the background. She was pretty sure Parker was humming to the vocals. As she rounded the corner, she saw that Parker was also swaying her hips back and forth to the music before picking up a spatula and using it like a microphone during a particularly powerful vocal arrangement. Ella couldn't refrain from clapping for her American Idol-worthy performance. Parker jumped a mile into the air, knocking a frying pan off its eye.

"Holy shit, you scared the hell out of me," she said, closing her eyes and placing a steadying hand on her heart. Ella couldn't stop the wide grin that took over her face. She moved to Parker then, taking the spatula and placing it on the counter, before pulling her into a kiss. Parker immediately wrapped her arms around her shoulders, increasing the intensity. They made out like horny teenagers for a few minutes, or an hour. Maybe even a week, before Parker stepped back suddenly. "The bacon's going to burn, hang on," she said, turning around to tend to the now past well-done breakfast delicacy. Ella wrapped her arms around her waist from behind and pressed her face into Parker's luxurious curls that still smelled amazing. Parker's perfume combined with the aroma of frying bacon, what could be better?

Parker leaned back into her as she continued to sort out their breakfast.

"How do you like your eggs?" she said, attempting to move around the kitchen with Ella leeched firmly to her back. Ella muffled 'anything' into the back of her neck. They both giggled before Ella dropped her arms and looked at the coffee pot. It was wonderfully full of the nectar of the gods, and Ella decided that she loved Parker even more for making a full pot. Then, she paused. There was that word again. 'Loved.' Parker. They made 'love' last night. Parker said she 'loved' her; granted, it was in the throes of passion, but could it still be valid? Everything was so wonderful and new, but potentially raw. There was just no need to upset that delicate balance with potentially distressing conversation.

"Oh, thank you for making coffee. Do you want me to make you a cup?" Ella went about Parker's kitchen like she'd been there for years.

"I've had one, but I'll drink another with breakfast. We're ready to go here. If you don't mind making me another cup, I'll bring our plates through."

This was all weirdly yet wonderfully domestic between them. Parker moved to a stool at the bar, carrying their plates of food. Ella moved in with their coffee, setting Parker's in front of her before placing her own next to her plate. She took a bite of the food and found the eggs to be perfectly over-easy. The toast was crunchy and buttery, and the bacon was…well, it wasn't completely charcoal.

"Yeah, sorry about that," Parker said, picking up a piece of bacon and sniffing it before wrinkling her nose and discarding it. "Someone was distracting me," she said and looked directly at Ella, who feigned innocence, placing her hand upon her chest.

"Me? Surely you don't mean me?" she said.

"*J'accuse!*" Parker said, bopping her on the nose. Ella looked completely affronted. She picked up Parker's rejected piece of bacon and ate it in one bite, trying her damndest not to grimace, but failing miserably. Parker laughed loudly at what must have been an interesting expression to say the least.

"Well," Ella said, picking up another piece of bacon and holding it up to the light. "Maybe you can market it as blackened when you open your first restaurant. Better brush up on your Cajun food, *ma chère*." Ella took a big bite of eggs and toast to get the taste out of her mouth and smiled at Parker, who was now looking at her longingly. When she set her fork down and stared down at her plate, Ella reached out to take her hand. "What's wrong?"

Parker sighed and looked up with a mixture of elation and sadness swirling in her almost-black eyes. "I just feel like this is a dream and I'm afraid I'm going to wake up at any minute," she said and looked back down. "It's silly, I know. I'm sorry."

Ella brought the back of her knuckles to her mouth and took the time to kiss each one in succession. "Stop apologizing for your feelings. It is perfectly normal to feel whatever you feel. Emotions aren't rational, sweetheart." She placed the back of Parker's hand against her cheek. "I'm here."

Parker nodded almost more to herself, as an answer to her inner dialogue, than to Ella. "Thank you, for everything," she said on a wistful exhale before turning back to her breakfast. They ate in comfortable silence, and when their plates were clean, Ella took them both back into the kitchen and began the process of cleaning up.

"What are you doing today?" Parker said, unable to hide her hopeful tone.

"Not a lot. I've got to grade some papers, and AJ and I planned on dinner and a movie tonight. That's our usual Sunday night celebration. How about you? I know you have to work tonight," Ella said, placing the last of the clean plates into the dish drainer.

"I do. But I was hoping we could spend some time together this morning and maybe some of this afternoon. If that's not too much, too soon. I just want to be with you for as long as possible," she said before looking down self-consciously.

Ella dried her hands and returned to Parker's perch on the bar stool, kissing her sweetly. "Of course. I was hoping to spend some time together, too. Let me just check in with AJ and let her know what is going on and when I will be home. I don't want her to worry." Parker nodded vehemently and kissed Ella on the cheek.

"Yes, please do," she said. Ella started toward the bathroom before Parker stopped her.

"Ella, did you mean what you said?" She turned to face her and awaited clarification. "When you said you want me to meet AJ. Did you mean that?"

"Of course. That's not something I would say lightly. I promised her I would introduce you if and when things got serious. I'd say this is pretty fucking serious, wouldn't you?" she said with a wink.

Parker chuckled, sounding relieved. "Yeah, I agree. I don't know that I have ever been more serious."

Ella smiled and started to turn back toward the bathroom before pausing again. "Hey, Parker?"

"Yeah?"

"Have you showered yet?"

"No, why?" Parker said, sounding distracted while looking at something on her phone.

"You wanna join me?" Parker turned to her, dropping her phone on the counter where she sat. She was out of her chair, ripping her shirt off, and passing by her before Ella knew what was happening.

***

After what felt like an hour-long shower that was not much of a shower at all, they decided to get out when the water started to go cold. Parker winced and silently offered up an apology to the three other tenants who shared the quadruplex's amenities with her.

Toweling each other off turned into another lustful dance, this time on the pile of discarded towels on the bathroom floor. It wasn't exactly luxurious, but Parker didn't care. Once she truly felt Ella's heartfelt affection for her, it was like every barrier inside fell in a heap of rubble. Her heart was once again a living, breathing organism no longer shrouded in memories of the past. Ella represented a present and, hopefully, a future. She felt healed, felt whole.

When Ella first returned from the date that never actually happened and they sat down and discussed their feelings, Parker wasn't sure exactly how free she was. But, when Ella wrapped her up in her arms and practically carried her to the bedroom, Parker shed her bonds with every step they took. Upon reaching the bedroom, she finally knew. She was ready. Ready to be touched and treasured. She wanted Ella to be the only one to bring her to her ecstasy because Ella made her feel safe. Ella made her feel loved.

Once Parker undressed and stood with her body and soul bared before Ella, for Ella, she knew everything was right with the world. There was no more fear, no shame, and no disgust. There was only her and Ella and the love Parker felt for her. She felt relieved to know that Ella didn't seem to hear her admit her true feelings as she came for what seemed like the tenth time that night. She couldn't stop the words from spilling over and flowing out of her mouth as she rode out her pleasure. Her mind was completely blown, and her body ached in the best possible way.

She could hardly sleep last night despite being utterly exhausted. After Ella went to sleep on the pillow next to her, she simply couldn't close her eyes. Every time she tried and started to drift, she would startle awake and have to reach out to touch Ella gently to make sure she was still there.

When she finally rose at the first rays of sun peeking through her curtains, the first thing she did was watch Ella sleep for a few wonderful moments. All felt right with the world.

Parker decided to make her breakfast in bed. While the coffee brewed, she opened her front door with the intention of basking in the early morning light, and almost tripped over the abandoned takeout from the night before. *Oh well, no big loss. I had something much better to eat.* She guffawed at her horrible joke before she could stop herself.

Parker walked around the house to the hill behind the apartment complex that displayed a beautiful array of wildflowers. She picked some pink and red coneflowers and dark purple bellflowers interspersed with Queen Anne's lace. Upon reentering the apartment, she pulled a small bit of ribbon from a utility drawer and wrapped up her bouquet.

She didn't want to chance waking Ella, so she pulled some clean and comfortable clothes out of the dryer for her. Creeping back into the room, she placed the clothes on the bedside table and topped them with the flowers. The faint sound of the coffee pot beeping reminded her of the dire need to get caffeinated as the previous night that was anything but restful.

After breakfast and hopefully only their first session in a love-making marathon, they had dressed themselves and moved on to the couch to find a movie to watch before Ella had to go back home. Parker sat back, and Ella's head was in her lap. She traced her fingers gracefully through her girlfriend's hair…wait, girlfriend? Surely that's what they were now, but that was a conversation they needed to have. It may be too much to discuss right now, but she had to be brave and push forward. She had to know exactly where they stood.

"Ella?"

"Hmm?"

"What does all of this mean to you?"

"What do you mean?" Ella said, sitting up to face her.

Parker joined their hands and placed them in her lap. "What am I to you?"

Ella looked taken aback. "You mean a lot to me. I thought I had kind of shown you several times last night and then once this morning…" she said provocatively.

Parker smiled but didn't laugh. This was something she needed to know. "I'm serious," she said. "I just need to know. How do we label this?"

"Honey, I'm serious, too. You do remember the part where I told you that I want you to meet my daughter?" she said, again trying to lighten the mood.

Parker could not be dissuaded. "Do you want this to be a relationship? I mean, I know I don't want to see anyone else. I don't know if I could handle it if you did," she said.

Ella shook her head. "I don't want anyone but you, Parker Chase. If you want to say we're in a relationship or you're my girlfriend or my partner, I don't care," she said, shrugging.

"Call it what you want, whatever makes you feel comfortable. Just know you're my one and only, okay?"

Parker visibly relaxed at the reassuring words. "Good. I just needed to hear you say that."

Parker leaned over to place another quick kiss on her lips before Ella dropped her head back into her lap. 'Girlfriend, partner, one and only' reverberated through her head and she couldn't stop smiling. Ella's phone began ringing, and she picked it up off the coffee table.

"It's AJ," she said, sitting up and suddenly looking slightly nervous. Parker nodded as if to say she would remain silent.

"Hey, baby girl," Ella said. She stood up to walk back and forth across the living room as they spoke. Parker tried not to listen in, but Ella didn't leave the room.

"Yeah, I am. Yeah," she said, laughing, "Pahhh, that's right. I'm here." Parker was confused with only one half of the conversation, but Ella seemed to be happy with the way it was progressing. She also could hear excited screaming on the other end of the phone as Ella pulled her phone away from her ear, probably hoping to not lose an eardrum.

"Yeah, she's here right now." A pause. "Right, I want you to meet her, for sure. I promised you, didn't I?" A pause. "I'll be home in a few hours, and we'll talk, I promise." Another pause. "Turn my camera on?" She looked at Parker with eyes the size of dinner plates. "You want to say hello?" Parker's eyes went just as wide as they had a very quick discussion with facial expressions and gestures that ended with Parker shrugging and smiling and Ella doing the same.

"Wait one second," Ella said, sitting down next to Parker. They both tried to smooth their rumpled hair, untended after their earlier shower and ensuing sexual romp. Ella pulled the phone away from her ear, finger poised above the screen's camera button. Parker leaned forward for a quick good luck kiss before Ella enabled the camera function. It seemed like years before a beautiful young girl who very obviously inherited many of her mother's features popped up on the screen, smiling brightly.

"Ohmygod, hi!" AJ said, making it all sound like one big word.

Parker felt her cheeks heat up as she lifted her hand to wave. "Hey, AJ. Nice to meet you, kind of," she said, and they both laughed.

"Yeah, you too. You know I'm supposed to have movie time with her tonight, right? Hopefully you haven't completely worn her out?" AJ said scandalously.

Parker's mouth dropped open, and Ella gasped. Now they were both blushing, and there was absolutely no way AJ didn't know what they had been doing.

"Anna Jean Gardner! Why…what…I can't believe you just said that," Ella said, with a choked laugh. AJ laughed maniacally.

"Mom, you already tend to pass out when we watch movies together. The last thing I need for you to do is come back home in a sex coma."

Parker seemed to choke on air while Ella laughed slightly uncomfortably.

"Yeah, so," she said, trying to change the subject, "you said you wanted to say hello, so let's try a little bit of that, shall we? AJ, this is Parker. Parker, my daughter, AJ. Although right now, I'm thinking I might put her up for adoption," she said. Parker seemed to find herself and waved at the screen again.

"Listen, all jokes aside, I'm so excited to get to say hi. Whatever you've done in the last few weeks, please keep doing it. You've made my mom very happy, and she deserves it," AJ said with reverence in her voice. Ella smiled openly at her daughter's image on the screen.

Parker's heart swelled to the point she wasn't sure her chest would be able to contain it much longer. "I," she said, then cleared her throat, "she's very special, that's true." She turned toward Ella and ran her fingers through her hair affectionately. "I have every intention of doing everything I can to keep her happy. I promise you both that," she said. Ella reached out to cup her cheek, and they stared longingly into each other's eyes until AJ cleared her throat.

"Well, that's exactly what I wanted to hear. I'm just going to let you guys get back to…whatever you were doing. Mom, I'll have my homework done in a few hours. I'll start dinner? And by 'start dinner,'" she said, using air quotes, "I mean I will call and order the pizza. Parker, do you have dinner plans?"

Parker, who had obviously just been staring dumbly at Ella, realized AJ was still on the line and had addressed her directly. When she didn't respond, Ella looked at her and winked.

"Parker has to work tonight, but I promise we will have a big hangout day after you finish with your big week. Time to say good-bye, AJ. I'll be home in a few hours."

"Good-bye, AJ," her daughter parroted before cackling. "See you soon, Mom. And, Parker?"

"Yes?"

"Thank you."

Parker blushed even hotter at AJ's appreciation. How amazing it was to have this sort of connection with Ella's daughter through a simple video call. Parker understood it would be just as easy to love AJ as it was to fall in love with her mother. "You don't have to thank me. This is special for both of us. And I look forward to hanging out soon. Good luck at regions!" she said and waved again. Ella waved at AJ who blew kisses before disconnecting the call. Ella stared blankly at Parker, who simply laughed.

"Kids these days?" she offered tentatively.

Ella shot her a withering stare. "Yeah, I don't know where that came from. She thinks she's funny, but she's not."

Parker knew exactly where it came from. AJ shared her mother's sense of humor and comedic timing. It made her absolutely irresistible. "Oh, she's very funny. She reminds me a lot of another tall, green-eyed blonde I know. Now, I wonder who that could be?" she said, tapping her finger against her lips.

"I have absolutely no idea to whom you may be alluding," Ella said, her tone completely deadpan.

Parker took Ella's chin between her fingers before leaning forward to place several quick kisses on her lips. "Let's get this movie and cuddle session going so you can go home to your girl," she said. Ella leaned in and kissed her again before returning to her previous position across her lap. Parker could only hope that one day Ella wouldn't have to leave her presence to go home. Ella was home to her. She sat back and relaxed into the couch cushions while stroking her hand through Ella's hair.

She intended to enjoy every minute they had together. Every minute she had with her girlfriend.

Ella heard "walk of shame" as soon as she entered the foyer. She looked down at the clothes that she had apparently now stolen from Parker.

"Hi, AJ. How are you today? Everything good? Yeah, great. You're grounded!" she yelled back as she entered the kitchen where her daughter was poised at the table finishing her homework.

"Hey, you can't just throw your mom-weight around just because you don't like me calling you out on being a dirty, dirty girl," she said playfully. Ella just shook her head and got a glass of water from the tap.

AJ got up and walked over to her mother, placing her arms around her. "She's really pretty, Mom. And she seems nice. I'm so happy for you," she said.

Ella pulled her a few inches down to place a kiss on her forehead. "Thanks, baby. I appreciate it. She's just," Ella said, shaking her head almost in disbelief, "never in my wildest dreams did I imagine I would find anything like this."

"You know, I totally get that," she said, draping herself over Ella's shoulder in a snuggle. "I felt the same way when I met Kat. Hey, have you told Dad about her?"

"I mentioned her in passing, and he seemed very accepting and encouraging. But I haven't had a real heart to heart with him about my feelings for her. It almost feels a little uncomfortable, you know?"

AJ nodded sympathetically. "I think you should. Or I can tell him. I know he just wants you to be happy."

"And I want the same for him," Ella said, patting her hand before moving from where she had been stationed with AJ draped over her like a shawl.

"I think he may be close to proposing to Rebecca," she said, popping a grape in her mouth from the fruit bowl.

Ella's steps stuttered, and she wondered if AJ was looking for a reaction. "Did he say that?"

"He talked to me about doing some detective work on what cut of diamond she likes, so I am guessing that's what it was about. I dunno," she said, shrugging and wolfing down fruit like a starving animal...or a teenager. They are one in the same.

Although it was kind of strange to think of Alex married to someone else, she was elated for him. This was her dream come true, for him to find someone who could love him as he deserved to be loved. "I think that would be absolutely amazing," she said, and she truly meant her words. "And yeah, you can tell him all about it. I'm going to movie super-hard with you for a few hours before I have to get some work done and head to bed. I'm exhausted. Did you order the pizza? I'm starving." Ella opened the fridge to find something to snack on while she waited.

"I figured you'd have had enough to eat before you came home today," AJ said sardonically. Ella knocked over a jar of pickles as she felt blood color her face. She leaned her head out to stare at her daughter.

"Seriously, AJ? I don't even know what to say, other than I am not having that discussion with you," she said in her serious mom voice before continuing in a much softer tone. "And I plead the fifth. And maybe the sixty-ninth." She heard AJ knock over her water glass before letting out a very loud belly laugh.

"*Touche*, Mom. That was a good one." Ella was a regular comedian. And apparently so was AJ.

Chapter 19

Ella and Parker talked pretty much non-stop for the rest of the evening on Sunday, culminating in Ella calling her to say a quick good night and the two of them being on a video chat for three more hours. By the time Monday morning rolled around, Ella had put together about six hours of sleep over the weekend and was suffering from a major need of caffeine to get through the day.

She checked her phone during her planning period, and sure enough, there were messages from Parker waiting for her. Ella's heart rate increased to a canter as she read Parker's sweet words. She started to type out a reply when she heard a knock on her door. As she looked up, Zeke stood there with a vase of flowers. Ella was very confused.

"Hey, Zeke, what's, uh, what's that you have there?" she said, hoping that he hadn't developed some sort of teacher-crush on her just because she was kind to him after class the other day. Mary Kay Letourneau she was not.

"Hey, Teach, I honestly don't know. I was in the central office when they told me to take these to your room since my next class was on the way."

"Oh, great, thank you. Just place them here," she said, indicating the side of her desk with no paperwork currently cluttering its surface.

Zeke walked in and sat the vase down. "Looks like someone has a crush on you, I think."

Ella looked up at him sharply before noticing there was a small card attached to the bouquet. "Ah, yes, well, thank you, Zeke. Are you ready to give me a summary on what you think the different colors meant in 'The Masque of the Red Death'?"

"Oh yes, ma'am. I have my presentation ready, note cards and everything." He smiled, looking as pleased as he could be. Ella smiled up at him before looking back at the card that was drawing all her attention like a moth to a porch light.

"Thanks for this," she said, motioning toward the flowers. "I'll see you this afternoon."

He simply waved as he backed out the door and headed to his next class. As soon as she knew he was gone, she attacked the card and practically destroyed the envelope trying to get to the information inside.

"Until I see you again, hoping these flowers can provide you with some of the happiness I have in my heart. I miss you —P."

Ella placed the card against her lips and smiled. She couldn't fight it anymore and she didn't want to. She had fallen head over heels in love with Parker, whether it made sense or not. She no longer cared. But how to say it out loud... She decided to take Parker out for a romantic dinner Saturday night and tell her then. She did a Trip Advisor search for the most romantic restaurants in her area and found a lovely tapas bar that had opened in a neighboring city. She called and made the reservation for eight before texting Parker.

Ella, 12:05 p.m.: "Hey so, someone sent me flowers. I hate to tell you, but this mysterious 'P' is seriously vying for my affection."

Parker, 12:07 p.m.: "Hrm. Well then. I'm going to have to track down 'P' and have a little talk with her about sending flowers to my girlfriend."

She just loved seeing and hearing that word. She had a girlfriend! It was candy and rainbows and puppies and all of that 'everything nice' stuff.

Ella, 12:08 p.m.: "I feel violence may not be the answer. Maybe you could attempt to out-gift her? I do love chocolate, you know."

Ella treasured their witty banter and knew exactly what kind of response she would get from Parker.

Parker, 12:10 p.m.: "If you say I don't need to kick her ass, then I won't. And I will make you something delicious with chocolate. Saturday night? My place?"

Ella, 12:12 p.m.: "Yes, we can do dessert at your place for sure, but I just called and made dinner reservations for eight on Saturday. Does that work for you? I should have checked with you first."

She knew Parker would be able to make something just as good at home, but she wanted them to have a date. She wanted to reaffirm to Parker that she was confident and that she believed in them. She wanted to show Parker to the world.

Parker, 12:13 p.m.: "Sounds great! Will you be able to come Friday to The Paper Tiger for my debut?"

Ella smacked her forehead with a loud slap. How could she have forgotten about that? She ran a mental check of her planner and was almost sure she was free.

Ella, 12:16 p.m.: "Of course, I will be there. Is it an all-ages club?"

Parker, 12:17 p.m.: "Why? Already trading me in for a younger model?"

Ella couldn't hold back a snort.

Ella, 12:18 p.m.: "No, I just thought I would invite AJ. I think she'd be into it."

Parker, 12:20 p.m.: "Ella, that sounds amazing. Yes, on Thursday and Friday nights, they let 16- and 17-year-olds in for live music nights. They just get that ugly stamp that indicates they can't drink. I think it's shaped like a donkey's ass or something."

That got a cackle out of Ella for sure. She could just imagine the look on AJ's face when a big, fat ass was printed across her hand. Er, a big, fat ass's ass? Either way…

Ella, 12:22 p.m.: "Sounds good. I will ask her. I hate to do this, but I have to go for now. I miss you and can't wait to talk to you again."

Parker's reply came almost immediately.

Parker, 12:22 p.m.: "I miss you more than you could ever know. Bye, darling."

Oh yeah, Ella liked Parker's terms of endearment—a lot.

⁓

When Ella arrived home Tuesday after school, she was an absolute bundle of nerves. It was the night for the regional championship game, and she could hardly contain herself. Her heart felt like butterfly wings fluttering in her chest.

She walked into the kitchen and poured herself a single shot of vodka, downing the liquid quickly. When that didn't immediately quell her nerves, she drank a second. Combined with ten quick deep breaths, she felt the anxiety drop to manageable levels.

"Hitting the bottle already? You know it's not a night for you to go clubbing, right?" AJ ribbed as she came downstairs.

"Sorry, I'm just so nervous. When I was a coach, I saw things so mechanically. But tonight, I'm just Mom, you know?"

Ella was overcome with mental images of AJ with her first volleyball when she was just toddling around the living room; AJ in her first middle school game and her first high school game. She had watched her baby grow up on the volleyball court right next to her, fetching balls and bringing drinks to the players when she was just knee-high. Her high school career was ending, whether it be tonight after a loss or in a few weeks after the team moved on to the state tournament. Ella smiled at the memories sadly. AJ wrapped an arm around her.

"Yeah, I know. I'm just glad you'll be up in the stands for me," she said, kissing Ella's temple. "Besides, remember you get to meet Kat tonight and I'm so excited! You'll get to see her tonight, too, before the game. They're going to cut the lights off and use a bunch of different colored lights as they announce the players from each team. We're both going to be announced last for our teams, so as soon as you see me go out, pay attention, because she will be next."

The high schools often did these celebratory acts for championship games, killing the fluorescents and using multicolored lighting effects and spotlights during introductions. It brought the level of excitement up several notches before the game even got started.

"That's great, honey. I will be paying attention so I can see her." Ella paused, remembering the gravity of the evening and how that must be playing on AJ. It wasn't just a regional championship volleyball game, but she planned on publicly telling Kat that she loved her for the first time. "You must be nervous too, though, right? With the prom-posal? I saw you had the poster laid out to dry in your room."

AJ tensed a bit. "Well, yeah, I am. I mean, it's hard telling someone you love them for the first time. I think she feels the same way, so, I'm not nervous she's going to say no to prom. But I guess it is kind of a lot to just kind of lay out on the line in front of both of our schools." AJ tongued her cheek in contemplation before looking up and locking eyes with her. "But she's worth it." AJ shrugged and turned to look through the pantry for something to snack on before the game.

Ella didn't understand why AJ's maturity and depth of emotion for her girlfriend continued to blow her mind, but it did. She wasn't a little girl anymore. She was an empowered young woman who knew what she wanted. Ella's mind was immediately filled with images of Parker. This was just more karmic reassurance from the universe that she was on the right path. "I'm so proud of you, Anna," she said with as much sincerity as she could muster. "Not just for volleyball, not just school and not just your maturity in your relationship, but for the complete person you have become."

AJ pulled her snacks from the pantry and butted the door shut behind her. Ella could see her eyes were wet, but she was obviously trying to keep her game face on.

"Thanks, Mom. I'm gonna—" she said, tilting her head to nod over her shoulder before moving toward the staircase to return to her room. Ella nodded.

"You do what you need to do. I didn't mean to get all heavy on you before the big game. I'll see you there. I'll be the one screaming her ass off up in the stands. You should be able to recognize me," she chided. AJ groaned. No player wanted their mom to act a fool while they were trying to play a game. Good thing it didn't matter what AJ wanted.

"Hey, you," Ella said, answering Parker's video call. "What time are you going to your parents' again? Are you nervous? How do you feel?"

Parker laughed and held her hand up as if to physically fend off Ella's barrage of questions. "I'm getting ready to leave now. Yes, I'm very nervous, but my sister has been very kind to set this up, so I'm just going to give it my all for her, you know?"

"It's going to be okay, babe. You've got this," Ella said. "I wish this was on a different day so I could go with you."

"You would go with me to my parents' house?" She looked absolutely floored.

"Of course, I would. I mean, I assume I'm going to meet them sometime, right? I'm not the kind of woman you just keep on the down low," Ella said, buffing her nails on her non-existent lapel.

Parker smiled the wide grin that lit up her entire face, the one Ella loved so very much. "I'd love for you to meet my whole family. And I can't wait to meet AJ, like in person," she said, blushing at what Ella assumed was the memory of their brief phone conversation. "She's…something."

"She is indeed. And yeah, I can't wait. I was talking to her about going Friday, and I think she's on board and wants to bring her girlfriend. Is that okay?"

"Yeah, that sounds great. If everything goes well, I'm going to tell my family tonight and see if they will come. I'm not holding my breath, though."

"Well, even if they decide against it, we will be there and I know you said a big group of your friends will be there, so you will not be alone." Then in a lower, serious tone, she added, "You'll have family there." She hoped that did not sound as cheesy as it did in her head.

Parker looked down and smiled. "Thank you," she said without looking up.

Ella cleared her throat. "So anyway, I just wanted to make sure to let you know that I've got my ringer turned off during these games. And then, I'm supposed to hang out for a few to meet the girlfriend's family. I don't know if we're doing anything after that, but I will check in with you as soon as we leave the school."

"That's fine. Don't worry about me. I have very low expectations and I will not allow anything to blow up into something ugly, so worse comes to worse, I'll just go home and cry along to some emotional rom-com on TV until you call," she said, grinning.

Ella made a gagging sound. "Ugh, I don't know how you can stand that. Maybe go home and watch a stress-relieving horror flick where the bad guy destroys everyone with a chainsaw? I'm thinking that will make you feel much better."

"Maybe. I've got to go if I'm going to get there on time. Wish me luck?"

"Always, but if it doesn't work out, know I'm here," Ella said, trying to reassure her as best she could to take away some of the stress.

Parker took in a deep breath, sighed heavily, nodded, and slapped a hand on her knee. "Thank you, babe, but I've got this. I'm ready. You make me feel strong, you know? Just knowing you're here. I just feel like even if it doesn't go the way I hope, I've got you and that makes it okay. I kind of sound pathetic, don't I?"

Ella shook her head vehemently. "No, that's actually very sweet. You can put all your trust in me. As long as you want me around, I'll be here."

Parker looked up at her with soulful eyes. "I believe you. And I believe in us and what we're building here. Ella, I'm all in."

Ella felt a tingle start at the base of her spine before it traveled across every nerve in her body. She felt powerful and absolutely whole. "Me too, Parker. I'll talk to you tonight."

After the call disconnected, Parker's heart was full, and her mind was relaxed for the first time in a long time. This was bliss. Love was just incomprehensible.

Chapter 20

The atmosphere in the gymnasium was electric. Both high schools were well-represented. There were plenty of folks dressed in Havenwood's colors of bright green and black, but this was the Lair of the Lady Dragons. People were packed to the rafters dressed in navy blue and gold. It truly meant a lot to have home court advantage, and tonight, Ella hoped the Lady Wildcats would understand what it meant to step into *The Lair*.

She met up with Alex and Rebecca in the hopes of finding seats together with a good vantage point of the match. She waved them over and they waved back before heading over to meet her.

"This is just crazy!" Rebecca said, obviously awestruck. Ella appreciated her excitement. These kinds of rambunctious crowds during a regional match were old hat to her and Alex, but Rebecca seemed happy to be here.

"Oh, just wait until the actual game starts," Ella said, doing her best to be heard over the din.

Alex bent over to kiss her cheek. "How are you doing, El? Did you already get us good seats?"

She motioned for them to follow her, and they were lucky to find seats a few rows up and very close to center court. Ella was greeted by a few other parents and took a few moments to exchange pleasantries. When she turned back around to address her seatmates, she nearly jumped to see Rebecca chose to sit next to her with Alex bookending them. *This is fine. Everything is fine*, she thought. She wasn't great at making small talk in uncomfortable social situations, but if this woman was going to be Alex's wife and AJ's stepmother, she was going to give it the old college try.

"So," she said, trying to think of something on the fly, "who's your favorite author? I'm a literature teacher, you know." She could have slapped herself and probably would have if it wouldn't have made her look even worse.

Rebecca's bright blue eyes lit up, and in the best news of the evening, she didn't even seem to notice Ella's awkwardness. "I absolutely love to read. I like a little bit of everything, but right now I'm into Shakespearean tragedies. I'm knee-deep in *MacBeth* and loving it." Ella was impressed. Most people in their age group would name Patricia Cornwell, Stephen King, Nicholas Sparks, but Rebecca cited Shakespeare as her current interest.

Maybe they could be friends? Would that be weird? Perhaps they could start small and join a book club together.

"Oh yes, *MacBeth* is one of my favorites. I want to eventually try to teach a class on it, but right now, I'm doing a big section on Edgar Allan Poe."

Rebecca squealed with delight. "I love Poe! Have you read 'The Gold-Bug'? That's my favorite of all time." Usually when people say they like Poe's writing, they mean they read "The Raven" in high school. But hearing that Rebecca's favorite was one of his lesser-known works ignited an excitement in her.

"Oh, I love that one. Have you ever read—" As Ella was talking, the gym lights went down, and the spotlights and strobe lights came on. Everyone started cheering, followed by the booming voice of the announcer over the loudspeaker.

"Welcome to the Region 3A championship volleyball game between the visiting Havenwood Lady Wildcats," the announcer said over a mixture of loud cheering and even louder boos from the home crowd, "and your home-standing Benton Lady Dragons!" When the home team was announced, the crowd cheered so loudly, it completely drowned out the jeers from Havenwood's fans.

Once the crowd calmed a bit, the announcer named all the non-starters for the night's game before queueing up Metallica's "Enter Sandman." Again, the crowd went crazy, and the spotlights were pointed at each team's bench where the starting players waited for their names to be called. A player from Benton was called out first followed by a player from Havenwood. And so, the introductions went down the line until it was just AJ and Kat remaining.

"And, finally, starting at outside hitter for the Lady Dragons, last year's Region 3A player of the year and a shoo-in to repeat, a 6-1 senior, A...J...Gardner!"

The crowd erupted, but none were as loud as Ella, Alex, and, surprisingly, Rebecca, who stood up with them and screamed just as crazily. That's it. She's family. She's definitely in. AJ ran across and high-fived all her teammates as they huddled in the middle of the floor for a pregame pump-up session. Ella looked to the remaining player on the opposing team's bench. Kat. She had long, dark brown hair that was pulled back in a pretty typical volleyball braid. Her face was the picture of concentration as she waited for her announcement.

"And for Havenwood, a 5-7 senior and all-conference setter, Kathryn Chase!"

Again, a mixture of cheers and boos brought Kat out on the floor. After tagging all her teammates' hands, they huddled on their side of the net and did a team cheer to rev them up. All the players had their game faces on, and the cacophony in the gym mellowed out to a rumble. Ella mouthed *Chase?* to herself as AJ took the ball and stepped behind the service line. The official signaled that the game was ready to begin while Ella shook off a particle of recognition in the back of her mind.

Parker pulled into her parents' driveway. She sat in her car, steeling herself for a moment, gathering up the courage to enter. She thought about calling her sister to say she was not feeling well, but that would have been kind of hard to do after Keeka had already opened the curtains and waved. Parker waved back sheepishly before heading in.

"Oh my God, it's so good to see you!" Keeka said, hugging her sister so hard she picked her up off the floor.

"Whoa, Kee, put me down. It's good to see you, too." It had been several months since Parker had been to her parents' house. There had been no birthdays since the big Independence Day celebration, so there was no real reason to go. Parker couldn't stop herself from peeking around her back, attempting to glimpse their parents.

"Parker, please come in," Denise Chase said in a very business-like tone.

Her sister took her hand and pulled at her when it seemed she wasn't going to move. She felt like a lamb being led to slaughter. "Hey, Mama," she said, waving. They didn't hug much anymore. "Where's Dad?"

"I'm here," a distinguished-looking, tall man with salt-and-pepper hair said. Carter Chase then entered the room looking solemn. "Hello, Parker," he said, nodding curtly. Parker nodded back.

"Hi, Papa," she said. Then, when an uncomfortable silence took over, her sister ushered everyone to sit down at the kitchen table.

"Okay, come on, come on," she said and ran around them like an excited herding dog. Everyone sat, albeit with obvious reluctance. Kee pulled a meat tenderizing hammer out of the utensil pot beside the stove and banged the flat side in the middle of the platter in front of her. When it split down the middle, she smiled sheepishly and pushed it aside. Everyone looked at her with wide eyes and confused expressions.

"I call this Chase family meeting to order," she said, setting the mallet down. "I will be presenting my case to everyone, and I expect you all to sit and listen. I will take questions at the end. Do you understand?" she said, looking around the table.

"Katie, you know we're on a time restraint here. You've got to get dressed and your mom and I have to get ready, too," Carter said. Kee sighed and looked at him pointedly, hating the fact that he was using her childhood moniker.

"Dad, this is more important. I miss my sister. I know you guys miss her, too. She's amazing. She's putting herself through college while working practically full-time hours. Did you know she was on the dean's list last semester?" Everyone looked up in surprise at this; Carter and Denise because they had no idea, and Parker because she had no idea that anyone knew. She didn't say anything to anyone in the family.

"Yes, Peeka, I know. I looked on the university's Facebook page and saw they had posted it. You had a 4.0. Is that right?"

Parker nodded, speechless.

"And this is your second-to-last semester, right? So, you're getting ready to graduate with a degree in music theory with a minor in psychology, right?"

Parker nodded again, feeling her parents' eyes turn toward her in disbelief.

"And if I remember correctly, you told me that not only do you want to work on your musical career, but you want to get your master's degree and teaching certificate which will enable you to teach music in schools if the music industry doesn't pan out, is this also correct?"

Parker looked down and nodded again.

"Why didn't you tell them any of this?" she said, indicating their parents.

Parker shrugged. "I knew that you guys didn't want me to go into anything having to do with music or art, so I just didn't bother."

Carter let out a small noise that sounded like a cross between a gasp and cough. "Parker, you're going to school full-time? You know we would help you with that. You don't have to work at that *place*." He spat out the last word like it was a bitter pill.

Parker looked up sharply. She remembered when she told her parents she was no longer going to take a full load at college. She would go part-time while she worked on her music. They were so upset at the concept, she never bothered to tell them she had changed her mind and had been working herself to the bone for the last few years trying to obtain her degree.

"You don't understand. I love making music, whether it's on my guitar, my keyboard or with my computer. It's all valid," she said, forcefully but not angrily.

There was no reason for anything to go down like it did last time. There would be no screaming matches today if Parker had anything to say about it.

"I'm going to graduate with honors this spring. I've worked hard and buckled down. It just took me a little longer to get my head on straight. I'd love for you guys to be there when I graduate, but it's your choice. If you support me, then you support me one hundred percent. I love making music and that's what I am going to do," she said resolutely.

Her parents looked at each other for a long moment before her father spoke. "Parker, why would you keep this from us? Why would you let us continue to think that you weren't doing anything worthwhile with your life?"

"Dad, our definitions of 'worthwhile' differ greatly. I am happy. I'll probably never have as much money as a doctor," she said, motioning toward him, "or a lawyer," she said, indicating her mother, "but what I will have is my life on my own terms."

Denise reached over to tentatively place her hand on Parker's. "Honey, we never wanted you to feel like you were less than us. We just wanted you to be focused on a career and on your future," she said, looking pleadingly at her husband.

"Parker, I'm very happy to hear that you've been going to school full-time. You're so intelligent and charismatic, everything about you screams success. We don't care what you get your degree in."

"But it's more than that, isn't it? If I weren't going to school and getting my degree, if I was just working at the bar and DJing on the weekends, then that's not a valid existence to you guys?"

Her father frowned, opening his mouth and closing it without saying anything.

Denise squeezed her hand. "Of course, my initial response is to say that is not a stable way of living," she said, and Parker started to get up out of her chair to leave. Her mother gave her fingers another squeeze. "Just hear me out, please." Parker sat back down without looking at her mother. "We're old-fashioned. It just doesn't sit right that someone with all of your intelligence and abilities would just throw her life away on a pipe dream. But," she interjected quickly as Parker looked at her in abject horror, "your sister is right. We miss you terribly. I hate that we had that ridiculous fight so long ago, and I hate that you feel like you can't just come around and be yourself anymore. If you want to pursue this musical career, that's what we want for you."

Parker looked up at her mother in disbelief. "I have a plan, Mom. I will have a degree. In the meantime, I still want to work on my music. If it doesn't become a career, it will always be a hobby. But it's not like I'm some wide-eyed dreamer with my head in the clouds. I know it's hard out there. I've not actually performed before, either. But that's about to change," she said. Her parents and sister looked at her expectantly. "I'm going to DJ my own mixes for the first time in a local club on Friday. I'd love it if you guys could be there to hear what I have been working on and see what I can do," she said.

Her sister immediately spoke up. "Hey, I'll go. Wait, am I old enough to go?"

Parker chuckled and nodded. "You'll just get a hand stamp that will let everyone know you're jailbait. Are you good with that?"

Kee cackled. "Yeah, I'll just be excited to tell everyone I went clubbing," she said, smiling brightly at Parker. Then her countenance turned serious as she looked between her parents. "You guys can go, too, right?"

She looked at her parents expectantly. Both of them looked like fish out of water, gasping for oxygen. Denise spoke first.

"Uh, well, I can definitely check my schedule," she said, looking expectantly at her husband. "Honey?"

Carter's expression had been inscrutable for most of this conversation. He looked down at the table before slapping his palm down rather loudly. Parker was terrified that the argument was about to begin. "Hell yeah," he said out of a still completely expressionless face. Everyone looked at him like he had grown an extra head. He shrugged. "Let's go. I want to see what Parker is so excited about." He turned back to her and smiled for the first time. "I want to see this performance of yours. You'd better be very impressive," he said, winking at her.

Parker's face was a mask of complete shock. She could not believe what she was hearing. "Uh, thanks, Dad. Mom? Can you come?" she said, turning back to her mother with a heart full of hope.

Denise nodded resolutely. "Absolutely, we'll all be there. Just send us the address and time we should arrive. Oh, I'll have to go buy something cool to wear. Katie, shall we take a trip to the mall?" she said, rising from her seat and putting on an apron to get dinner going.

"Hell yeah," she said in her gruffest voice, an obvious imitation of her father. Everyone laughed.

Parker's mind was blown. Was this actually happening? Did her parents and her sister just tell her they would come to watch her perform? She couldn't refrain from pinching herself to make sure she was still awake.

"Parker, do you mind helping me prepare these vegetables? I'm sorry we're having to eat so early, but we have to hurry," Denise said, looking down at her watch. "Damn, we're already running behind. I want to make sure we get a good seat."

"Mom, I ate a big salad when I got home, so I think I'm going to wait until afterwards to eat. I need to get over to the school," Keeka said, then she slapped her forehead and looked at Parker. "You can come, right? I know I told you to clear your evening, but I didn't even tell you why. Are you free?"

Parker was confused, and it probably showed on her face. "Sure, what's going on?"

"I've got volleyball tonight. We're playing in the regional tournament championship game against Benton. The winner moves on to state and the loser goes home. This could be my last high school game, Sis. Please come!"

Parker figured this was the same volleyball game that Ella would be attending to watch AJ play. How cool would it be to run into her there! She could introduce everyone and get that part out of the way. She typed out a text to Ella, letting her know she was attending a regional volleyball game at Benton. Even though she knew Ella would have her ringer off, she was hopeful she might check her phone at some point. But probably not. Ella was serious about this volleyball stuff, and AJ was playing. Oh well, she'd keep an eye out for her in the meantime.

"Yeah, sure. I did clear my evening for family stuff," she said, and the words still felt weird coming out of her mouth. "I'll go."

Keeka jumped up and down and grabbed her sister up in a huge hug. "Yay! I'll see you there. I'll be the one out on the court kicking ass," she said before she grabbed up her duffel bag and headed out the door. Parker was now alone with her parents, but it didn't feel as uncomfortable as it usually did. She picked up a knife and a carrot and looked at her mother questioningly.

"Yes, chop those. Chop all of these. We have to be there in time to get good seats," Denise said, settling in next to Parker and slicing the chicken breast. "It feels good to be doing this. I've missed you," she said.

Parker felt tears prick the back of her eyes. Looking up at her mother, she saw her eyes were wet as well. "Me too, Mama."

They resumed prep in double-time fashion. After eating dinner, they loaded into Carter's SUV and barreled down the highway on their way to the school. Denise fretted at the time.

"Oh, darn it all. We're going to miss the introductions. She was so excited about those," she said.

Parker attempted to alleviate any stress. "Maybe someone will get it on video? Anyway, the important part is we'll see all the game," Parker said.

The gym was absolutely packed when they arrived, and they were forced to settle for sitting in the nosebleed section. The score was 5-4 to Havenwood in just the first set. The family settled in to watch their Lady Wildcats battle the Benton Lady Dragons for the Region 3A championship.

Chapter 21

"Come on, AJ, you've got this!" Ella screamed between her cupped hands. The Lady Dragons dropped the first set 25-15, but they were charging back in this second set and were up 24-20. The rotation happened to come around so that AJ was serving the game point after the team picked up the penultimate point on a side out. She could see her daughter bouncing the ball in an attempt to still her mind and focus, just like Ella taught her. The Havenwood student section were being as loud as they could be, doing everything they could to disrupt AJ's concentration.

AJ delivered a powerful jump serve that skimmed the top of the net and looked like it was going to fall before Kat dove and bumped the ball back into play. With their setter down, the Lady Wildcats couldn't set up for a proper kill, so they settled for a volley. Benton's libero was in perfect position for a dig, and when the ball was set by their setter, AJ took two quick steps off the serve/receive line, jumped, and demolished the ball back over the net. One of the Havenwood defenders was able to get to the ball, but it careened off her outstretched fist and landed in the first row of spectators. The Benton crowd went wild as the game was now tied at a set apiece.

Any momentum the Lady Wildcats carried over from their first set victory went the way of all flesh after that. The Lady Dragon defense was on point, fielding seemingly every ball that came their way. The setter placed the ball exactly where it was supposed to be, and AJ and her hitters consistently demolished the ball across the court, directly down to the floor. They also faked kills only to lob the ball over to where there were no Lady Wildcat defenders, and it seemed like there was nothing the Havenwood team could do about it. Kat was having a rough night because if your defense is not on point, the setter cannot properly position the ball. And AJ and her crew were making mincemeat of the Lady 'Cat backline.

In the fourth and what would end up being the final set, the Lady Dragons were one point away from victory. Kat served the ball over the net, but Benton's defense was there and bumped the ball to the setter. Another Benton hitter tried to deliver the kill, but Havenwood's libero got a good dig on the ball. It went back to Kat, and she set the ball for one of their hitters who got an angle on her spike. But AJ and another blocker timed it perfectly, jumping up and forming a wall that the ball could not penetrate. It bounced off their hands back to Havenwood's side and slammed into the floor. The game was over. They had beaten the Lady Wildcats three sets to one, and the Lady Dragons celebrated on their half of the court as the crowd went wild.

Havenwood's seniors dropped to their knees in defeat, their high school careers over, and were surrounded by the underclassmen offering comforting words and a shoulder to cry on. Kat was inconsolable with her face buried in her hands as she practically curled herself into a ball on the floor. Once AJ saw her, she left her team's celebration, ran across the floor, and slid under the net on her knee pads to take Kat in her arms. She wrapped her up and held her as she cried. The rest of the Lady Dragon team followed her example and crossed the center court line, offering their consolation to the other team. Cheers rang out in the gym at the display of sportsmanship, but AJ and Kat never moved in the several minutes it took her to settle down.

AJ bent her head to talk to her, and Kat started nodding her head. AJ got up and held her hand out. They embraced again, and Kat had started to laugh through her tears. It was at that time that AJ pointed to the scorer's table and Rhianna's "Only Girl (In the World)" began to play over the sound system.

The dispersing crowd began to turn their attention back to the court to see what was going on just in time to see several members of the junior varsity squad rush out onto the floor. They all had on T-shirts that were painted to look like tuxedos, but the conformity of their dress did not at all make up for how out of sync they were in what looked to be a poorly rehearsed dance routine.

Two of the varsity players joined in then, spinning and jumping across the floor. One held a large poster board while the other carried a microphone. The mass of people still didn't quite understand what was going on, but laughed along with the girls and their display. Once AJ had the mic in her hand, the lights were lowered again, and a spotlight hit her and Kat where they stood. A still teary Kat looked thoroughly confused, but that changed to elated surprise as AJ got down on one knee in front of her. The girl with the poster stood by while AJ began to speak.

"Kat, you mean the absolute world to me and ever since I met you this summer, you have made me feel like I *am* the only girl in the world." This was apparently the cue for the girl with the poster, and she held it up over AJ's head as she continued. "I just want you to know," she said, but paused as she choked up a bit. Ella felt her own tears flowing freely as she looked aside to Rebecca and Alex, who were also crying. After regrouping for a few moments, AJ reached out, took Kat's hand, and kissed it before continuing.

"I want you and everybody here to know I love you. Would you now make me the happiest only girl in the world by going to prom with me?"

A few cheers went up with a whole lot of 'aww' permeating the atmosphere. Kat was crying again, for a completely different reason, as she nodded vehemently to deafening applause. The house lights came up and the spotlights went off as the girls embraced on the center court, just like something out of a movie...sans the awkward, but very much appreciated, dancing volleyball players.

"She's just a star," Rebecca said, wiping her eyes and turning to Ella. "You have done such an amazing job."

Ella was truly touched at the sentiment. "Well, we're a team, you know," she said, nodding toward Alex. "But there's definitely room for more members on this squad if you're willing."

Rebecca was now crying in earnest. She couldn't do anything but embrace her, right? Alex mouthed 'thank you' over her shoulder.

"Let's head down there and meet this girlfriend!" Ella said, rubbing her hands together in anticipation. Alex and Rebecca followed as she weaved her way through the throngs of people on the stairs.

The Chase family cheered their team on vehemently, but when it was obviously going to end in the fourth set, Parker couldn't wait any longer. She had to find a bathroom.

"I have absolutely got to go pee. I'll be right back," she said in her mother's ear.

Denise didn't even turn around as she screamed encouraging words to the girls on the court. "Okay, just hurry. We have to go down on the court as soon as the match is over."

Parker had no idea why she was emphasizing this fact. She knew her sister would be crushed and would need their support. She had every intention of getting back in time to console her.

As she climbed the stairs, she heard what must have been the final point as the home crowd went wild. She cursed under her breath but couldn't put off the call of nature any longer. After completing the mission and washing her hands, she heard more cheering coming from beyond the door. When she walked back out into the gym area, the crowds were moving toward the exits. Her parents were still in the same place, probably just waiting on her to get back. As she made it back to her seat, she saw that her mother had been crying.

"Mom, is everything okay?" she said with concern. Her mother laughed as she blew her nose into a tissue.

"Did you miss all of that?"

"All of what?"

"The prom-posal!" she said, turning away as she and Carter made their way down the stairs. Parker could only follow. Denise kept talking, but with the crowd being so loud and her speaking in the wrong direction, Parker could hardly hear her. Denise grabbed her hand and pulled her up to them as they nudged, ducked, and shimmied their way down the stairs toward the court.

"Katie just got asked to prom!" she said as she and Carter wrapped up her little sister in their arms.

"Mom, stop calling me Katie. It's Kat. Just Kat," she said, red-faced and still teary from the extreme lows and highs of the night. Kat broke away from her family to hug Parker.

"Oh, Parker, did you see? Don't I have the most romantic girlfriend ever?"

Parker, who was still somewhat confused, could only agree until more information was made available. "Yeah, for sure. I'm happy for you. I didn't know you had a girlfriend!" she said, wrapping her sister up in another hug.

"I do! She goes to Benton, but she's still good people, I promise," Kat said with a laugh. "I'm so happy you're here. Mom and Dad are meeting her parents for the first time tonight. And now that you're here, they can meet my whole family, and, well, everything is just perfect," she said excitedly, looking over

Parker's shoulder while waving and motioning for who she could only assume was her girlfriend and her parents.

"AJ! Come on, hurry up, bring them over," she heard Kat say, but then her ears started to ring, and her vision got a little fuzzy around the edges as things came together in her mind. Kat's girlfriend is AJ, who plays volleyball. Ella was supposed to be meeting AJ's girlfriend's parents tonight. Her stomach began to revolt, and her guts began to churn. Parker was sure she was going to faint. She didn't want to turn around.

"Mom, Dad, you know AJ, of course," Kat began. Parker reached out to steady herself, but there was nothing to grab on to. "These are her parents. This is her dad Alex and his girlfriend Rebecca and her mom, Ella."

There it was. The final nail had been hammered in. All the blood had either rushed to her head or drained to her feet, Parker wasn't sure which. She hoped she was at least still breathing.

"Mr. and Mrs. Gardner, Ms. Bridger," Kat continued, "these are my parents, Carter and Denise Chase. And I am so excited to announce that my sister has joined us tonight. Please meet my favorite person in the world, my sister, Peeka. But now since I am no longer a baby and can pronounce it correctly, we'll just call her Parker."

Ella, Alex, and Rebecca made it to AJ and took turns embracing and congratulating her, not only for playing an amazing game, but for an astounding, thoughtful gesture. AJ spotted Kat and her family across the floor and urged them along.

Kat waved openly to them after releasing the embrace she had on someone who was probably commenting on how sweet the prom-posal had been. As Ella approached, she saw that Mr. and Mr. Chase were probably in their late forties and very distinguished. But she was quite used to being much younger than AJ's friends' parents. They both wore broad smiles and appeared very welcoming.

As the girls got on with the introductions, she saw that the woman Kat had been hugging earlier hadn't turned around or moved from her spot. She had beautiful, flowing raven hair that made her think of her Parker. *Wow, I must be in love.* She shrugged it off before moving in to shake hands with Kat's parents. Then, Ella was sure her hearing had failed her. Kat said her sister was there. And she used that childhood nickname. Peeka. Surely that was just a coincidence. But then, she was almost sure she heard the name 'Parker' over the blood rushing in her ears. She held on to that as long as she could, until her new girlfriend turned around to face them.

Ella couldn't make her vocal cords work. Nothing would come out except a small croaking sound. Parker was white as a sheet and looked like she just might fall on the floor at any moment. She held out her hand to Ella, who just looked at it dumbly as if she couldn't remember what hands could do.

"Nice to meet you," she said as Ella took her proffered sweaty left hand with her right hand, shaking it with an unwieldy up and down motion. She still couldn't talk, nor could she avert her eyes from Parker's. The others were looking around at each other trying to decipher what was taking place. AJ muttered 'holy shit' somewhere in the background. It was something Ella felt palpably.

"Mom, you already know Parker, right?" AJ's voice sounded like it was booming through a speaker. It was too loud and rang like feedback in her ears. Ella winced at the sound. AJ reached out and placed her hand on the small of her mother's back. Ella whipped her head around, startled at the contact. AJ nodded at her. There was no judgment in her eyes, just an indication that she needed to deal with the situation at hand.

"Yeah…yes," she said, clearing her throat as very little sound was coming out. "Yes, I do. We know each other quite well." She finally released Parker's hand and watched it fall to her side. She still looked like she was halfway between vomiting and fainting. Ella looked at the floor before clearing her throat to get rid of what felt like gravel in her vocal cords.

"How do you know Parker, Ms. Gardner? Do you frequent her club?" Denise said and laughed good-naturedly. Her husband joined in. Kat was laughing. Alex and Rebecca were laughing. AJ winced. Parker and Ella were not laughing. Parker put her hands over her face, and Ella slowly closed her eyes and ran her tongue along the back of her teeth. They didn't know it, but they were effectively laughing at her. Why would a teenager's mom try to pick up twenty-five-year-olds at a bar? *This one, this one right here,* she thought to herself and sighed.

"The truth is that we did meet there initially," Parker chimed in, finding her voice out of nowhere. "But, uh, we've been—" She stopped to look at her sister, who looked back and forth between her and Ella and then to AJ, who put an arm around her girlfriend and pulled her off to the side and out of earshot. "We've been seeing each other."

The Chases gasped while Alex looked at Ella with an intense protectiveness, like he wanted to just change into his superhero suit and whisk her away to safety.

"Seeing…each other? What does that mean, 'seeing each other?'" Denise said.

"Mom, we're a couple," Parker said before looking back to Ella for back-up. Ella looked away and ran her hand through her hair.

"How old are you, anyway? And what are you doing in a bar? You know she's only twenty-four, right? You're a mother, for goodness' sake," Carter said. Ella looked completely stricken while tears started to stream down Parker's cheeks.

Alex, however, stepped up and put his hand on Ella's shoulder. "There's no need to be rude, Mr. Chase," he said, fire behind his ice-blue eyes. "They are both adults, so let's leave them to their adulting, shall we?" Alex's fingers flexed reflexively on her shoulder. Ella placed her hand on his, hoping to draw some of his strength, because what little she possessed was fading quickly.

"Hey, let's just all go home and cool off and we can all talk about this in the clear light of day," Parker said. Her parents simply turned and started toward the exit.

Alex squeezed Ella's shoulder one more time before looking between her and Parker. She nodded to let him know he could go. He bent forward to give Parker a quick hug. "It was nice to meet you, Parker. I look forward to getting to know you in the future," he said, directing the last few words at Ella. Her best friend always knew what she was thinking, and he knew what she was getting ready to do.

Parker looked up at him and smiled through her tears. "I hope so, too."

Alex took Rebecca's hand and led her toward the exit. Parker wrapped her arms around herself, and Ella gnawed at her nails nervously.

"So," Parker started. Ella looked up to meet her eyes, but quickly looked at the gym floor. "Can we go somewhere and talk?"

"I don't think that's such a good idea right now," Ella replied, putting her hands in her back pockets.

"You don't," Parker said, nodding to herself and looking at her shoes. "What do you suggest then?"

Ella stared at the ceiling for a few moments before finally looking back at Parker's tear-streaked face. "I think we probably need to take a little time and get used to all of these new…developments," she said, searching for the right word for the predicament they were now in.

"So, you're just going to walk away again after you promised me you wouldn't," Parker said.

"Parker," Ella started, shaking her head, but Parker cut her off.

"No, don't *Parker* me. You promised me! No one could have seen this coming. But we can't run away from each other now."

"Yeah, well, maybe I want to," Ella said, sounding harsher than she meant to. When Parker's face dropped, Ella stepped forward with an instinctual need to pull her into her arms. Instead, she stopped short and grabbed her shoulder in a very platonic gesture.

"I'm sorry, I just…I need to talk to AJ, and I think you need to talk to your family. We just need to revisit this when the dust settles."

"And how long is that going to take, Ella? A day, a week…a year? You heard them. They're upset and will probably try to do everything they can to try to keep us apart. Now is when we need to have a united front. Now is when we need to be strong. Together," she said.

Ella felt a tear spill down her cheek, but she scrubbed it away and shook her head. "I don't think I can be strong, Parker. Not right now. I just…I've got to go," she said, doing an about-face and turning her back on the only woman she had ever truly loved.

Chapter 22

Ella called in to work the next day, hoping the school had sufficient time to find a substitute. Last night, after leaving Parker standing in the middle of the gym, she walked directly to her car, drove straight home, and went to bed. She had been there ever since.

AJ texted to let her know she was going to stay with Kat overnight, but she didn't say much else. Ella sent back a thumbs-up and that was the end of her phone activity for the night. She was quite surprised that she hadn't heard from Parker and was currently processing the dichotomy of being relieved and being overcome with a soul-shattering sadness that made it hard to even exist.

Ella was pretty sure she had only managed small naps throughout the night, but those seemed to end around four in the morning. She couldn't cry. She could barely breathe around the knot in her stomach. She stared at the ceiling while sad music played from the speaker on her bedside table. Morning eventually happened as the sun peeked through the curtains. She was going to have to get up and get some water.

In the kitchen, she debated back and forth with the idea of coffee on an already sour stomach and opted for some chewable antacids instead, grateful that she had the house to herself. Ella knew she would have to face AJ soon, but she wasn't quite ready to take that on. Then, she heard the front door open and close. *Oh well, here's to ripping off the bandage*, she thought.

AJ tiptoed into the kitchen, obviously trying to sneak in without having to face her mother. But now they stood face-to-face for a very uncomfortable few beats of silence.

"Hey," Ella said breathlessly.

"Hey," AJ said, twisting her hands in front of her. Neither moved nor said anything for a moment. Suddenly, Ella couldn't stifle the tears that had evaded her all night. She sank to her knees, incapacitated and inconsolable. AJ put her keys on the table before dropping down to embrace her mother while she sobbed.

AJ ran a comforting hand up and down Ella's back as she held on for dear life while she cried. After a few minutes and with everything in her completely spent, Ella wiped her eyes and looked at her daughter apologetically.

"I didn't know. I'm so sorry," she practically choked out. AJ, who hadn't shown any signs of being angry at her, nodded her head sadly.

"I know, Mom. I didn't know either," she said.

"Did you not see family pictures at their house when you were there? I know you only saw Parker over that video call, but I just don't understand how you didn't know."

"They took all the family pictures down after they had that big fight," she said. "God, I didn't even know her real first name. I thought it was a strange name, but I wasn't questioning it. She explained to me last night that she started calling her Peeka because she couldn't say Parker when she was little," she said, as Ella quoted the last part along with her. AJ looked at her surprised and then with sympathy.

"I guess you got the story, too, huh? From Parker?"

Ella nodded, sniffed, and wiped her face with a paper towel. "Yeah, she started calling Kat 'Keeka' as a way to bond. According to Parker, they never use their real first names unless they are mad at one another." AJ now quoted the last few words along with her mother. They shared a chuckle before returning to the mood at hand. Another long beat of silence hit before AJ sighed and helped her mother to a chair, then she moved to make coffee.

"What did Kat say to you? Does she hate me?" Ella squeaked out.

AJ shook her head vehemently. "No, no. Not at all. I mean, she was confused. We both felt dumb that we didn't figure it out beforehand, but I want you to know that if you're both happy, Kat and I are all for it."

Ella's head snapped up to look at AJ almost hard enough to give her whiplash. She couldn't stop herself from rubbing the back of her neck as she thought about her daughter's words.

"I will admit it is kind of weird. I'm not going to lie. But, last night, I was telling her that I had never seen you so happy," she said, and Ella started sniffling anew at her sweet, supportive words.

AJ put a hand on her shoulder. "She said that when they were having that family meeting yesterday, she saw something different in Parker. She seemed stronger and more confident than she had ever been. Mom, that's because of you. You guys make each other happy and bring out the best in each other, you know?"

Ella sobbed harder into her hands. AJ held her again. Once Ella had settled somewhat, AJ stepped back to pour herself a cup of coffee. She offered one to Ella, who just held up her hand in refusal.

"Wow, you know things are shitty when you don't want coffee," AJ said, trying to lighten the mood.

Ella tossed her a sympathy smile in appreciation for the attempt at levity. "What about Mr. and Mrs. Chase?" she said.

AJ froze momentarily before resuming her coffee prep. "Well, they were angry with Kat and me because they didn't understand how we didn't know. But I guess we looked convincing in our explanation because they kind of relented in the end. They absolutely blasted Parker, though. It was awful," AJ said, shaking her head sadly. Ella listened raptly as her heart broke a little more for her love.

"Apparently Parker didn't drive there and had to ride back with their parents because we left before they did. She told us that the arguing was constant for the entire trip. Then, when they all got back to the house, no one was saying anything. Kat and I heard them come in and went into the living room to talk to everyone, but Mr. and Mrs. Chase just went upstairs. They didn't come back down until after Parker left."

Flashes of Parker's dejected face just before Ella abandoned her ran through her mind. Parker had wanted to fight for them. Ella couldn't, whether she wanted to or not. All of her mental stamina drained from her body when she saw it was Parker who turned around to meet her during introductions.

"Parker picked up her keys and sat down at the kitchen table for a minute, so we went to check on her. Kat just kind of held her while she cried but didn't ask a lot of questions with everything being so stressful. She came over to hug me and apologize before she left. I told her she didn't need to apologize to me for anything, but it didn't seem to be the time for a deep conversation. She just looked so…defeated," AJ said, finding the word she was searching for.

"Kat was trying to get Parker to stay, just telling her how much she loved her and that everything would be okay, that we were going to still be there for her. She told her that she and I would still go to watch her perform on Friday, which we will," she said, looking expectantly at Ella who was staring off into space. "Then, she just left. After the door shut, the parents came back downstairs and were all angry with us until we explained everything on our end. Kat tried to defend Parker with the whole 'love is love' argument, but that didn't seem to fly. Even though the age difference isn't that huge, they seem to be pretty much hung up on the fact that you're my mom and you're dating their daughter."

AJ got herself a bowl of cereal and looked at Ella with raised eyebrows as if to ask if she wanted one, too. Ella shook her head and got up. This was way too much, and she just needed to sleep. She stopped in the doorway.

"I'm sorry you had to be a part of all of this. I'm sorry about the way this went down," she said, turning to walk out again before AJ's voice stopped her.

"Mom, you're still going to be with Parker, right? You've waited too long to find someone to love." When Ella started shaking her head slowly, AJ approached her and turned her around. "Dammit, don't you dare give up on this. It's so obvious that you guys are in love. And you'd just walk away? Over two people's opinions? Kat and I were shocked, yes, but we support you one hundred percent. Obviously, Dad is in your corner. Who's left? And honestly, what the fuck does it matter if you're both happy. What would you tell me to do in this situation?" AJ said, folding her arms across her chest.

Ella looked at her sternly for the extreme swear but was only truly fazed momentarily. She was right, of course. Ella would always tell her to follow her heart. But this was so much more and felt so different. She could only shrug as she turned to go back upstairs to the sanctuary of her bedroom where she could shut out the world.

∽

Ella stared at the ceiling for most of the day, which was going by fast and slow in equal measure. Time simply had no meaning as she played the previous evening's events over and over in her head, trying to figure out how to fix everything. She was worried about Parker more than she was upset for herself, especially knowing Parker had just started to build herself up.

Kat had even told AJ that she seemed stronger and more confident. That's the kind of thing that happens when you're in love. But why didn't she feel the same power? Why had she folded like paper in the wind while Parker stood strong through the shock and tried to defend them? She didn't have the answers yet.

It must have been sometime after three because she heard AJ knocking on her door. "Mom, can I come in?" came the muffled request. Ella wasn't even sure her voice was working but chanced an admittance. Ella scooted up in the bed as she blew her nose and wiped it with a tissue. She waved AJ in, but AJ hesitated. Ella looked at her skeptically.

"Mom, I know I didn't ask you ahead of time, but Kat wanted to talk to you," she said as the youngest Chase sister stepped around her and through the door hesitantly. "Don't get mad. I just didn't know if you would let me bring her."

Ella had nowhere to go. There was no escape route here. She relented, sighing heavily and motioned them both in.

"Ms. Gardner, hi, we didn't really get a chance to say hello last night," she said, perching on the very edge of Ella's side of the bed. AJ stood behind her, placing steadying hands on her shoulders. Ella smiled sadly.

"Yeah, it went pretty badly, didn't it?" Ella said. Kat chuckled and nodded. "I know AJ said you aren't upset, but I want to tell you I'm sorry. Parker—" she said, practically choking on her name, "Parker and I were still new as I'm sure you know. We hadn't discussed all the family specifics." Ella stopped talking as she noticed Kat looked stricken. Jesus Christ, what had she said or done now?

"You said *were*, as in past tense. About you and my sister." Ella closed her eyes, looking completely defeated. "I hope you don't mean that. I've never seen my sister so sure of herself when dealing with our parents. She was like a different person when she came to our house for dinner. I'm guessing that you had something to do with that," she said and placed her hand on Ella's, who looked up to meet her eyes.

"I've tried to call her since she left that night, and she won't answer. She's returned texts, but it's the bare minimum. I was hoping," she paused and looked up at AJ, who nodded reassuringly. "I was hoping you would try. I'm worried about her. I don't want her to be alone right now."

Ella started to immediately say no. Parker would not want to see her, and Ella still wasn't sure how they could push forward together. But the words wouldn't come. Kat looked so forlorn. She made it seem like Ella was her only hope. And maybe if she could see Parker again, the universe would tell her what to do, as that very celestial cluster had seemingly guided them from the first moment they met. "Of course. I'll go. She won't head in to work for a few hours. Let me just get a shower," she said as she grasped Kat's hand. "Don't worry, honey. We'll figure things out."

Kat sniffled and nodded. "Thank you so much," she said, standing up and taking AJ's hand, linking the three of them. "You know, everything started to look up yesterday after our family meeting. I thought I was getting my whole family back, but now," she said, choking on her words with a voice riddled with emotion. "Anyway, we're going back to my house and try to talk some more sense into my mom and dad."

Kat led AJ out of the room, but not before AJ turned around to mouth her thanks and her love to her mother. Ella smiled as convincingly as possible and winked at her. Once the bedroom door was shut, she got to her feet and pulled out some gray joggers and a tattered hoodie without a second thought. She wasn't interested in what she was wearing anymore.

Chapter 23

Ella pulled up to Parker's apartment, relieved to see her car was there. She walked up to the door and knocked, pulling the cuffs of her sleeves down over her hands to try to ward off the chill. When no one answered, she tried again, this time pounding on the door. She heard movement inside followed by the unlatching of a deadbolt before Parker stood before her for the first time since the volleyball game. She was wearing the same clothes and her normally impeccable appearance was disheveled. She said nothing and did not invite Ella in, but merely stood in the entryway with her arms crossed.

"Hey, I just wanted to check on you," she said. Parker's facial expression was unchanged. "Kat, er, your sister came over and said you haven't been returning her calls and she was worried."

Parker shifted to lean against the doorway, but this was her only movement. "I'm fine. Can I go back to bed now?"

"Don't you need to get ready for work?" It was a knee-jerk response that she didn't think out clearly to a question she wasn't expecting.

Parker was obviously not pleased with her taking those liberties now. "I don't think that should matter to you anymore."

Ella met her eyes. They were red-rimmed and a bit puffy, probably from crying. But there was no emotion in them. "Come on, Parker. It was shocking, don't you think? Can we just sit down and talk about where we go from here, please?" she said, taking a step toward her domain. Parker stepped in front of the doorway, effectively blocking her from entering.

"No, we can't. You said everything you needed to say when you chose to leave me standing there last night. You said you would always be here, but you were quick to turn tail and walk away when things got hard," Parker said, but it seemed like she was just winding up. Ella was going to let her have her say. She deserved everything that was coming to her.

"I defended us," she said, forcefully patting her chest. "I stood up to my family to defend our relationship. And you only got to see part of it. On the way home, even after you abandoned me, I continued to defend us. By the time I left my parents' house, I had nothing left in me. I was completely depleted. I just came home, went to bed, and cried myself to sleep because the person who I wanted to run to more than anyone else in the world wasn't there. The person I love—" she said, closing her eyes, obviously not intending to have given away that information. "The person I love wasn't there. And I was right back to where I started. Alone."

Ella felt a maelstrom of emotions swirling around in her chest. Here it was. Parker was admitting that she loved her right here, right now. The warmth spread from the top of her head to the tips of her fingers and all the way down to her toes. This is what something felt like when it was worth fighting for. She'd just explain it to Parker. She got scared and ran. But they had AJ's and Kat's support. Mr. and Mrs. Chase would have to get used to it…or not. It was their choice. But Parker would understand that she was here now. She'd just have to.

"I'm so sorry I ran away," she said, reaching out and attempting to take Parker's hand. Parker jumped back at the contact like she had been shocked. She stepped back and rammed her hands into her pockets, pushing on. "I was scared and walking away was a stupid move. I don't even feel like I was in my right mind when I made that decision. It was like I was on autopilot. But that doesn't matter. I did it. I ran. I accept responsibility for that. I left you there to fend for yourself and I would give every penny I own to be able to take it back. But I can't. I can only hope you'll just give me a chance to fix everything. To fix us."

Parker began shaking her head before Ella had even finished her spiel. "No, don't you dare. You don't get to come crawling back to me after you left like you did. That's the one thing, the only thing that you couldn't do. You could have been scared. You could have stayed silent beside me while I handled my parents and we explained everything to Kat and AJ. We, Ella. We. We should have done this together. We should have been together taking care of one another after last night's shit show, but you took yourself out of the equation."

Parker paused to take in a breath, and Ella decided to seize the opportunity during the temporary cease fire. She stepped forward and tried to take Parker's hand again. She didn't resist her, but looked at Ella with a cold, exhausted gaze. She looked utterly defeated. Ella couldn't stand it any longer. The warmth flared deep in her belly as it gained strength until the three words she had been holding onto climbed up her chest before spilling out, no longer willing to be restrained.

"Parker, I lo—" But she didn't get to finish her declaration of love as Parker placed two fingers on her lips, effectively silencing her while staring at her in disbelief.

"Are you serious? You think this is just going to be fixed because you come over here and say…that," she said, almost like Ella's words left a bad taste in her mouth. She once again pulled her hand back before taking another step back into her apartment.

"Goodbye, Ella. These last few weeks have been nothing if not eye-opening. Please tell my sister I will call her tonight. Actually, never mind. I will just text her," she said and closed the door in Ella's face.

As soon as the door was shut, Parker leaned backwards against it as her knees would no longer continue to support her weight. She slid down, jelly-legged, until she sat on her welcome mat. She was so tired, so bone tired, of trying to stand tall. After everything that happened last night, she just didn't have it in her. Now was the time that she was supposed to be getting support from her partner, but Ella had left her to fend for herself. And she did. Now that the most recent battle was over, she had no strength left.

The tears overtook Parker then, and she sobbed quietly to herself again. She was surprised there was still any water remaining in her body after the amount of crying she had done in the last twenty-four hours.

The next thing she knew, there was soft knocking at her door. "Dammit, Ella, I do not want to see you," she said under her breath, but then realized her apartment was almost dark now. She checked her phone, unsure how much time had elapsed, and noticed she had received several texts from her sister through the hours that passed. She tried to stand but found her lower body and back to be very stiff after falling asleep sitting in the foyer. After a few moments, she rose to open the door for who she now assumed would be Kat and AJ. She assumed very incorrectly.

"Parker," her father said with a nod of greeting. Her mother stood next to him, looking very distraught. Parker was completely speechless.

"Can we come in?" Denise said.

Parker still said nothing but stepped to the side and allowed them to enter. They had never been inside her apartment before. She would normally be worried about what they thought about her working-class way of living, but today, she just didn't care. When they entered the living room, she gestured to the couch as she walked toward the kitchen.

"Do you want something to drink? I think I have some juice," she said, opening the fridge to find the remains of the jug of orange juice. A bottle of vodka rolled around on the almost empty top shelf like a pebble in a can. Ella's vodka. She contemplated pouring the expensive liquor down the drain this instant, but something was stopping her. She had a love/hate relationship with the idea of seeing it there every day when Ella would no longer be around. It could stay for now. She retrieved three bottles of water from the bottom shelf before closing the door with her foot and heading back to face off against her parents for the second time in as many days.

She handed them their drinks and opened her own to take a long swallow from it before sitting in her shabby armchair and waiting for them to start. They both took drinks from their bottles and looked at each other without saying anything. The silence hung heavy in the air like a suffocating fog.

Carter took one more sip and cleared his throat. "I'll go first," he said. It took him a few moments to continue, and Parker awaited his forthcoming words. "I, we, want to apologize to you for our reaction and behavior last night."

Parker was sure she had misheard him. When it looked like she was going to say so, he held up his hand to stop her.

"Please, just let me get this out," he said. His voice was shaking ever so slightly. "When we found out that you had been dating Ms. Gardner—"

"Ella," she interrupted. "Her name is Ella."

Her father looked at her and cleared his throat before continuing. "I can imagine that you would understand it was quite a shock."

"Yeah, it kind of was for me, too," Parker said sarcastically.

He looked wounded but continued. "Kat and AJ have done a lot of damage control today and explained more of the situation. The age difference is still fairly vast, but not out of bounds. We had no idea that Ms. Gardner—Ella—was such a young mother and our reaction came from a place of love for you."

Parker eyed him suspiciously. "How exactly do you figure that?"

"Honey, we were worried you were being preyed upon," Denise chimed in when Carter's words seemed to falter. "You're an impressionable young lady, and when we heard Kat's girlfriend's mother was your girlfriend, well, we just reacted without thinking. I also want to apologize for my actions. Can you please forgive us?"

Parker took another long sip from her water bottle before tucking her feet under herself in an attempt to stall for time. "I honestly don't know, guys. This whole situation has probably just destroyed my relationship, and I don't know how we come back from that," she said, looking them directly in the eyes.

Her mother shuffled uncomfortably in her seat. "From what Kat says, you have only known each other for a couple of weeks," she said. "Are you sure you don't just want to move on?"

Parker scoffed at the notion. "You may not understand it. Hell, neither of us get how it happened so quickly. But she was my perfect fit. She completed me. She felt like the other half of me, and right now, without her here, I feel like I can't even breathe. I feel like my soul is going to search for hers for the rest of my life, even though my brain knows she's gone. I'm going to go the rest of my life feeling incomplete and I'm so mad at you guys; I don't know if I even want to be a member of this family anymore," she said resolutely. Parker couldn't cry anymore. She wasn't actively angry. She was completely numb and just stating the facts as they stood. Her parents looked at her with wide eyes before glancing at each other. Her mother began to cry softly. Her father took his handkerchief out of his pocket and handed it to his wife.

"Please, we're very sorry for the way we reacted," he said.

"You know," Parker said, looking down at the almost empty bottle, watching the water move back and forth as she tilted it this way and that, "I'm sick and tired of people who supposedly care about me telling me they are sorry after letting me down." She upended the bottle and drained the contents. "I do blame her, though, don't worry. She chose to abandon me instead of standing with me. But I can't help but wonder if she would have stayed and worked it out if you hadn't basically accused her of robbing the cradle or 'being predatory,'" she said, using air quotes to place emphasis on the last phrase.

"Can't you just talk to her and fix everything?" her mother said tearfully. Carter nodded hopefully, placing his arm around his wife to support her.

Parker nodded, indicating his comforting gesture and laughed sardonically. "See? That right there? That's what she didn't do. She didn't put her arm around me in an uncomfortable situation. She didn't put a steadying hand on my back while I cried as my parents dressed me down. It's the simplest thing in the world when you truly love somebody. She walked away and you held the door for her. Maybe you did me a favor and maybe, one day, I'll thank you for it, but today is not that day," she said, keeping her tone completely even as she got up to throw her bottle away. Then, she walked toward the door and opened it.

"Thanks for stopping by, but this is not repairable. My life is broken in so many ways, including with both of you. I will be seeing my sister as often as I want, and you will let her come over here anytime she wants. But you are no longer welcome here and I would appreciate it if you would leave now."

Her parents looked at each other again, not knowing what to say or how to react. Tears now streamed freely down Denise's cheeks. They both rose to their feet. Carter's face had gone ashen. He looked like he wanted to say something, but only nodded at her as he walked past. Her mother stopped in front of her.

"Parker, I am so, so sorry. We will do anything to fix this. Please, just tell me what we can do," she said. Parker shook her head sadly, but she couldn't stop an errant tear from tracking down her cheek.

"When things are this broken, I honestly don't think there is anything you can do. You just have to sweep the pieces in the trash and start over and I'm getting to that as soon as you are gone," she said, looking away. Denise placed her hand over her mouth as choking sobs came to her in earnest. She moved past Parker to join her husband. They didn't turn around as Parker shut the door and locked it behind them.

Chapter 24

Somehow, Ella made it through the next few days. She was in full TGIF mode when three o'clock rolled around on Friday; relieved to finally have some time off to go home and get caught up on sleep. Parker's visage haunted every dream and most of her waking moments, but she was an adult and had responsibilities. She forced herself to keep pushing through.

When Ella pulled in her driveway after the drive home from school, an unfamiliar car was parked in her spot. She pulled up behind the large, black SUV and parked. Kat and AJ came out the front door and met her as she was getting out of the car. AJ reached into her back seat, got her attaché and lunchbox, and carried it in for her.

"Well, curbside service is now something teenagers in this house offer. I like it," she said, although her snarkiness had suffered in its magnitude as of late. Kat wrapped an arm around her waist as they walked toward the door. Ella placed her arm around her shoulders and kissed the top of her head, accepting the kind gesture. AJ reached out to get the door for Ella, who walked through appreciatively. That is, until she walked into her kitchen to see Carter and Denise Chase at her table. She immediately froze where she stood.

"Now, Mom, we're all just going to talk, okay?" AJ said, like she was a lion tamer in a den full of, well, lions. If AJ could have been physically burned by the intensity of Ella's stare, she would have been sporting redness in the second or third degree.

"Mr. and Mrs. Chase, welcome to my home. I hope my daughter has been hospitable and that you have enjoyed visiting with her because I have a feeling she will be grounded for so long after this, she might not see the light of day until her thirties," Ella said.

AJ knew she was only partially kidding. She and Kat retreated to the head of the table while indicating Ella should sit across from the Chases.

"Is Parker coming, too?" Ella said, unable to stop the hopeful tone from entering her voice. AJ put her arm protectively around Kat's shoulders as her face dropped. Mr. Chase cleared his throat.

"That's actually why we're here," he said. "We went to see Parker the day after…everything happened. She blames us for causing the problem and fears your relationship is destroyed. Is it true?"

Ella bit the inside of her cheek before shrugging noncommittally.

"I went to see her, too. Kat was worried about her. She wouldn't let me in. We talked for a few minutes on her doorstep, but when she finished reading me the riot act that I very much deserved, she practically shut the door in my face. So, yeah, I'd say destroyed is probably a good descriptor," she said.

The Chases were silent for a few moments but had the good decency to look down. AJ and Kat looked back and forth between the two sides of the table like watching a tennis match at Wimbledon. A very uncomfortable, tense tennis match.

"Firstly, we want to apologize to you. We have already apologized to Parker, but you deserve that much at least. We were very thrown by the situation, and we reacted badly," Denise said, trying to catch Ella's eye, hoping to convey the depth of her conviction. Ella saw and felt it on so many levels. She nodded once.

Denise looked relieved. "I honestly don't know what we can do to fix this, but we will do anything we can to help. Parker is a different person since she met you. She's never stood up to us the way she has over the past few days. She has a confidence that I've not seen from her before. We were out-of-line bullies that night, and she didn't take it. There must be something good between you two," she said.

Ella muttered 'was' under her breath.

"Pardon?" Carter said.

"There was something good, no, absolutely life-altering between us. I came into my sexuality a lot later than most. I have had a good life, but a loveless one. Meeting Parker and getting to know her has really shown me everything I have missed in the past and every single thing I want for my future. But she wouldn't even discuss the other night with me. She came to the door, and we talked, but she wouldn't let me in, not like she did before. She's completely shut down and to tell you the truth, I'm very worried."

Ella knew the walls that she and Parker had taken down between them over their few weeks together would leave her raw and exposed emotionally. She didn't want her to have to go through that on her own. She wanted to be there, but the barriers felt insurmountable now.

"It doesn't make sense, I know. It doesn't happen very often that two people will fall in love after only a few weeks, but we did. I think I loved her from the moment I laid eyes on her," she said wistfully, reaching out to grab a napkin from the holder so she could dab at her eyes. "I'm not apologizing for how I feel anymore. If there was anything I thought I could do to get her back, I would do it," she said.

AJ and Kat looked at each other. AJ nodded and Kat began. "So, that's why we wanted to get you all here today. We want to help you get her back. You know she's playing at that club tonight. We're still going," she said, indicating herself and AJ. "They're still going," she said, pointing to her parents. "The big question is, are you still going?"

Ella furrowed her brows in confusion. "I don't think she would want me there, Kat. So, no, I hadn't planned on going."

"Mom, you're going and you're going to put together the most amazing prom-posal ever. And we're all going to help you," AJ said.

Ella thought about how preposterous the whole idea was, but what the hell did she have to lose? Parker had made it clear she was no longer interested in trying to work it out. She decided that she would hedge all her bets and wager her entire heart on Parker, because she was in love. Truly, madly, deeply. And she wanted her back. She wanted a future with Parker.

Ella felt hopeful for the first time in days as she smiled and nodded her agreement at the girls and then at the Chases, motioning to everyone to huddle up over the table like a volleyball team discussing their strategies. "So, what exactly did you girls have in mind?" she said.

Chapter 25

AJ and Kat came up with the idea to put a song together. Parker had gifted Kat some DJing software last Christmas, and she had figured out the basics. All Ella had to do was come up with the ultimate get-Parker-back song and then they would mix it with whatever type of beat she wanted. After going back and forth on what worked the best, the girls agreed that Ella had created a masterpiece. Once they put on the finishing touches and laid down the track, Kat put it on a jumpdrive.

Carter called The Paper Tiger and got the owners on the phone. After explaining the situation and offering a hefty sum, they agreed to play the new track before Parker left the stage after her set.

"Apparently, he thought people in the bar would enjoy a truly sentimental moment because they would drink more," he said, shaking his head.

Ella smiled softly at him and walked over to offer her hand to him. "I can't tell you how much I appreciate you making that call."

He looked down at her momentarily before taking her hand between his two larger ones and held it between them.

Denise walked over and placed a tentative hand on her shoulder. "All we ask is that you treat her well and make her happy," she said.

Ella looked at her with determination. "If I get another chance, I promise you I will," she said.

The girls walked back in the room and cleared their throats while the adults sprang apart like they had been caught with their hands in the cookie jar. "Mom, we've got to get you dressed and get your makeup done. And since it's such a special occasion, I'll let you wear something from my closet," AJ said.

Ella painted the fakest grin possible on her face. "Oh, ok, great, honey, thank you. That's very kind," she said, following them up the stairs.

AJ and Kat pulled out various outfits, setting them on the bed next to Ella as she waited for directions. They talked amongst each other without ever consulting her opinion. She was happy to leave them to it. They knew what they were doing.

"I think we've got it," AJ said, holding up a fashion-forward patterned blouse and a stylish pair of designer jeans. Why had she never worn those before, she thought to herself, but refrained from saying it out loud. AJ held up a pair of her shoes, but Ella shook her head.

"I love the outfit, but I have to be me tonight," she said and left the room. AJ and Kat looked at each other when Ella came back holding a pair of high-top, black Chucks. The girls smiled and nodded as they left the room for her to get changed. When Ella announced she was ready to be surveyed, they came back in. AJ looked shocked, and Kat whistled at her.

"Oh yeah, we're amazing, AJ. This outfit works." Kat signaled for Ella to sit down as she preheated curling irons and laid out more makeup than Ella had ever seen in one place.

"Um, Kat? I don't normally wear this much makeup."

Kat waved her away. "The point is to make you look like perfection without looking like you have anything on. Trust me, I've got this."

Ella held up her hands in surrender, trusting herself to the two young ladies who had worked so hard to try to make this happen.

Almost an hour later, they announced they were finished, and she looked in the mirror, hardly recognizing herself. Kat was right; it didn't look excessive. Her angles were highlighted, and imperfections were masked. She definitely looked the part. Now, she would just have to convince Parker that her feelings were real.

"Mom, are you ready?" AJ said with love and adoration in her eyes.

Ella looked in the mirror one last time, running her hands over the clothing and gently fluffing her hair before nodding resolutely. "I think I am. Here goes nothing," she said, before looking over at AJ who had her arms wrapped around Kat's middle and her chin resting on top of her head. She checked her watch and saw that they needed to leave soon.

"Don't you guys need to get dressed, too?" she said. They looked at each other and down at their effortlessly cool outfits and shrugged.

"Yeah, of course you guys always look great," she said and felt her eyes start to well up again. "Thank you so much. Even if this doesn't work out, I just appreciate what you've tried to do. I love you both," she said.

Kat's 'uh-oh' was punctuated with her quickly grabbing a tissue from the nightstand and rushing it over to dab at Ella's eyes. "I'm telling you, if you ruin this face before you even get there, I'm going to be very angry with you," she teased.

Ella allowed her to clear away any residue before nodding that she was good to proceed. She wrapped Kat up in a warm hug and kissed the top of her head before moving to AJ and placing a kiss on her cheek.

"Wish me luck!" she said, smiling. They both returned the sentiment before Ella rushed out the bedroom door.

∽

Parker had resolved that no matter how bad she felt, she was going to put on her brave face and head over to The Paper Tiger. She had been waiting on this moment for what seemed like forever, and she sure as hell was not going to let anything or anyone stop her. Not her parents and not Ella. Not anymore.

Rack had stopped by to help her get ready. She had talked to him a lot over the last few days, explaining everything that had gone down. He had been by each day to make sure she was eating and taking care of herself.

"Listen, from what I've heard of what you're going to play tonight, it's some good stuff. People are going to flip their shit, for sure. You might even get offered a regular gig," he said, leaning across the bar in the kitchen.

Parker desperately wanted a single drink to settle her nerves, and even though she knew she didn't have anything else, she went through every cabinet and even some drawers. When she discovered nothing, she sighed and looked at the refrigerator where Ella's vodka remained. Opening the door, she took out the orange juice and set it on the counter before staring at the bottle.

Just because Parker drank her vodka did not mean she forgave Ella or even cared what she was thinking or doing right now. She didn't wonder how her day had gone or how her classes were progressing or anything like that. Or so she told herself. She took out the bottle and slammed the door shut before unscrewing the top and tossing it angrily to the side. Skipping the orange juice, she drank several swallows straight from the bottle before slamming it back down to the counter and wiping her mouth with the back of her hand.

"Did that bottle do something to make you angry?" Rack said with a smirk. ~~chidingly~~. "Or maybe someone reverse-Jesused it and turned your vodka into water?"

Parker looked at him, trying to stay mad, but she was no match for his wide smile and twinkling eyes. She choked out a laugh. "No, this is what she left after the first night we—" She cut herself off, swallowing hard against the memory. She grasped the edge of the counter like she was trying to hold on to a fragment of her sanity. Rack rounded the bar and embraced her from behind, placing a scruffy kiss on her cheek. She leaned back into the comfort of his friendship.

"Listen, I know you're angry. You have every single right to be. But, be honest with me, which feeling is stronger: being mad at her or missing her?"

Parker stiffened in his arms and tried to walk away, but he held firm. She struggled a moment before resigning to allow herself to be loved on. "I don't know," she said honestly. "I'm fucking wrecked. I mean, I've lost her and my parents and that's an awful lot, don't you think?"

Rack released his hold on her and turned her around to face him. "Uh-oh," she said humorlessly.

His expression remained serious. "I was happy to be here for you; to hold you and comfort you and keep you from completely falling apart. You're like my little sister and I love you very much," he said. She smiled lovingly at him and started to give him a hug when he continued.

"But—" he said, holding up the forefinger of one hand and giving pause for emphasis. She retreated and looked up at him with curiosity. "Knowing what I know about her and how terrified she was at your age difference to start out with, I can't imagine the level of shock that went through her. And I honestly think if it were me, I also may have just needed a minute. And isn't that what she said, that she needed some time? She didn't tell you she didn't want to be with you, did she?" he said.

Parker thought back to the moment in time and realized that Rack was right. This situation was so unexpected for her, but what about for Ella? Had she ever taken a moment to think about what Ella had said to her? Had she thought about how this might have affected her, standing in the middle of a gymnasium meeting her daughter's girlfriend's parents and potential in-laws all at the exact same time? And the way her parents had spoken to Ella, like she was some creep who was trolling for young ass at every club in town? Ella looked absolutely crushed that night. She remembered her face: a dark mixture of fear, embarrassment, and utter sadness.

They just happened to meet the first time that Ella even went to a club. She wasn't a monster, just a late-bloomer at the very worst. And Parker clearly remembered that she came on to Ella. *She* pushed for more time together. *She* pushed for a relationship. Her parents couldn't have known that Parker was the aggressor. And even though she was angry at the way they had spoken to Ella, on some level, she had to appreciate their protectiveness.

All three came back to her the next day proclaiming their love. Well, she assumed that was what Ella was going to do when she refused to let her speak and shut the door in her face. She remembered the look of hurt in her eyes just before the door closed and finally came to the horrible realization that she put it there.

"I know, Rack, but my heart was broken when she just left me there. I don't know what to do."

"Do you love her?"

"God, of course I love her. That's never even been the question. But how do I know she won't just leave every time things get tough with us?" she said, looking up into his dark eyes.

"Honey, I think these were some extenuating circumstances. I'm not saying what she did wasn't wrong. It was. But don't you just want to cut her some slack? Don't you want to feel that love again? From what you say, she obviously wants to give it to you. Are you strong enough for both of you to show her you can carry her when she's weak?"

Parker thought back to their lovemaking. She thought about the look in Ella's eyes and her own tears the first time she tried to touch her, when she didn't know about the abuse. Ella cried with her, took care of her, and stayed until Parker had calmed. Then they talked about it. Ella was there for her that night.

Then the second time, Ella was prepared. She came in with the idea of a safe word. She moved so slowly and carefully with Parker, and when the touches turned out to be too much again, she wasn't angry. She lay next to her and soothed her, surrounding Parker with her love. She had never felt safer and more secure than when she was in bed naked with Ella, their bodies pressed together, and their arms and legs intertwined. Whether they were making love or talking into the early morning hours, it didn't matter. It was her very presence that made things right. It was her.

And then last weekend when Ella had been able to touch her for the first time, even though she hadn't said anything, it was because of Ella's love for her. Because of their love for each other.

Once she was able to get through the initial phase of anger and hurt, she couldn't help but wonder to herself, who had abandoned whom in this situation? Ella was clearly floored and just asked for time to gather herself, and Parker couldn't give her a minute to just catch her breath? Then Ella came to her and tried to explain, tried to tell her she loved her, and Parker was, what, too proud? Too indignant and drunk on righteous anger to just sit down and have a discussion?

"I should text her, shouldn't I? I mean, I should give her a chance?"

"Yes," he said, patting her on the head. "But time is of the essence here, so make it short. You have to get to the club and get everything set up." He retreated toward her front door.

"Dimitri and I will be there front and center watching for you, but for now, I have to go get sexy," he said over his shoulder.

Parker seemed to not be paying attention to his joke. "All right, yeah that's great," she said, typing frantically on her phone.

"Don't sprain your fingers. I have a feeling you're going to need them to be in tip-top shape very soon," he said suggestively. Parker never looked up from the screen.

The environment in the club was already hopping when Ella and AJ arrived with the Chases in tow. They paid the cover charges at the coat check area, and Carter asked to speak with the owner to hand over the money and pass along the jumpdrive. AJ and Kat tried to sneak past the bouncer without getting their hands stamped, but Ella grabbed them both. They pouted, but then quickly ran off to get some dancing in, promising they would reunite with everyone just before Parker's set. She was then left with Carter and Denise and a lot of uncomfortable space to fill.

Ella looked at the Parents Chase and thought about how she felt her first time in a bar only a few weeks ago. They looked around wide-eyed and tentative, holding on to each other like they were afraid someone would try to sex them up.

"Can I buy you guys a drink?" she said. They looked back at her almost like they had forgotten she was there.

"Uh, yes, that would be lovely," Denise said. Ella motioned toward the bar and waited to make sure they were following. When it was her time to order, she went with her standard vodka soda with lime. Carter ordered a beer while Denise took her time looking at the drink menu. The cute little butch bartender apparently found this particularly appealing and offered to make Denise her specialty drink. She looked delighted with her hand over her heart as the bartender mixed and poured, finally pushing a fruity-looking drink toward her. She sipped and her eyes popped open before slamming shut as she took another long drink out of the straw.

"Oh, my goodness, this is delicious! Carter, try this," she said, shoving the drink at him. He held up his beer and shook his head. She took another big drink before leaning over to speak.

"What do you call this delicious concoction, my dear?" she said, holding the straw between her fingers before taking another drink. The bartender ran her hand through her short hair before she leaned forward and all but leered at Denise.

"It's a Panty Dropper," she said with a grin and a wink. Denise began to choke. Ella could hardly hide her smile as she gently patted her on the back. "You should give me your number. I'm Pax," she continued. Boy, could this go any worse?

Denise collected and steadied herself as she blushed, only partially from the alcohol she had drunk so quickly. "I'm flattered. But I'm just here with my husband and my daughter's girlfriend. My daughter, Parker, she's going to DJ tonight," she said. Ella was shocked that she had just referred to her as Parker's girlfriend without pause. She was so hopeful she'd be able to pull all of this off and make that dream a reality once again.

"Oh, right on," Pax said. "I heard her doing a test run on her equipment before the bar opened. It sounds pretty fucking awesome," she said, then her eyes went wide, realizing what she'd said in front of a respectable lady. "It sounds really good, I mean," Pax corrected herself.

The surprises continued as Denise smiled widely at the youngster. "My daughter *is* pretty fucking awesome," she said. Pax laughed and reached across to give her a fist bump. Denise placed her hand on Pax's fist for a moment before squeezing. It was the cutest thing ever.

She and Carter smiled at each other as they sipped their drinks, both watching the interaction between Pax and Denise.

When his wife returned, Carter seemed to relax a bit more. They looked around for a free table and finally found one. Parker's parents sat together and across from Ella, who had absolutely no idea what to say. Small talk was not her forte.

"So," Carter said out of nowhere, "you say you met Parker at the bar where she works. Tell us about your first meeting."

Ella decided she should probably go ahead and finish her drink for this one. "Well, let's see. I had this drink pulled up on my phone that I was going to ask for because it was something I had never had before. But, when I first caught sight of Parker, she literally took my breath away," she said, wistfully staring off into space. Carter and Denise gave her their full attention as she continued. "She was absolutely the most beautiful woman I had ever seen, and I felt like I couldn't talk. Anyway, I had accidentally scrolled off the screen and couldn't find the drink I wanted so I ordered something...different," she said. Ella was not saying the name of the drink out loud to Parker's parents. "Anyway, I ended up going with my regular," she said, holding up her drink for emphasis, "and it was the best one I had ever had. So, I went back for more drinks. And the rest is kind of history," she said, leaning back in her chair. The expressions on both faces staring back at her were cautious but produced small smiles in her direction.

"Don't forget to tell them that the next drink Parker made for you was called a Sex with the Bartender. Talk about foreshadowing," AJ said, sitting in the one free chair and pulling Kat onto her lap. Ella could have died right there. It was Carter's turn to choke on his drink now.

"AJ, honey, don't you need a drink? From that convenience store we passed a few miles out? If you leave now, you'll get there before they close," Ella said, turning a shade of beet red she was getting used to when AJ wanted to poke and prod at her.

AJ beamed a huge smile at her mother. "They have homemade grenadine here, so I'm going to go get us a couple of virgin Shirley Temples. I'll just tell them to put the drinks on your tab, shall I, Mom?"

Ella checked her watch and saw it was five minutes till Parker was due on stage. Her pulse kicked up, and suddenly, she had a crazy case of cottonmouth. She shook her head at AJ. "I need a bottle of water. I'll get them. Mr. and Mrs. Chase, do you need anything?" she said. They both shook their heads and smiled at her, noticeably warmer now. As she started to walk off, AJ gave her a cheeky grin. She mouthed "behave" at her, and AJ just rolled her eyes.

Ella stood in line waiting to order drinks when she heard a couple of familiar voices coming toward her from the side. She turned to see Tally and Danna holding hands and laughing at their own shared joke. She cleared her throat, and they both looked up. Eyes that were previously rather normal-sized went extremely wide. Ella finally figured out why Danna had been being so sketchy.

"Hey, guys," she said, smiling wryly.

"Uh, hey, Ella. It's good to see you," Danna said. She looked at Tally and then back to Ella. "How have you been?"

"I'm good. Looks like you are, too, huh? Listen, I'm not mad. No one did anything wrong here. No one was committed. If you guys fell for each other, I wish you would have just been honest. I'm happy for you," she said. Both visibly relaxed at this.

"Good. I was terrified you were going to be mad at me. But Danna and I talked a whole lot that night at Sparkle and then after that, we just kept talking," she said, looking at Danna lovingly.

Danna was without her normal bravado but smiled back at her. "Yeah, I just pretty much figured you were going to end up with Parker and this just kind of happened. I hated avoiding you, but neither one of us knew how to tell you," she said.

"Umm, recommendation for the future. Just tell me. I'm a pretty straight shooter. I'd like to receive the same level of honesty from my friends," she chastised, looking back and forth between them. "And we are friends, right?"

"Yes, definitely. Oh, I'm so relieved," Danna said. "And again, I'm so sorry."

"It's fine. So, when I call or text, you'll answer next time? I just want to make sure I'm clear…" Ella said with a wink.

Danna chuckled. "For sure. Hey, we have a game night in a few weeks. Let me text you the details and maybe you and Parker can swing by."

Ella felt her smile dissipate. "It's a long story, but for now, I'll say maybe. Send me the info." Ella looked at the couple appraisingly, giving her nod of approval. "This," she said, signaling between them, "I like. Very much. Now, go be cool kids and dance to Parker's tunes." They both nodded and gave her quick hugs before heading on their way.

It was at that time the spotlights came on and pointed toward the DJ booth. A crowd started to gather on the dance floor waiting for the beats to kick in. And then, Parker walked onto the stage.

She looked like an absolute dream. She wore a skintight black T-shirt with a white phoenix screen-printed on the front. Ella recognized it as the exact same drawing she had tattooed across her abdomen. Directly under the drawing, also in white, was what Ella knew was her stage name: DJ Feenyx. That fit her perfectly. She wore the jeans that she had let Ella borrow for her 'date' last weekend. She also had a black-and-blue plaid flannel tied around her waist as a nod to the 90s grunge she was using for her mix-ups. Her hair was combed back flat against her head on one side and the other side was the normal voluminous curls she was used to seeing. It was a very chic look for her.

Before she started her show, she first checked several settings and effects on her board before signaling to the lighting tech that she was ready to start. She picked up her headphones and put them on her head before making the first couple of effects. The crowd cheered in anticipation. When she finally dropped the beat on Pearl Jam's "Even Flow," which had been layered over a driving dance beat, the crowd went crazy.

Ella couldn't stop watching. She was completely enthralled by Parker's movements and hyping up of the crowd as she scratched and looped. When the first song was winding down, she faded in Nirvana's "Smells Like Teen Spirit" that was almost unrecognizable as a grunge song past the opening guitar chords. Parker had developed a beat for this song that was a cross between dubstep and techno and even more people moved in to dance.

Ella must not have moved because when she felt a hand on her shoulder, she was no closer to the bar and their drinks than she had been when Parker started. She turned with a start to see Denise standing with her.

"The girls wanted to go dance and Carter wanted another beer," she said in explanation. "And when you stood frozen to the spot watching my daughter like a woman in love, I thought I should come help you carry everything back," she said, smiling warmly. Ella sniffed and smiled back before returning her gaze to Parker.

"I do, you know. I love her. She's amazing," she said simply.

Denise nodded, placing a reassuring hand on her bicep. "I don't understand the music, but what she is doing really does take a lot of talent. I had no idea. And look at the way these people are reacting. They love her," she said, looking at Ella pointedly.

Ella couldn't tear her eyes away. The crowd bobbed and bounced as Parker waved her hand back and forth. "Yes, they do," she said, looking back at Denise and smiling. It was at that point that Ella truly felt the acceptance she was looking for from the Chases. Now, if only Parker would accept everything she had to give as well.

Ella knew that Parker's set was set to go on for one hour exactly. When she looked down at her watch and saw there were only a couple of minutes until Parker's music would end and Ella and the girls' attempt at a song would begin, she felt the nerves start to kick into high gear. Her hands went cold and sweaty, and she felt her heart hammer in her chest. AJ and Kat came out of the crowd and ran up to her screaming.

"Mom, are you nervous? I'm so nervous," AJ said, flapping her hands back and forth to alleviate some anxiety.

"It's just got to work, Ms. Gardner. It has to," Kat said, showing everyone that she had all of her fingers crossed as well as crossing her thumbs.

Ella couldn't talk as she waited. Her mind was full of visions of Parker and their time together. The feelings those memories brought were all encompassing, and she could only nod at the girls.

After the final song finished, Parker took off her headset, waved to the crowd, blew some kisses, and started off. Then, the opening piano and gentle beat of "A Sorta Fairy Tale" by Tori Amos came on. Parker looked very confused and started fiddling with her equipment. After the intro, the lazy soporific beat with which the song was spliced began driving a deep, slow rhythm.

The girls did their jobs well as they made it to the DJ booth. When Parker saw them, she bent over and helped them climb up. Ella watched her grab both her sister and AJ in a tight hug and kissed them each on the cheek. It warmed her heart. They were looking out in the crowd trying to find Ella. When Kat spotted her and waved, Ella waved back tentatively. Kat got Parker and AJ's attention and pointed to Ella in the crowd.

Parker's face went from overjoyed upon seeing the girls to completely blank in the space of a moment. Ella couldn't stop her own face from falling, but someone shoved a microphone in her hand. She looked at the owner who shrugged and walked off. She then found Carter in the crowd. He smiled and held his beer up in support and solidarity as he put his arm around Denise.

"Hello," she said quietly into the microphone before a blast of feedback almost deafened everyone. Apparently, she was supposed to wait for the house DJ to lower the song as he was now eyeing her down from his permanent booth to the side. She waved in apology.

"Hi, my name is Ella. I wasn't quite expecting to talk to everyone tonight. This was unexpected to say the least," she said, clearing her throat. "But I'd like to tell you a story. I guess it is a sort of fairy tale. It's one of those girl meets girl, girl freaks out over their age difference, girl works it out with girl, and then girl finds out she's dating her daughter's girlfriend's sister…you've heard that one before, right, guys? Tale as old as time?" The crowd tittered. Well, at least they weren't throwing rotten fruit yet.

"Anyway, I met an amazing woman. It's been a complete and total whirlwind and it's only been a couple of weeks. So, I can't even imagine how deeply I am going to feel for her over the next fifty years or so." Ella chanced a look at Parker. Her expression seemed softer, and AJ and Kat were crying all over each other.

"What I am trying to say here in front of my daughter and your sister," she said, indicating AJ and Kat, "and your parents," she said, motioning to where they stood. Parker looked at them, surprised. They waved at her and at the smattering of applause from the crowd. "What I am trying to say, Parker Chase, is that I love you. And I just want to continue this fairy tale with you," she said, dropping the mic to her side. The crowd looked expectantly to Parker, who climbed down out of the booth and walked purposefully toward her. Ella wasn't sure if this was a good thing or a bad thing as her face gave nothing away.

When Parker was standing directly in front of her, she stared meaningfully into her eyes. Ella dared not move or look away. Suddenly, Parker grabbed the microphone out of her hand and brought it to her mouth.

"I love you, too, you dork," she said and smiled that real, spirit-warming Parker smile that Ella had missed for so long. The crowd cheered and applauded.

Ella grabbed the microphone back from her. "I think this is where we kiss," she said.

Parker nodded, wrapped her arms around Ella's neck, and pulled her down into a searing kiss. This time, the crowd went insane. AJ and Kat finally made their way over and practically fell into them, laughing, crying, and hugging Parker and Ella, thus breaking the kiss.

"I think this is where we begin again. Right here, clean slate. Remember our first meeting? Heck, we can do introductions again," Ella said, holding out her hand. "Hi, I'm Ella. This is my first time at a gay bar. I'd like to order a drink from the sexiest bartender I've ever seen. Oh, and it's nice to meet you."

Parker took her hand and smiled that wry smile that meant she was up to no good. "So, we're starting over. From the beginning. And we're replaying our first meeting?" Parker said, and Ella nodded vehemently.

"Parker," she said, taking her hand. "It's nice to meet you, Ella," she said, leaning in to whisper in her ear in that scandalous tone Ella loved so much. "Did you still want that Screaming Orgasm?"

Epilogue: One year later

"Parker, pass the eggplant, please," Carter said as everyone sat down at the table where Parker, and to a lesser extent, Ella, laid out a spread of several different types of curry. Ella didn't think it was possible for her food to get any better, but it had. Parker always wanted to try out a new dish on Ella, and her hips were showing how much she appreciated the delicious food.

"Guys, this is so good," Kat said. She and AJ were home from college for fall break. AJ had gotten a full ride for volleyball, and Kat had her tuition covered by academic scholarships. They were also sharing a dorm room, which Ella was sure would have been detrimental to their relationship, but they were still together and seemed to be more in love every time she saw them.

Parker looked up at her and winked as she handed Ella some of the spinach and cheese curry that was her favorite. She rewarded her girlfriend with a quick kiss on the lips.

Alex and his wife Rebecca sat on the other end of the table. They had gotten married in a beautiful ceremony early in the spring. Not long after that, Alex called Ella to tell her the good news.

"Hey, pass everything down here. Yes, that, too. Please pass it all this way. I know I'm eating for two, but I feel like I'm eating for an army," Rebecca said, rubbing her baby bump.

"She's not kidding, folks. Please send the food this way," Alex said, moving his arms like an air traffic controller helping a plane to land. "If you don't, she's likely to start on my forearm." Rebecca gave him 'the look,' and he lowered his eyes and began to behave himself.

"You guys are such nerds," AJ said, but she couldn't stop smiling. She was very excited at the prospect of having a new baby brother or sister to fawn over. Kat bent over to kiss her cheek, but she hadn't wiped her mouth beforehand. Now, AJ sported a large swath of sauce over one cheek and looked completely affronted. Kat grinned as she chewed, and AJ wiped her cheek with her napkin.

Carter and Denise dug into the chicken Tikka Masala and were making the most provocative moaning sounds.

"Get a room," AJ and Kat said at once, and everyone laughed. Ella felt a squeeze on her thigh and looked back over at Parker.

"Are you happy? You look happy."

Ella nodded. "I never thought I could be this happy. I love you so much," she said.

Parker smiled but kept looking over at Kat across the table. They were communicating back and forth with their eyes. Ella looked between them trying to decipher the code. When Parker finally nodded at her sister, Kat tapped her fork on her water glass to get everyone's attention. Ella looked at Parker with furrowed brows. Parker would only divulge a wink.

"I'd like to make a toast," Kat said, getting up from the table. Everyone quieted down and looked at Kat expectantly. Everyone except Parker who smiled knowingly.

"What's going on?" Ella leaned over to whisper to Parker.

"You're going to be even happier in a minute," she said, signaling that Ella should pay attention.

"First of all, I'd like to say thank you to my parents who are the most amazing people. I wouldn't be the same person without you. I love you." Denise and Carter smiled and raised their glasses.

"We love you, too, honey," Denise said.

"I'd also like to thank my sister and her girlfriend. You guys have been there for us so much over the last year. AJ and I don't know what we'd do without you," she said. Parker just nodded. Ella blew her a kiss. "Mr. and Mrs. Gardner and Baby

Peanut, you guys have been such a source of strength for us to reflect upon. We are learning a lot about family from you guys." Rebecca, who was full to the brim with the pregnancy hormones, was already crying. Alex was at the ready with a travel pack of tissues.

"That brings me to you," she said, turning toward AJ who was midbite. She looked up at Kat expectantly. "Look at our family. Look at all these examples of love we have around us," she said, motioning around the table. "I promise you that I want to continue to grow with you. I want to take all these lessons we have learned from everyone at this table and apply them to our lives every day," she said, tears streaming down her face.

AJ stood up to hug her. "Of course we will, honey. Where is this coming from?"

"I promise you that as long as I am on this earth, I want to be part of you and I want you to be a part of me," she said, pulling out a ring box. Ella gasped, and Parker's smile grew even wider. Rebecca now boohooed, and Alex pulled out a handkerchief as the flimsy tissues weren't going to cut it anymore. AJ's face was a mask of utter surprise. Kat kissed her softly on the cheek and got down on one knee.

"You once told a room full of strangers that you loved me. Well, Anna Jean Gardner, I am telling a room full of people who love us, our family, that I love you. I want to be with you for as long as you'll have me. Will you wear my promise ring?"

Carter and Denise now joined in with sniffling of their own, while Rebecca was probably going to need some electrolytes and a nap after this was over.

"Oh, my—baby, of course! I would love to wear your ring! Did you buy this for me?" AJ said, her voice breaking as Kat slipped the white gold band on her finger. The small diamond sparkled in the light. She pulled Kat up into her arms and they cried into each other's shoulders, mouthing words of love and murmurs of assurance. The room erupted in applause and the tapping of glasses in response. Ella looked over at Parker and her smug smile.

"Why didn't you tell me?"

"Kat asked me not to. But I promise that's the extent of anything I'll ever keep from you again," she said and leaned in for another quick kiss.

Ella looked over at AJ, who smiled and held up her hand with the ring. Ella smiled broadly at her daughter before lifting her eyebrows in question. AJ nodded vehemently. Now it was Parker's turn to look between them to try to decrypt their signals. She wouldn't have to wait long.

"It damn well better be," Ella said, pulling the ring box out of her jacket pocket.

About the Author

Kellan lives in the deep south with her wife and a cadre of kids and pets. She enjoys the finer things in life like quality dark roast coffees, ice-cold lagers, and world peace (in that order).

You can often find her listening to an audiobook while heavy metal blasts on Spotify and a scary movie plays on TV (hello ADHD), or just trying to catch some downtime (napping) from her crazy, busy, wonderful life.

@KellanMcKnight

Kellan McKnight

kellan.mcknight.author@gmail.com